Kelly imm... large blue-a... crime scene... all of their ... ...scope, a more portable, yet still powerful, version of the CS-16.

Dan watched as the team set up their equipment. He seemed a little bit annoyed for having been called in after quitting time.

Before the lights were switched off, I checked the floor. There were no fresh marks gouging the beaten wood. All of the dismembering had happened at the pier—or at least not here.

"All set," Kelly said. She handed each of us a pair of reddish-orange tinted goggles.

I slipped mine on and the orange from the streetlights turned to fire.

Kelly flipped a toggle switch, and the CrimeScope projected its bluish beam of light. She ran the beam over the floor, and the blood we had seen before under the faint coating of Luminol now glowed brightly.

Joshua emitted a thin whistle.

Smaller specks that had not been visible with the Luminol appeared before us. The area of blood evidence was even greater than we had originally thought. Kelly slowly moved the light over the wall where the newer paint was, and it glowed towards the bottom. Through my goggles, I could see whitish-blue patches marking blood splatters.

A couple of small oblong droplets shot out towards the floor. Long streaks extended from more centralized splotches as if a bottle of ink had been thrown against the floor and wall several times. The beating had been more severe than I could have ever imagined.

"Well," I said dryly to Joshua, "looks like we found the other crime scene."

EDGE OF DEATH

MAURA SHERIDAN

LEISURE BOOKS NEW YORK CITY

A LEISURE BOOK®

April 2005

Published by

Dorchester Publishing Co., Inc.
200 Madison Avenue
New York, NY 10016

ISBN 0-8439-5533-3

Printed in the United States of America.

Visit us on the web at www.dorchesterpub.com.

A special word of thanks to:

Cynthia Manson, Don D'Auria and everyone at Dorchester Publishing, Jack Kappler, Kurt Crawford, Special Agents James Margolin and John Fiore, Officer Daniel Valenza, Alvin Carter, John Ingram, Greg-O Cohen, Dr. Carol Scherczinger, and the 14th Street Crew. Did I mention Cynthia Manson? John and Ruth Walsh, Ann McCormick, Ellen Wallace, Richard, Carolyn, Clare, and Neal.

EDGE OF
DEATH

Prologue

In my dream I could see her, pure and clear as the white moonlight that surrounded them. She was slim and attractive, and she seemed so peaceful looking up toward the starless heavens. He was standing over her, staring down upon her motionless body. I was so close to them, but I was just an observer. I felt almost dirty—like a voyeur.

I followed her disconnected gaze toward the moon, which was a white ball of pure light signaling like a beacon through the dark sky. The heavens shined upon him, offering their approval in the lunar glow. Someone was whispering his name.

I watched as he gently knelt over her and put his ear close to her mouth. No, it wasn't her. It was the water lapping against the pier, murmuring a hushed, inaudible warning—too late. His face was so close to hers. The closest it had ever been. He brushed his cheek lightly against her lips, and she flinched: an unexpected action that startled him. There was no time to lose.

The ax fell with a deafening thud, and the initial sight of her blood struck him in a curious way. Another *whack*, and another. Her right arm was cut off, and he stared in horror at the gross cross-section of the limb. No—my arm was cut off. I opened my mouth to scream, but only silence. He quickly scurried to the other side and raised the ax again. His actions no longer required thought as he lashed out in a frenzied hatred based solely on animal instinct. He needed to catch his breath. The sharp end of the blade dropped and nested itself within the rotting planks of the battered pier, as he leaned against the handle of the ax. Sweat beaded along his hairline, and he wiped it away with his sleeve, leaving a long streak of my blood beneath his shaggy bangs. He stared down at me, his eyes wide open. His expression was wild while he searched the darkness, but in the desolate confines of this nightmare no one could hear my screams.

Chapter One

We had decided to nap. The telephone rang at 3:00 PM, which was an hour too early. Without moving my body or even acknowledging consciousness, I groggily picked up the receiver off the nightstand. The mid-afternoon sun pouring into my tiny bedroom seemed to have targeted only my eyes, and I squinted in response to the annoying intrusion.

I spoke meekly, as I was suddenly overcome with the inexplicable urge to check that my arms were still attached to my body. "Hello?"

"Agent Brantley?"

My eyes popped open, and I shot to an upright position. I was more startled by the name by which I was addressed than the familiar voice at the other end of the phone. The nightmare I had just awakened from was now a distant memory, washed away into the depths of my subconscious.

"Joshua?" I questioned, knowing full well that it was.

"Yeah, Meredith! How are you?"

"I'm . . . I'm, uh, fine." I nervously drew the sheet up around my neck as if he might be able to see me. "How did you get this number?"

The connection was tinny and wavered like he was drowning in water. I guessed that he was on his cellular phone.

"Hey, I'm with the goddamned FBI. I can find anyone."

I rolled my eyes. "Seriously, this is a new and *unlisted* number."

"I kind of get the feeling you're in hiding," he said.

"So how did you find me?"

"I called NYU and spoke to someone in your department."

I grimaced. "The staff has been instructed not to give out personal numbers," I commented suspiciously. "Only in cases of family emergencies . . . Oh, Joshua, you didn't."

"I kind of made up a little story."

Fury rose inside of me as I bit down on my lower lip. "I can't believe you would do something so underhanded."

No longer in the mood to loaf about in bed, I sprang to my feet. The air was only slightly cooler than it had been the day before, but the cold hardwood floors startled me.

"I'm sorry, Meredith, but I really needed to get in touch with you."

"Fine, what's done is done."

Grumpy and still groggy, I brushed a hand through my shoulder-length, ash-brown hair, which was now stringy. I avoided the large antique mirror that hung over the bureau. I did not need to be reminded that my blond highlights were in desperate need of a touch-up.

At five-feet-ten-inches, I was the result of a union between Irish and British genes. Historically, these two nationalities were bitter enemies, and growing up it was once again a proven fact. For ten years, my childhood Christmas wish was for my parents to get a divorce. And yet, they were still together.

There were bags under my eyes. I angrily threw on a pair of gray shorts with FBI ACADEMY printed on the left leg, and a navy blue T-shirt, which turned my gray eyes blue. My once-muscular frame was now giving way to small areas of fat that were collecting along my somewhat-lean body. I had not exercised for even a minute since taking my leave of absence from the FBI nearly two years ago. However, my late-thirties were fast approaching and my metabolism was slowing.

I touched my fingers to the saggy pouches that had developed under my eyes. Nothing that a little bit of makeup couldn't conceal. Or perhaps my secret weapon: a dab of Preparation H.

Kyle and I had slept very little last night.

"Hold on a minute." I pressed the *hold* button and placed the receiver back in the cradle.

As I leaned over the bed and gave Kyle a light kiss on the cheek, he quietly moved about in his sleep. I sighed softly and gently pulled the sheet over his naked body. The cotton percale settled lovingly over his long muscular frame.

"Damn. What a way to start the weekend," I muttered, glancing at my watch: a habit I had developed while working as a cashier during my high school summer vacations.

I made my way down the hallway of my small one-bedroom apartment and stubbed my big toe on the front wheel of one of Kyle's Rollerblades.

"Son-of-a—"

I swiped the cordless phone out of its cradle and had barely turned it on before barking into the handset, "What the hell do you want?"

"Wow, I thought maybe you fell back asleep. Sorry if I woke you. Didn't know you'd be sleeping so late."

I hobbled into the kitchen and began filling the coffee carafe with filtered water from a pitcher.

"So, Professor Brantley, how's school life? Criminology 101, right?" he asked, with a tinge of sarcasm.

The rich aroma of coffee with a hint of cinnamon and nutmeg began to fill the air, and I took a deep breath, allowing the sweet aroma to calm my nerves—temporarily.

"Let's cut the chit-chat. What do you want?"

"Well, it seems you've adjusted well to your new pedestrian lifestyle," Joshua huffed. "You're your usual charming self."

"Look, I kind of get the feeling that this isn't a social call."

I walked over to the refrigerator and poked my head inside. He was hesitating, and I could feel my muscles tense, bracing for what was coming.

"First I want you to know," he began, "that I wouldn't have called unless it was absolutely necessary."

"What?" I asked without masking my lack of enthusiasm.

"There's a case—"

"No! Absolutely not! Not now, when I finally have some stability in my life."

"Please, Meredith, just hear me out. I wouldn't have called unless I thought that you could be of assistance."

Had he not heard me?

"Don't ask me to do something that I'm not prepared or willing to do." The fact that my voice was slightly pleading repelled me.

"You don't have to travel anywhere, the case is in Manhattan."

"Manhattan; L.A. Nashville, Butt-fuck, Indiana—the answer's still, no."

"Nice language."

My mouth opened, but Joshua did not allow me to respond.

"Look, Meredith. You're good—"

"Used to be," I firmly reminded him. A horn blared loudly through the phone. "Where are you?"

"I'm in a cab on Broadway. I just flew in from Quantico. We only got the call late this morning. I know very little of the situation, as it is. The body of a young woman—"

My eyelids fell and my shoulders shuddered. I could see them. The faces I had seen so many times before: in person, in my dreams, and in my nightmares. Ten years with the FBI and these haunts still controlled my life. Bloodied body parts, faces of victims and grieving families came back to remind me that no one ever forgets.

"Look, Meredith, I don't have time to argue with you or cajole you. I need to see the body before they remove it from the crime scene. If you'll do this, meet me in half an hour in front of the main entrance of the field office."

My tone softened as I dug my fists into my eyes, trying to rub the images away. "I've already told you."

Joshua sighed as if admitting defeat. "Like I said: meet me in half an hour. But please, Meredith, please consider this."

There was sincere desperation in his voice, and I felt a surge of pity, but thankfully, caught myself from screaming "yes" into the receiver.

"You didn't send me a Christmas card last year," I said, before slamming the handset into its cradle.

Maura Sheridan

* * *

"Damn him!"

I briskly walked to the bedroom and peered into my closet, slowly thumbing through a stock of drab, earth-tone suits. Thirty minutes was hardly enough time to make this kind of decision. I stopped.

"What the hell am I doing?" Back in the kitchen I stared at the mess I had created. I pressed my fingertips against my temples. There was a sickening feeling churning in the pit of my stomach and small streaks of light shot sharply before me. My body slid down the jamb of the kitchen doorway and I rolled myself into a tight ball, bracing for the migraine.

With my head held tightly between my fists, I alternated lifting and lowering it, hoping that a change in elevation would drain it of the pain. I was in desperate need of an Imitrex. On my hands and knees, I crawled down the hallway to where I had dropped my purse the night before. After struggling with the childproof packaging, I gulped one of the pills and swallowed without water, hoping the pain wouldn't last more than fifteen minutes.

I gazed up toward the moulding running along the right angle where the wall and ceiling met, and was suddenly intrigued by one of the framed photos hanging with geometric precision against the peach-colored paint. It was a photograph I had passed everyday, yet this afternoon it looked different.

With the palms of my hands, I pulled myself up along the wall, and stared at a photo taken on the day I graduated from the FBI Academy. There I was, proudly standing next to then-FBI Director William Sessions, my brand-new credentials—or creds—and gold shield between us. I began tracing the ornamentation around the picture's frame, and fondly remembered that glorious day. Sixty-four graduates lined against the wall of the auditorium waiting to step up to the stage and officially receive the title of *Special Agent.* Pride and honor had enveloped the auditorium in a thick cloud of idealism that had consumed the hearts and minds of all those who stood along the putrid orange-brown wall. But for me, it had been a bittersweet moment filled with disappointment. When I had looked out upon the glowing face of my younger brother, Ethan, I could not dismiss the hurtful emptiness of my parents' intentional absence. They had refused the invitation to come to Quantico. They had refused to offer their support on my proudest day.

I gazed pensively at the image of my younger self. My face was so full of energy and idealism. In ten years, how had I allowed myself to become so cynical? I slumped to the floor. The Imitrex was not working.

With my head bent forward, I slowly crawled back to the bedroom, muttering, "Damn him."

Chapter Two

There was a burning on the inside of my hands as I breathed on my reddened fingertips. I silently cursed myself for not having the foresight to bring a light pair of gloves. The city was caught in a seasonal limbo where the days were still somewhat mild and the evenings frigid. The Thanksgiving break was two weeks away, but nary a leaf had turned yellow or orange. The fall foliage in the Big Apple had two stages: green and dead.

"Wheh tu, ma'am?"

I climbed into the cab and was immediately over-whelmed by the stagnant odor of sautéed onions. The passenger door had barely closed when the meter displayed the initial charge of $2.50 in glowing red numbers.

"Twenty-six Federal Plaza."

"Oooohh. Yooh mahs be vetty eemportahnt pehson." The cab sped across East Twelfth Street and began its journey downtown along Broadway. I could see his right eye giving me the once-over in the review mirror, and thought he might suspect me of being INS.

"Ah-ha!" The driver emitted a nervous, yet hearty laugh.

I only smiled in response, hoping to discourage conversation. The talkative man's accent was very thick, and I had difficulty understanding him. Eventually, his voice faded into the endless noise of the city, and I was relieved to find a moment of solace in what was turning out to be an annoyingly eventful day.

The smell of the cab's vinyl interior combined with the driver's incessant overuse of the gas and brake pedals, was making me nauseated. I cracked open the window. Dirty air was better than no air.

While a student at New York University pursuing my undergraduate degree in psychology, delving deep into the criminal mind became my obsession. I read and studied as much literature as I could get my hands on. Something from my past made it a necessity. And now, ten years later, I was very near regretting my stint with the Investigative Support Unit, which eventually became the Child Abduction Serial Killer Unit, and finally, the National Center for the Analysis of Violent Crimes, or NCAVC.

I laughed lightly. The FBI liked to play the name game.

Forty-eight agents, working tirelessly to understand why human beings lash out and react violently toward others. Sometimes I felt as if I would never find the answers.

The cab pulled up to the imposing Federal building, which was guarded by two rustic red monolithic sculptures. Recently, impenetrable cement barriers had been stationed around the perimeter of the block, protecting the building from the threat of a terrorist car bombing.

"Wait here," I ordered as I stepped out of the cab.

Maura Sheridan

In my career with the FBI, I had spent many weeks at the Jacob K. Javits Federal Building. Standing as a civilian before the grayish stone and darkened windows, I held a much different perspective. I took a deep breath, and through two large potted shrubs spotted Joshua's tall silhouette waiting at the front entrance. The late afternoon light created ominous shadows that cut across his sharp features.

I smiled when the cab driver cleared his throat nervously at the menacing figure.

Joshua was in his usual finely pressed suit of an inexpensive cut, but he still filled it out like a *GQ* model. It was what I called his "uniform." And I never saw him out of it. Well, maybe once—or twice—or a few times. . . .

"Meredith!" Joshua shouted, as he bounded up the small flight of stairs and ran over to me, clutching an expandable file. His warm disposition and gregarious nature were the complete opposite of his conservative appearance. "It's so good to see you!"

He hugged me with such enthusiasm that I was lifted off my feet. My nose was pressed against his shirt collar, and I was overwhelmed by the smell of cologne.

Although ten years my senior, Joshua's youthful personality sometimes made me feel as if he were decades younger. His normally ageless face looked only a bit more tired and worn than usual. The years were slowly catching up with him. From experience, I knew that he must have been floundering in an unforgiving workload. But those stark features that looked so dangerous in the shadows revealed a handsome angular face set against a set of "bad boy" movie-star brown eyes. The corners of my mouth turned up into a grin. *Dangerous either way.*

He ran a hand gently through my much-too-layered

12

hair, and down the side of my face. "You look great, Meredith. I knew you'd show."

My eyes narrowed, wondering if I had been too predictable or if he had been too presumptuous. But my sattention was quickly drawn to the rectangular identification card that hung casually from his neck on a silver chain. On the front was his picture, laid over a sketchy illustration of the Statue of Liberty. On the back of the ID was a magnetic strip that served as a keycard and allowed access through all of the secured doors in the field office.

"I won't be able to get you an ID until tomorrow," Joshua said almost apologetically.

"I'm only temporary," I reminded him. "I don't need an ID."

The cab driver pressed on his horn, and Joshua grabbed me gently by the wrist and pulled me inside. His cologne immediately waged battle with the sautéed onions.

"Twenty-sixth and the West Side Highway." His right eyebrow arched as he considered something. "And there's an extra twenty if you run the lights."

Without hesitation the driver floored the gas pedal, throwing us up against the back of the seat.

Joshua looked over at me with a gleeful expression. "I love New York!"

Chapter Three

As we neared the West Side Highway, red, yellow and blue lights swirled rapidly and bounced off the water and nearby buildings, filling the already orange sky with an ominous foreboding. Royal blue wooden police barriers marked POLICE LINE DO NOT CROSS NYPD, were being used to block off the area between Twenty-fourth and Twenty-eighth streets, which only served as a catalyst in generating a macabre curiosity in the nosy onlookers gathered along the sidewalk. As the workday came to an end, a light stream of tourists, attracted by the commotion, trickled in.

Excitement mounted when our cab slowed at the police barricade on the southeast corner of Twenty-sixth Street. I climbed out while Joshua paid the fare, and a prerecorded voice of a celebrity personality reminded him to ask for a receipt. He displayed his leatherbound creds to a young uniformed officer, and we were motioned through the police line.

A few resourceful teenagers scurried past the blockade and were pressed up against the cement Jersey barriers that lined the roadside. Necks stretched and people sat on shoulders in a futile attempt to gain a view of what horrible sight lay below.

The Channel 4 news van was blocking vehicle access to the area, and the crew argued tirelessly with four officers, who demanded adamantly that they remove it, while the reporters argued that they be allowed access.

I walked briskly toward the scene, shamefully acknowledging that my own curiosity was now piqued. But my normally confident stride quickly dissolved into tentative baby-steps as I followed Joshua along the centerline of the highway. My heart began to race and blood pounded in my ears. The faces from the past were coming back. Who would be the new victim to add to my catalog of horrors?

Several officers stopped us again when we reached the parking lot of the nearby restaurant, but waved us through when they saw Joshua's gold Department of Justice shield hooked over the breast pocket of his coat. A passing paramedic lifted the yellow plastic tape marked CAUTION CRIME SCENE DO NOT ENTER, and I ducked under. We walked over to the edge of the paved road, the dilapidated pier just coming into sight.

The ground below slowly disappeared and the murky waters of the Hudson came into view. The embankment and the abandoned pier were swarming with plain-clothes detectives and crime scene technicians in dark jumpsuits. There was still enough daylight to illuminate the area, but large halogen floodlights were being unloaded and lined up along the roadside, just in case.

I leaned against a stiff wire-mesh fence lining the edge of the paved area. The cool air that came from the water was biting, and I drew my coat tighter around my body. Normally deserted, this part of the river was now clambering with activity.

I shook my head lightly. "This is eerie."

Joshua moved closer and placed a comforting hand on the small of my back. I shivered as he tightened his hold. My nose wrinkled, and I unbuttoned my coat. I was suddenly feeling quite warm and felt my cheeks flush. I quickly took a couple of steps away from him. Our eyes locked on to one another for a brief moment before I turned and stared out toward the water.

There were several remnants of old piers no longer in use. What had once been planks of healthy wood, were now gray and weathered. The run-down, rural quality of the scene was quite beautiful in a sad, picturesque way. Under any other circumstances, the setting may have appeared to be something out of a photography book meant for someone's coffee table.

I inhaled deeply and walked to the end of the fence. An officer held us there for a few minutes as a technician finished taking photographs. We watched as he continually fired a high-intensity strobe flash, each time a few feet closer to the victim's body. He was finished several minutes later, and we were allowed to enter the crime scene.

When I slid down the manmade embankment, I lost my footing on the loose dirt. Joshua reached out to catch me, but his hand merely brushed my shoulder. As I skidded, my ankle caught on a brick and I tripped, landing ungracefully on my butt. It was the worst entrance to a crime scene ever executed. An officer packing up a video camera chuckled, as I sprang to my feet and brushed myself off, my face red with embarrassment.

"You could've caught me," I scolded Joshua under my breath.

A tall, lanky man in khakis and a pine green rugby shirt underneath a black Gortex hiking jacket, came toward us.

He thrust out his hand. "Joshua." He looked at me curiously. "Meredith?"

"Hi, Chris," I replied, shaking his hand. Chris's smile was warm.

Special Agent Chris Schills was the Profiling Coordinator for the Manhattan Field Office, serving as a liaison to the NCAVC. It was his job to analyze the complexity of the cases and determine whether the troops from the Academy needed to be called. When I had been in active service, New York City, the surrounding counties and New Jersey had been the regional area to which I had been assigned. After taking my leave of absence, I had decided to move to the city. There was just something about this city; it was much too easy for someone to disappear and become anonymous.

"We miss you," he said. Chris rubbed the point of his chin with an index finger. "I'm glad you got here so quickly."

"It sounded urgent," Joshua replied.

"Well, I was able to hold the body because thankfully, our lead detective isn't adept enough to learn a three hundred-dollar computer program that would assist him in drawing the crime scene." Chris closed his eyes, openly displaying his impatience. "What should've taken two or three hours, took four and a half."

We were interrupted when a slightly paunchy man in

17

his late thirties, wearing a wrinkled navy suit and a gray coat, sauntered over.

. I immediately read his predatory gait, and stiffened with an air of defensive officiousness.

Chris leaned over and quickly whispered, "That's him, the lead detective. Name's Sergeant Daniel Grissard. He's a shit. Just ignore him and let it roll off your back."

"Yous duh profilers?" Dan asked in an almost accusatory tone, enhanced by his strong Flatbush accent.

His dark hair was slicked back and his beady eyes looked as if they had no pupils. He chewed on a wad of gum that must have contained several sticks, since it bulged against his cheek, exaggerating his already saggy jowls.

I bit the inside of my lower lip. "Yes, we're the . . . profilers."

It was a term I detested, due mainly to Hollywood's overzealous interest in the subject. But "behavioralist" had too many syllables and I found it difficult to say after three shots of tequila.

"Sergeant Grissard, NYPD." He did not bother to offer his hand. "I've got an Oriental girl over here. Some busboy from the restaurant called nine-one-one. Found her when they was getting ready to open for dinner."

Joshua was looking around. "Where's the body?"

"Which part?"

Joshua and I looked at Dan. There seemed to be a gleam of pleasure in his eyes.

"Forget it." He motioned for us to follow, and climbed up to the pier on a short, four-foot wooden ladder that the NYPD had placed there.

I positioned my hands on the edge of the pier's rotting wood, balancing myself for the last rung of the ladder.

We walked toward the body as the water smacked into the stilts with short, forceful waves. Salt hung heavily in the air and burned my already dry eyes. I rubbed them gently, but the fishy smell was proving to be more of a nuisance. I quickly counted five evidence markers: a low number for a crime such as this. I turned and looked back toward the roadside. It had disappeared. There was no way anyone could have seen down to the pier unless they were standing right by the fence. It was the perfect choice for a crime scene.

An officer from the Crime Scene Unit, or CSU, handed us each a pair of Latex gloves.

I squirmed my hands into them, my middle finger missing and sliding into the hole meant for the index finger. After ten years and countless crime scenes, donning a pair of Latex gloves was still a two-attempt process.

Dan stopped before a huddle of investigators. He pointed. "The torso, legs and the head."

I eyed him warily. There was a disturbing pleasure in his tone as he described the violent scene.

He pointed to the far end of the pier. "The arms." He tapped an investigator on the shoulder. The sarcasm was thick when he said, "Come on, guys. The *profilers* are here. Let them see."

I shot him a look before bending down beside the corpse, careful to avoid the blood and not touch the victim. I could feel the heavy weight of stares as all eyes fell upon Joshua and me. I had probably seen more gruesome murders and autopsies than any of these officers would see in their lifetimes. This was nothing different.

Dan's description of the victim had been misleading. Much to my relief the woman's head and torso were intact, but her arms had been dismembered and presum-

19

ably placed at the end of the pier as he had so eloquently described.

Dan pointed to a yellow four-inch-by-eight-inch placard with a bold black numeral 5 resting upon the victim's stomach. "Hair. Not hers."

I began to wonder if he was able to compose a sentence more than four words in length.

"Now, Sergeant, don't tell me you already know the DNA results."

He held out his hand, and a young man in a dark blue jumpsuit handed him a paper envelope sealed with a bright orange sticker marked *Evidence.*

"Black hair," Dan said pointing to the victim. He thrust the envelope at me and said smartly, "Blond hair."

My expression never faltered as I turned and leaned in close to the body. The fully clothed young Asian woman could not have been more than twenty years old. The stylish black stretch pants and tight mock turtleneck were now soaked with blood, and dirt and gravel clung stubbornly to the moisture. Though the early evening was beginning to chill, the day had been warm. Rigor mortis had set in and had already begun its slow process of leaving the body. Her skin had turned a grayish color and was covered with light scratches that were consistent with her body being dragged. Some light bruising had developed under her chin and neck, but that seemed trivial compared to the marks left by the heavy beating the victim had endured. Whoever had done this horrible crime had not only dismembered her, cutting directly through the clothing with erratic and messy blows, but had also struck her several times with some kind of object that left strange U-shaped markings upon her face and body.

"Most of these marks are near her face and neck." I moved my head from side-to-side, studying the wounds from different angles. "The offender had to depersonalize her and make her an object."

It had been several hours since the diligent blowflies had detected the smell of death and begun regenerating their cycle of life.

"Is there any ID?" Joshua asked.

"Nope," Dan replied. "Just another Jane Doe." He snorted. "I guess, Jane Chow."

I reached out and swatted one of the flies away as it flew by my nose, pretending that it was Sergeant Grissard.

"Interesting that the offender decided to leave her eyes open," I said with a calm casualness. "There was no real sense of guilt. He had total control right to the end. He made her see him."

The victim's belongings were missing, but with what the young woman had endured, robbery was definitely not the motive. Often a violent offender who kills will take some of his victim's possessions as souvenirs or trophies, depending on what the attack meant to him. Souvenirs allowed him to relive the fantasy. Trophies gave him the triumphant satisfaction of making a kill.

Starting near the feet, my gaze slowly traveled along the young woman's body.

For these types of inhumane creatures, it wasn't the actual killing that they took pleasure in, it was the plotting, the strategizing, the enticing—the entrapment. Then it was the mutilation and the arrangement, or disposition, of the body, all of which was a sexual charge for them. Then it was the reliving of the fantasy they had concocted—over and over—until that no longer satisfied them, until they had to kill again. And then, finally, the mind games and feelings of superiority when the police couldn't decipher the clues fast enough. It was the only way they knew how to place value on their existence.

I had just reached the neck when a voice rang with a familiar scraggly coarseness.

"She's probably been here since eleven-thirty last night," someone said from above the huddle.

My head snapped up, and I smiled at the familiar voice.

"Anthony!" I jumped to my feet and hugged my dear friend. "And how's New York's finest Deputy Medical Examiner?"

"Ecstatic, now that I see you've come to your sense and reinstated yourself."

Joshua smirked and nodded his head in agreement.

I cringed, and with my forearm, nervously brushed away a few errant strands of hair from my eyes, taking care not to contaminate my gloves.

"I'm here as a consultant."

"Can't say that's not a disappointment." He looked over at Dan, and seemed agitated.

I stared down at the body. "She's been here since last night?"

"It's not an exact science, but that's my best guesstimate."

I knew that Anthony Montello's best guesstimates were as precise as a finely crafted Swiss watch. Just as Joshua and I could in some mystical way read into the minds of victims and criminals, Anthony could read the stories left behind with the dead.

"Come here," he said. "This is very disturbing."

There were four officers keeping a watchful eye over the severed limbs, a blue wall between the evidence and any photographer with a high-powered lens. I looked back at the highway. This far out the pier was within view of the highway, but fortunately, unless you had binoculars, there was little to see.

"Christ, this thing's like a football field," I muttered before kneeling down.

The victim's arms, with the sleeves rolled up three-quarters, had been seemingly dumped at the end of the pier. They had not been placed, just dropped like pick-up sticks or some worthless trinkets. The wrists were still tied together with the same basic store-bought twine used for recycling newspapers. I followed the path of the ligatures. Four passes had been made around her wrists. They were amateurish. She gave little resistance.

My curious gaze studied some scars on the victim's arms that were only partially visible and mostly covered by the sleeves. It was something that would be addressed in the autopsy, for touching the body went against crime-scene protocol.

"Are you dealing with any cults in the area?" Joshua asked.

Chris turned to him. "No, not since the Children of Mercy. Or at least, not that we know of."

"Can it be linked to any other murders in the area?"

"Not that I know of. But once we're done here we can forward it to VICAP."

Through VICAP, or Violent Criminal Apprehension Program, the NCAVC was able to identify and link sexually motivated cases with similarities, subsequently notifying local and state authorities. If a crime was left unsolved, details were forwarded to the NCAVC on a VICAP form, and processed for future cross-referencing.

This was particularly important when a criminal crossed state borders to commit his crimes.

"There's nothing ritualistic about this," I said with a matter-of-fact air.

Chris cleared his throat. "Well, I thought there might've been some kind of cult influence, and Grissard did, too. What, with the dismembering and all."

I concentrated my gaze on the torn body parts.

"Grissard has probably never encountered a dismembered body," I said. "Beheaded, blown to bits, knifed, shotgun blasts, but limbs intentionally severed, I doubt it. To the untrained, this could seem like the doings of a satanic cult. But to the trained—" I eyed him with my Professor Brantley look, and Chris lowered his head—"It's not."

"Sorry to have wasted your time," he said.

I was immediately consumed with a gnawing guilt. "No, Chris, we should've been called, because obviously there are some disturbing factors here." I placed my face close to the limbs. "There's a definite deliberateness behind the dismembering and picking up the limbs and dumping them twenty feet from the body."

Dan lumbered over and joined us.

"What about the cuts?" Chris asked.

"Damn cults," Dan said gruffly.

I looked at him askance. "These cuts are not from a cult. They're not patterned in any specific way and appear random. There's nothing symbolic about them."

I leaned in closer and studied the double knots at the ends of the ligatures.

"Same double knots my kids use on their sneakers," Joshua said.

"Not the best kind you could use," I said. "At least we know he's never served in the military, or sails."

"And he ain't no Boy Scout," Dan commented with a sour face.

I turned my attention to a couple of detectives questioning a crowd of nervous restaurant employees. It was doubtful the offender was an employee, or worked anywhere so close to the dump site, but he was definitely familiar with it. Perhaps he ate at the restaurant or drove to work every day along the West Side Highway.

Joshua leaned back on his heels. "Anthony, your best guess. How easy is it for someone to cut through a person like this?"

He began to chuckle. "Not very. Look how difficult it is to cut through a chicken wing."

Anthony cleared his throat when he caught Joshua's stern expression. "It would've taken some time, even if the instrument used was a very sharp blade."

Speaking about victims of violent crimes was an impersonal, often cold process, but it was never done with the intention of sounding malicious or heartless. It was a job. And like any other occupation, analyzing ruined bodies was just daily shoptalk.

I listened with an attentive ear to the ideas and information being brainstormed. It was how I worked best: as an observer. People will tell you almost anything if you say nothing.

"What about a power tool?" Chris asked.

Anthony shrugged. "It'd be faster. But from the looks of it, this was a hand tool coming from above. There are many cuts in the skin off the line of dismemberment, as if whoever did this was hacking rather violently and fell off his mark a couple of times."

"There are deep cut marks in the wood of the pier near the victim's shoulders," I said, still staring at the arms. "They're fresh and just the right size for the edge of an ax blade."

"Besides," Anthony continued with a decidedly unprofessional vocabulary when he noticed Dan hovering over us, "look how messy and ripped the insides are."

Dan scrunched his face and turned his head slightly away.

"That's some sick shit, huh?" he remarked with forced machismo. "Reminds me of this gang fight. One side took an ax to this guy. Found him, head cut in two. Right in half. Down the center of his head, ear-to-ear. Like an orange. Clean cut. Face was undamaged. Looked like he was sleeping. Strangest thing."

I allowed his voice to fade out, as I stared back at the victim and absorbed a panoramic view of the crime scene. It would have been easy for us to immediately dismiss the potential complexity of the murderer's mind, but we knew there were no "crazies" when it came to this type of organization. No, people who thought like this were most definitely sane and even more dangerous—they were intelligent, unlike the offender who made an orange out of Dan's gang victim.

When I quickly stood, I could hear my knees crack in protest.

"We need to know more about the victim," I called back to them as I retraced my steps along the pier.

Heavy boots reverberated off the pier's rickety planks as everyone caught up to me.

I stared down at the young victim. "This is not the first time he's committed this type of murder."

Joshua nodded his head lightly, and Chris sighed wearily.

Dan grunted, refusing to believe a serial killer had just been discovered making the rounds in his precinct.

"You don't think it's isolated?" he asked with an almost pathetic hint of desperation.

"All of this would've taken time," Joshua explained. "The violence, the abuse was all unhurried. He's done this before."

I knelt and leaned over the young woman's face, when I was suddenly hit with a mild case of déjà vu.

The victim's eyes were glassy and a light film of lifelessness had glossed over them. The young woman stared upward, her eyes left focused on one final image. I wondered what the woman had seen as she released her last breath. I followed the deadened gaze and looked into the sky.

"Sergeant Grissard, haven't you restricted the airspace?"

With a stern expression, Dan looked at me, but sounds of chopper blades soon filled the air. Everyone looked up as the Channel 4 news helicopter hovered gently out over the middle of the Hudson.

"Oh, shit!" Dan jumped down from the pier and raced over to one of his officers. He muttered something using animated gestures and an equally lively vocabulary.

An officer down at the water's edge yelled something about finding a wallet. But his words were almost lost in the excitement happening overhead.

I watched in complete rapture, as in a matter of seconds an NYPD helicopter descended upon the other, creating a barrier between it and the crime scene. The two aircraft hovered effortlessly for a moment before banking left and flying upward and away from the area. I had always marveled at man's ability to thumb its nose at one of Nature's most steadfast rules. For me, the ability to fly in the open skies was more than a thrilling adventure; it was a freeing of the soul. My gaze was drawn to the young, beaten face resting at my knees. Is that what this victim had felt? In her final moments, had she wished to fly off and be free of whatever nightmare was being inflicted upon her? Is that what Sumi had felt?

I froze, and every nerve in my body tingled.

"I said, you finished?" Dan was standing above me.

I had not heard him the first time.

"It's getting dark. We need to finish up."

I sprang to my feet, my face almost ghostly.

Joshua reached over and inconspicuously clutched my forearm, steadying me when I began to waver slightly.

As the last of the orange sky faded into the horizon, my haunted stare was reflected in his eyes, sending a chill up my spine.

"Joshua, I know this girl."

Chapter Four

It was just after 7:00 P.M. when Sumi Miyaki's body arrived at the Medical Examiner's office on First Avenue.

On the front steps of the ME's blue-tiled building, I held a paper cup as if it were the last of my worldly possessions. Venti: the mother of all coffee cups—from Starbucks. I frequented the coffee chain enough to know the proper phrasing for placing an order. If not worded correctly, the employees there had an annoying habit of "reordering" your drink. My love affair with the Java bean was no secret among my friends and colleagues. Down at the FBI Academy it was almost legendary.

Joshua was attached to a cigarette and stared aimlessly at the sidewalk. We waited out in the cool night air. There was no rush. Sumi's parents were inside the morgue identifying her body.

"I thought you quit," I said with disapproval, all the

while keeping a scrutinizing eye on the two vans with TV network logos parked across the street.

He looked up. A fresh cigarette clung to his lower lip and bounced rapidly as he spoke. "And I thought you were switching to decaf."

I raised my eyebrows. "Touché."

"Could be the reason why you get all those migraines."

I glowered at him.

We stopped our schoolyard tiff when the main door opened and a tall, distinguished, well-dressed Asian man stepped through. He turned slightly and offered his arm to a small, almost waiflike Asian woman, who relied heavily on his strength to steady her.

My coffee cup dropped to my side and I stared, suddenly overwhelmed with compassion—Sumi's parents.

A reporter and cameraman clambered from each of the vans.

"Mr. Miyaki," yelled a blonde wearing heavy makeup before she was even on our side of the street. "Mr. Miyaki. How do you feel right now?"

The Miyakis passed, ignoring the glare of the camera's lights and my stare.

How do you feel?

I felt like punching the woman in the face.

The small, red LEDs were flashing on the front of the cameras, indicating that they were filming.

The Miyakis slowly made their way to a dark sedan waiting at the curb, and the small gathering of the media, in a surprisingly empathetic turn, decided not to follow. Perhaps it was the brutal nature of the crime. Though we had kept the crime scene secure and managed to keep the information flow in a holding pattern, reporters had good instincts and could detect a sensational story even in its most basic form. But for a brief moment in this ugly night, they exhibited compassion.

The blonde stretched out her arm as her cameraman unwound the mike cord from his leg.

"Your daughter, Mr. Miyaki!" she yelled.

I did say brief.

A hot, bright-white light popped like a strobe, and I instinctively placed myself between it and the Miyakis, providing them a clearer path to the car.

The driver held open the door, and with careful attention he gently helped Mrs. Miyaki into the backseat. The door slammed with a deep *thud*, and the driver scurried behind the steering wheel. Then, as quickly as the Miyakis had appeared, they sped off into the night, the dark sedan disappearing into the city.

"Yes, thank you, Jane," the blonde said into the camera lens positioned four feet from her fake-bronzed face. Her eyes never blinked as she stared into the light.

"Wealthy and powerful businessman, Taekishi Miyaki, of the Noyitsu Corporation, and his wife just left the City Morgue. In fact, they *just* left." She pointed toward First Avenue. "Just drove off into the night. It has neither been confirmed nor denied that the victim was in fact their daughter—their only daughter—who was found murdered over by the West Side Highway."

I stared at her profile. She was trying desperately to sensationalize the mundane. Even though no one really knew who the Miyakis were, Noyitsu was a big deal in the business world. The New York Stock Exchange would be in turmoil at the start of the opening bell Monday morning. But your everyday citizen would not recognize either the Miyaki or Noyitsu names. At home, tired faces would be staring at their TV sets, glassy-eyed and barely registering another story of a murdered woman. Which was fine with me. Publicity was *not* what we wanted to give the offender.

The blonde looked at me.

I checked the camera. The red light in front was still flashing. I grabbed Joshua's elbow, and we hurried inside.

Chapter Five

Anthony Montello always had a soft spot for me, mainly due to the strength of my ironclad stomach. In the ten years he had been a forensic pathologist and his six years as Deputy Chief Medical Examiner for New York City and the borough of Manhattan, Anthony took great pleasure in welcoming new faces to his refrigerated office. Furthermore, he took even greater pleasure in holding casual conversation over international cuisine—or anything slimy and repulsive—during the decidedly more gruesome aspects of the autopsy. I was only one of six people who never had to excuse themselves from one of his autopsies.

Joshua and I lingered just inside the main entrance and watched the blond reporter. We were taunting her.

Ha-ha. Here we are in plain sight, but you can't come near us.

Oh, it would come back and screw us, but we savored the moment.

Forty minutes of irrelevant small talk went by before she climbed back into the van with her cameraman and drove off.

"Thank God," Joshua said, rolling his eyes.

He stuck his head out the door and lit a cigarette.

"Just one puff," he mumbled as he sucked air.

I grabbed the back of his collar and pulled him inside. The cigarette flew from his mouth and landed at the bottom of the steps.

Joshua and I slowly made our way down the deserted corridors, a foul odor weighing heavily in the air. Industrial cleaners and deodorizers failed to cover the nauseating smell of death. We stepped into the chill of the autopsy suite, where seven tables were empty and cleaned, ready for tomorrow's workday. But the eighth, glinting under the green tint of fluorescent light, seemed ominous and frightening. Two stainless steel carts, containing surgical instruments that resembled something out of a horror movie, rested next to the waist-high autopsy table. One of the technicians from the lab was fiddling with the CrimeScope, an ALS—or Alternate Light Source—which, with the assistance of fluorescent technology, picked up fibers, hairs and bodily fluids that under normal conditions would be invisible to the naked eye.

Sumi's body was laid out, and a forensic photographer had just finished a shot. Her arms had been placed upon a separate surface. X-rays of Sumi's lifeless body were clipped to a light box hanging on the wall. For the next four hours, her body would be poked and prodded. But Anthony was a good man, and no matter how quirky his personality, he was always respectful of his "patients."

Now in his scrubs, Anthony, with his graying hairline

peeking out the edges of his cap, moved his finger about the torn insides of Sumi's limbs, examining the damage. There were several markings on her bones. Markings that would prove important in determining the type of weapon used.

"Hey," Dan commented.

He held a bread knife in his hands. With its thirteen-inch blade, it was arguably the pathologist's most important tool.

Dan poked it through the air, emphasizing every other syllable. "We thought you was chickening out."

I frowned. It was going to be a full house tonight.

"Ah, there you are," Anthony declared jovially from behind his face shield, as he snatched the knife from Dan and placed it back on the cart.

Dan merely shrugged and wandered over to the counter where Sumi's personal effects had been laid out.

Lined up beside her possessions were several plastic evidence bags and paper envelopes. These appeared empty, but upon closer examination they revealed the tiniest of hairs and fibers. Two bags contained fingernail clippings.

I grabbed two gowns and handed one to Joshua. With ease I tied on a disposable plastic apron over my gown and put on a face shield. Once again, I struggled with the Latex gloves as Joshua awkwardly attempted to pull the rubber boots over his Rockports.

Anthony watched, shaking his head in amusement.

In the many hours I had spent in the cold autopsy rooms, I had come to learn that the assistants—or deniers—were something of an anomaly in the morgue population. They seemed to belong to some unusual subculture of their own making. The basic protocol of the autopsy room was that you never really spoke to the deniers, and they never spoke to you.

Roth, the denier on call tonight, was a small, dark man of slight build. I had often wondered about the strange men I occasionally saw him speaking to in the shadowed corners of the corridors. There were many unfounded rumors that deniers notified funeral homes when a new body was wheeled into the morgue, and sold the names of the families of the deceased to the highest bidder.

I watched him with interest but could not see it in him.

"Whoa, easy, boy," Dan said condescendingly as Roth expertly zipped a pair of surgical shears up Sumi's clothes.

Roth continued about his business as if Dan did not exist.

The forensic photographer began taking detailed shots of all the injuries that covered Sumi, as Roth assisted by holding a scale rule graded in centimeters to each wound. Film rolled through the camera for what seemed like an eternity.

When he was finished, Anthony began collecting more items from the body: a fiber here, a piece of grass there, some gravel.

"The debris is fairly consistent with the crime scene," Anthony said. "Most of the fibers aren't out of the ordinary and are probably from rugs and fabrics at her home."

"We'll check the fibers against her home," Dan assured us.

I watched intently as Anthony curiously poked at one of the U-shaped cuts.

"What is it?" I asked.

"Oh, nothing," he mumbled. "These wounds are

strange. Not consistent with any weapon I'm familiar with."

With his middle finger, he picked out four shiny specks.

"Glitter?" Dan asked.

I looked across at Joshua, and he met my disgusted look with an equally annoyed expression.

"Doubtful," Anthony said with kindness. "Probably a metal alloy from whatever was used to make these wounds."

He inspected more of the U-shaped cuts for the specks.

"Only four near the left shoulder have them." Anthony looked at me, "Containing four, four, two and three. Two on the right shoulder have three and one, respectively. None in the wounds on her face."

"He's right-handed and started at the left shoulder," I said, standing over Sumi with my clenched fist raised over her. "Then he moved to the right and made his way up toward the face."

"Mm," Dan said.

"There's no drastic change in angle," Anthony said.

Joshua moved in closer. "She didn't move much while he was stabbing her. Very little resistance, which is consistent with the simplistic ligatures."

"Or she just gave up," I said.

With a long, thin, brownish hose hooked up to a spigot, Roth rinsed off Sumi's body. A light flow of water streamed steadily as blood and grime washed quickly down the slanted table. Then Anthony set to work on the external examination, taking careful notes of all outward injuries.

"No signs of sexual assault," he said.

I inhaled deeply, Anthony's words alleviating my greatest concern.

"Tissue looks normal." As a matter of course, he picked up three thin, long cotton swabs from one of the carts and took samples of bodily fluids. "But with the magic of science we did find seminal fluids on her body."

I smiled at his charming reference to the ALS.

The ME's office had incorporated into its crime-fighting inventory the CrimeScope CS-16, a heavy black box with a tunable light source generated from a Xenon bulb. In ultra-violet mode, and with the assistance of red magnetic powder, the CrimeScope could pick up latent prints on human skin. Turn the wheel to any one of the ten filters, and you could detect semen, sweat, blood, urine, feces, vaginal secretions, saliva, gun residue, drugs, fibers, paint, grease, even bite marks.

An image of Sumi glowing like a Christmas tree came to mind, as I concentrated heavily upon her detached limbs. "No semen on her arms, right?"

His eyebrows arched. "Right."

My head bobbed in tight little nods. These types of killers who mutilate and brutalize get off on the violence, not on the sex, because sex confused them and in some cases scared them.

"Heyyyy."

I cringed at the sound of Dan's voice.

"There's something written inside this ring."

"What does it say?" Joshua asked as he walked over to the counter.

"Nine-two-five. Could be a date."

I rolled my eyes. "Is the ring silver or gold?"

"Silver."

"Nine-twenty-five is the mark for sterling silver."

"Hmm," Anthony muttered.

"What is it?" I asked, thankful that my conversation with Dan had been brief.

Anthony was hunched over Sumi's bare, dismembered parts. "In addition to the abrasions there are lacerations on her arms."

I stepped over to him. "Defense wounds?"

"No, some are newer, but they aren't fresh enough to have been inflicted in the last twenty-four hours. Most of them are old and scarred."

"Old defense wounds," Joshua said.

There was silence as Anthony examined the arms more closely.

"No. See how the wounds are all over her arms?" Then suddenly and without warning, he snatched up the long bread knife from the cart and lunged across the table at Dan. "Hiyaa!"

With lighting fast reflexes, I caught Anthony's forearm just as Dan stepped back and protectively raised both of his arms. Although I doubted that Anthony was looking to harm him, I reacted purely on instinct.

"What the—"

"Freeze! Don't move!" Anthony was pressed up against the table, a bizarre fire glinting in his eye.

Like a deer caught in the headlights, Dan was still.

"Anthony?" I said slowly and calmly, as if I was talking down a mentally unstable patient who had just turned on his caretaker.

A mischievous grin spread across Anthony's face and his arm relaxed and dropped to the table. "Don't move, Grissard. Hold that position."

Perhaps out of fear or maybe confusion, Dan did as he was told.

I moved in protectively as Anthony leaned over toward him.

"Don't worry," he assured me. "I had no intention of hurting our friend, here."

An awkward smile spread across my face, but I was still tense as I watched Anthony draw mock knife wounds with his index finger along Dan's forearms.

"See, Agent Luker? Where would all the defense wounds be?"

"Uh, along the underside and outer edge." Joshua's voice was trembling slightly. "It's elementary forensics."

Dan lowered his arms and appeared offended. "Shit. That's rookie stuff."

I tried in vain to stifle a grin. "Kind of dramatic means to make your point."

Anthony shrugged. "What can I say? I need some excitement around here." He returned to Sumi's arms. "So you can see why these aren't defense wounds. They were—"

"Self-inflicted," I grimly stated.

"Also," Anthony continued in a serious tone. "These are far too long and carefully placed to be arbitrary." He began shaking his head and continued his examination without saying a word.

I flexed my hands, squeezing them into tight fists, causing small pockets of air to gather underneath my gloves and squeak in protest. If no one knew of Sumi's secret in life, there was no way to hide it in death. Very little could be taken to the grave.

"I guess they *were* symbolic," Joshua said pensively. "Her own little ritual."

The thought of Sumi sitting alone in her room with a sharp blade, slowly cutting into herself made me nauseous with pain.

"What about her neck?" I asked, eyeing the bruises, trying to distract myself from the arms.

Without turning from the arms, Anthony paraphrased

what he had already recorded onto tape. "Those bruises are superficial and there's no evidence of petechia hemorrhaging in the eyes. When we get to the windpipe we'll find that it is neither damaged nor fractured. She was knocked unconscious and then bled to death."

Joshua lingered over the arms. "With no defense wounds, she either knew her attacker, or felt safe around him—that he wasn't a threat."

Dan pulled at his lower lip, his gaze concentrated on a shiny pair of pick-ups, or forceps. "He had to catch her by surprise. Whatever he used to immobilize her didn't seem dangerous. Or it was something that wouldn't have seemed in character if he was holding it."

We all stared at him inconspicuously. Even Roth had to give pause, surprised that Dan had actually said something observant, and used the word "immobilize" in the same sentence.

"These wounds are very strange," I remarked, leaning in close to examine one of the open U-shaped marks covering Sumi's face. "She was obviously beaten with some kind of tool."

Joshua put on his reading glasses and placed his face next to mine. "Maybe some kind of—I don't know—kitchen utensil."

I squinted and turned my head, our noses almost brushing. "Obviously, Kirsten does all the cooking."

"Hey, who knows, maybe it's some kind of weird European tenderizer."

Dan sauntered over to the table. "Looks like a gun butt."

"Yes," I nodded my head. "But the butt of a gun wouldn't leave an *open* U-shape *cut*, it would be a solid bruise and unlikely to break the skin." I looked up at Anthony. "How deep are these cuts?"

"They vary between a one-quarter and one-half of an inch."

"Too deep."

"Maybe he hit her really hard," Dan fired back.

He *had* hit her really hard, but still: "Most semis are mostly plastic and too light."

"Could be an older one."

I let my head drop as I shook it exhaustively.

"I've seen a lot of marks left by the butt of a gun," he continued with an arrogant tilt of his chin.

"And have they looked *exactly* like this?" I countered. "Josh, give me your sidearm."

He tentatively eyed me and then Dan.

I rolled my eyes at him. As much as I might have wanted to, I was not going to shoot the sergeant.

Joshua took out his Glock 23—he had not upgraded to the Colt 1911, yet—and handed it to me. I held it a half-inch above one of the cuts.

"Too big," I said sharply, tracing the outline of the grip along the cut. It extended about a quarter-inch beyond the wound.

"Could be a different gun," Dan angrily stated.

With a quick flick of the wrist, I spun the sidearm around so that Dan was looking at the bottom surface of the butt.

"Run your finger along that," I ordered.

Dan was stone; his eyes were like black slits.

"Smooth," I declared, quickly brushing the palm of my hand along the bottom. "Nothing to gouge, or cut."

Dan had no reply, but he muttered some unsavory comments that were mostly inaudible to me. I didn't care; I had been called worse by much better people.

I handed the gun back to Joshua, and he quickly holstered it.

"Let someone in Toolmarkings figure it out," I said, as

I checked my watch. It was a large Casio Pathfinder with an altimeter, thermometer and compass. It did nearly everything except brew my coffee in the morning.

"It's ten PM," Anthony joked, never taking his eyes from his work. "Do your parents know where their daughter is?"

I smiled politely. My parents didn't give a crap where I was.

"Actually, two tools were used," Anthony said, as he studied a mark left by blunt trauma. "This item with the sharp edge, and something that didn't break the skin." He studied it further. "Could be anything, really. But from the circular shape, perhaps the end of something. It's an inch in diameter; approximately the size of a quarter."

Dan put in his two cents. "Like a hammer?"

Anthony shook his head slowly with short movements. "No, it's the right size for the rounded head of any number of hammers, but an angry man wielding a hammer would cause a lot of damage. There's no broken bone underneath these bruises."

"Maybe the handle end of the sharp tool?" Joshua suggested.

He nodded. "Whatever it is, it's slightly rounded." Anthony pointed to one of the bruises on her cheek. "See how the edges aren't clearly defined and seem to fade? That means the edge didn't make much contact with the skin."

"Then definitely a handle of some sort."

Anthony ran his fingers along the underside of Sumi's head. "Your guy whacked her really hard back here with something. The X-rays show that there's a fracture underneath it. When we get to the brain there'll be a bruise."

"Coup injury," I muttered.

Anthony looked up with admiration. "Very good, Agent Brantley."

"Ms. Brantley," I corrected him, my voice low and out of everyone else's earshot.

"Yeah, whatever."

He lifted Sumi's left hip and poked at her underside, revealing where blood had settled itself into purplish patches.

"These patterns indicate that the victim died lying on her back," Anthony continued, like we were pathologists in training. "But they aren't entirely consistent with the disposition of the body as it was found at the crime scene. Do you all agree?"

Everyone looked, but only gave Anthony's findings a cursory exam. There was never any need to double-check his work.

"So, Agent Luker, what does that mean?"

Joshua's eyelids popped open. "Huh?"

"What does that tell us about our victim and subsequently our killer?"

"Oh." Joshua stiffened as if he were addressing a news conference, his hand motioning before him like a politician trying to win votes. "The victim was moved after death. The crime scene is not the death scene."

I stared at Sumi's body as if in a trance. "He beat her someplace else, before bringing her to the pier."

Anthony watched me with interest. "What else tells us that the body was moved?"

"There's debris stuck to her open wounds." I traced one of the U-shaped injuries. "He hated her. He hated her more than anything in the world."

"The weapon used to dismember her was brought to the crime scene, and he took it with him when he left,"

Joshua added. "We should understand that the offender had his crime planned and knew exactly what he was doing step-by-step."

"Question is, will he do it again," Dan remarked.

Everyone looked at him. It was the second semi-intelligent thing he had said. But it was short lived.

"What 'bout the crazy shit with the arms?"

Joshua and I were silent.

"If you ask me, it's some crazy cult." Dan went over to where Sumi's arms were. "All that crap she did to herself. Then this nutty stuff with her arms at the pier." His voice was surprisingly determined. "Has to be a cult. I don't give a rat's ass how rich or important someone's family is. It don't make a difference. A rich girl can worship Satan just like a girl from a trailer park. Everyone has a darker side. Everyone's up to no good."

I watched Sergeant Dan Grissard with a newly found interest. My original assumptions of him may have been accurate, but he was also a cop who for many years had walked the streets getting to know the grimier side of humanity. His understanding of the darker side was just as finely tuned as mine was, if not more so. I watched him as he began to chomp on his gum with large open-mouthed chews. When he caught my gaze, he winked and swaggered over to us.

Thoroughly repulsed, I threw him a disgusted look and turned back to the autopsy table. Whatever redeeming qualities I had found in him quickly dissipated.

"What about the abrasions?" Anthony called out to anyone who would take his little pathology quiz.

"Also indicative of the body being dragged," I replied, running a finger lightly over Sumi's shoulder.

"But these abrasions exist on her arms as well. Joshua, your turn."

He cleared his throat. "That means the offender didn't dismember her until they were up on the pier." He paused and stared at Sumi's entire body. "The victim's slim and slight in physique."

"She weighed in at 102 pounds."

"The offender is small and not particularly strong. It would've been easier and less awkward to carry her down the steep embankment. That is, if he had the physical ability."

Dan squinted and rubbed his eyes. "Maybe he was just tired."

We all were.

"Or maybe he just felt like banging her around some more," Dan said.

"No," I said in a hollow tone, as if no one else was in the room. "He's weak. He's very weak."

I knew the type. For nine years I spent all my waking hours hunting and analyzing; interviewing and caressing their egos, all in the name of finding out why people kill, rape, beat and torture.

I had an image in my mind. Like the paper dolls I had played with as a child, I always started with a flat, two-dimensional shape that had no features, no clothing and no identifying markers. As the pieces came together, so did the image, and I could place whatever new elements I needed to add with the small square tabs, just as I had done with my little paper dolls. Until finally, in the end, I'd see his face just as I had so many times before. Just as I had that winter night—

Roth lifted Sumi's upper body and allowed her to fall upon the body block; a plastic brick-shaped block that forced her chest to be thrust forward, allowing Anthony easier access to all the organs during the internal exam.

The killer was slowly evolving. He was a weak man, perhaps physically, but definitely emotionally. He sought to control the elements that in his everyday life he could not. Powerless to stand up for himself, but he built his confidence by lashing out at someone weaker and smaller. Throughout his whole life, he had been made to think and feel that he was inferior, and he lived up to this image. But alone and in the darkened cover of the night, he became the master of his own demons.

"Hey, don't I get a question?" Dan pouted sarcastically like a spoiled child.

Anthony barely paused before asking, "How much does a human brain weigh?"

Dan was excited and quickly replied, "Eight pounds."

Anthony froze and bit into his lower lip. "Head. That's a human head."

Joshua's shoulders were trembling and he turned away in order to hide his laughter.

"Brantley, go for it."

I replied in a monotone, detached from the moment. "Fourteen hundred grams."

With a large scalpel, Anthony drew a precisely curved Y-incision starting at Sumi's shoulders and under the breasts, then extending straight down to the pubic bone, making a slight detour around her bellybutton.

Dan's gum chewing grew more intense as Anthony peeled away the skin, the flaps lying freely along the outer edges of the table, the upper section practically covering her face. When Roth pulled out the bone cutter, which looked more like a pair of long curved pruning shears, Dan strolled uneasily toward the counter and joined Joshua as they uncomfortably occupied themselves with the evidence bags.

A loud cracking filled the air, as Sumi's ribs were cut and the chest plate removed. My reaction was in marked contrast to both Joshua and Dan's. I leaned in closer to Sumi's insides: almost as if I was testing myself. Death was nearly tangible to me, like the smell of raw meat smothering my face. I let it consume me.

Anthony eyed me curiously and with a mild sense of concern that I barely noticed, as he cut open the pericardial sac, but I never wavered. I watched with a fiery intensity as if all the answers lay waiting within Sumi's body cavity. Anthony removed all Sumi's organs with his precious bread knife. As he examined, weighed and took samples of each of them, the photographer documented them. Roth took the body block and placed it under her head.

I slowly turned my gaze toward Sumi's expressionless face, as I recalled the last time I had seen her alive.

Tell me about Charles Manson.

Sumi had asked me about Manson for a paper she was writing for a psychology class.

I leaned in close to her beaten face. Who did she dream about at night? What kind of goals and ideals did this young woman have? What about her hopes and dreams?

A shadow was cast over Sumi's head, and I looked up to see Anthony standing above her with a scalpel. It was time to cut away Sumi's face. My eyes were unblinking and I stepped back. He leaned over, scalpel poised, as I gasped and ran for the door.

"Ha," I heard Dan snicker. "Knew she was chicken."

But just as I stepped into the hall, I caught a glimpse of him lurching when Anthony made the incisions from ear to ear and across Sumi's crown, and peeled away her face.

* * *

48

Joshua found me halfway down the corridor, with my forehead pressed against the cold cement wall. My apron was smeared with Sumi's blood. My shoulders rose and fell with a rhythmic ease, matching the heels of his shoes clicking gently along the floor. With a soft and considerate touch, he placed a hand upon my shoulder and I moved with a start.

"Are you okay?"

My head rolled against the wall, my laughter tainted with a sharp cynicism. "I'm just like a trainee at her first autopsy."

"Except, from what I've heard, you never ran from your first autopsy." Joshua smiled and stroked the small of my back. "It's harder if you have a connection with a victim."

My eyebrows drew together and I could feel large wrinkles creasing my forehead. "Connection? What connection?"

"She was one of your students."

"Don't be ridiculous. She was one of nearly one hundred in that lecture hall. The only reason I remembered her was because we spoke briefly that afternoon."

"We've been doing good work tonight. Why don't you just take a little breather? Come back in when you're ready."

I shook my head. "No, I can't."

I slowly turned and looked back at the autopsy suite as the sound of the Stryker saw began to whir in distance.

"You were right. I looked into her eyes when they were full of life. It's never been like that before. We're not supposed to know who these people were in life. They're strangers, unfortunate victims, but always strangers."

I watched him as I felt a passion rising inside of me. My

eyes were wide and I was filled with an unwavering determination. "I want him, Joshua."

The sound of the Stryker saw grinding through bone echoed in my ears.

"And I'll get him."

Chapter Six

The *new message* light was flashing rapidly on my answering machine when I finally arrived home sometime after 2:00 in the morning. Three new messages, but I did not bother to play them. I felt drained. After the autopsy was complete, Joshua and I had grabbed some food near his hotel at the Bull Moose Saloon on West Forty-fourth Street. We spent the rest of the evening drinking and catching up with all that was happening in each other's lives.

I headed for the bedroom and kicked off my shoes before allowing my exhausted body to fall onto the bed. Kyle muttered something in his sleep about a small bit on the five and six o'clock news that may have been what I was investigating. I kissed him gently and didn't make the effort to undress before slipping into a deep and fitful sleep.

* * *

51

In the darkest corners of my mind, I envisioned bodies covered in blood and gore. Some of the corpses I recognized as victims from past cases, and I unconsciously prayed that the others were not premonitions for the future. The poor souls were crying out to me, pleading for help. People without faces, people with only half their faces. All mutilated and wronged in some monstrous way. Joshua's voice cried out from an unfamiliar face, as events from the day melded with the horrors of the night.

Professor Brantley, I need to know about Charles Manson. Please tell me about Manson, the voice of Sumi pleaded.

I felt my heart racing as I turned to run. My legs were pumping furiously, but I was not going anywhere. A face that I recognized—evil and frightful—appeared before me: begging and pleading for his life. And in my dream, I raised my Sig Sauer, the 9mm bullet tearing through his heart, the casing landing at my feet with a mocking accusation that echoed through my nightmare, just as the face of evil morphed into Joshua's dying expression.

Broken bodies hovered above me, until I could see nothing of the outside world. Nothing of *my* hopes and dreams: my ideals. All I saw were desperate victims. I collapsed into a huddled ball of despair, fists pressed up against my ears, trying to block the sounds of their pleas, but the voices only grew louder, until I slammed my hand down upon the alarm clock at my bedside.

Chapter Seven

I looked up from a small article on the discovery of Sumi's body written on the front page of Section B in *The New York Times*. The Saturday paper was always the thinnest. It had been the same case with the *Daily News*. A short, four-paragraph article on Sumi, with two pictures: a family portrait, and one of her parents looking grave as they left the Medical Examiner's Office. There had been no official news conference given by either the mayor or the NYPD, not until Monday. The weekend had bought us some time with the media.

When Joshua and I entered the Federal Building, we were required to use the non-employee entrance on Duane Street since I was technically Joshua's guest. Security was strict at the Federal Building and even tighter with the FBI.

After we passed through the revolving doors, Joshua simply waved the metal strip of his ID card over a scanner, but his cell phone set the alarms squealing and two security officers immediately descended upon him. He showed his ID, and they waved him through.

While I waited in the slow-moving non-federal employee's line, I plotted in my head how I would tactfully request an ID for myself without allowing Joshua the satisfaction of feeling that he had been right all along.

When it was my turn, I laid my purse and coat on the conveyer belt for examination under the X-ray. This morning I wore a trendy, bluish-gray light wool skirt suit. It was the new color of the season, and probably the most vibrantly colored outfit I owned. I caught up with Joshua over at Elevator Bank A. The elevators that stopped at any of the seven floors the FBI occupied were enclosed behind protective bulletproof glass.

We waited in silence for the express elevator to reception on the twenty-eighth floor.

Joshua had called me very early in the morning, a few minutes after my alarm had gone off. The NYPD had retrieved the security tapes from the apartment building of the Miyaki residence. But somehow, within four hours' time, the FBI wound up with them. The FBI held no legal right in the standard homicide case, so politics must have been involved because of Taekishi Miyaki's prominent status in the international business community, or there was something about the investigation that I was unaware of that placed it within Federal jurisdiction. Either way, the competitive and territorial lines were quickly being drawn. Dan was going to be a real pleasure today.

We stepped off the elevator, and Joshua walked over to the receptionist, who was enclosed behind a large bulletproof window. He muttered something to her, and she pointed past the main doors of the waiting area.

I looked around and inhaled deeply. It was all coming

back to me: the smells, the familiar sensation. In some bizarre way, it was almost comforting. I smiled lightly. Perhaps my stubbornness over the past two years had been more of a hindrance than a personal statement.

"There's someone I want you to see," Joshua said, as he touched the numeric keypad to the left of the main door of the reception area. Red digits popped up, and he punched in his seven-number code. The door clicked, and we exited through the glass doorway.

We walked by the main elevator bank and toward the large letters spelling out CRIMINAL DIVISION. As we turned the corner, we passed vending machines before being stonewalled by another set of secured doors.

Joshua punched in his code again, and the doors clicked open.

Blue. I had forgotten how blue everything was—royal blue, grayish blue, bluish gray. We passed by small offices and interview rooms on the left before Joshua led me into the squad room. It would have been more appropriate to call it the "squad floor." The expansive room was neatly divided into hundreds of cubicles, each with its own number assignment. Agents were paired and shared whatever workspace the royal blue partitions permitted.

The twenty-eighth floor of the Federal Building was at its usual pace for a Saturday morning. The few agents and civilian support staff, who had voluntarily sacrificed their weekend, were locked in a valiant effort to cope with the ever-growing crime rate. There was no overtime in the FBI. Everything was structured on what the government called "Availability Pay": a ten-hour minimum workday, and everything above-and-beyond was free to the government.

I followed him to the north side of the squad room, where the VCMO—Violent Crimes and Major Offenders—unit was located.

"Meredith Brantley! How the hell are you?"

My jaw fell and an enormous smile lit my face.

Cheryl Anderson was one of the few female agents with whom I'd had the pleasure of working. She had been one of the first women to receive the gold Department of Justice shield, back in the days when the Bureau was still riding on the reins of Hoover's G-*men* mentality. Recently, she had been promoted to Assistant Special Agent in Charge in the New York Office. A small, frumpy looking woman made up of mostly skin-and-bones, she looked deceptively weak and docile. But I knew from firsthand experience that Cheryl's skills with a baton were deadly, and her highest scores on the Tactical Firearms Course were within the top percentile of both male and female agents.

"I heard you became an ASAC," I said, pronouncing it *a-sack*.

I looked guiltily into the eyes of my friend. Since my hasty departure from the FBI, I had failed to maintain communications with the woman who had been such a source of mental and emotional support. One of my failures due to an inherited gene called stubbornness.

"Yes, they did. Put me with VCMO. They finally managed to make me responsible," Cheryl joked pleasantly. "Now, I hope that this handsome guy hasn't dragged you in on one of our investigations," she said, taking a playful verbal jab at Joshua.

"Hmmm," he replied with a grimace.

"The Miyaki case," I added.

Cheryl's expression darkened. "Brutal and very disturbing. Did you see the crime scene?"

I nodded. "Why is the FBI getting involved?" I asked point-blank. "The NYPD isn't known for admitting defeat so early." And then added, "They're pretty capable of doing this sort of thing."

The NYPD was one of the few agencies in the country well equipped with all the newest advances in forensic technology to handle investigations on par with the FBI. I had the greatest respect for them, even if we did not always get along.

"Okay, let me introduce you to our case agent," Cheryl said, avoiding my question as she lead the way through the maze of cubicles.

"Who is it?"

"Mackenzie Gorham," Cheryl replied.

This time it was my expression that darkened.

Chapter Eight

Agent Gorham, or Mac, as everyone called him back when we were trainees at the Academy, was hunched over his desk. He had been given the enormous task of "collaborating" with the NYPD in the Miyaki investigation. Based on what I remembered of him, it was highly unlikely that he was pleased with the situation. Wisps of reddish-blond hair fell over his weary eyes, as he attempted to make sense of who might want to murder the daughter of a prominent businessman.

As we neared I heard Dan grunt, "UNSUB," using FBI jargon for Unknown Subject. In this age of political correctness, no one ever used the term perp—only TV shows and news reporters. And even then, the perp was always "alleged to have been" something-or-other.

"Here comes fun," Dan remarked, before returning to his small Styrofoam cup of coffee and a pumpernickel bagel covered with cream cheese.

Mac's eyes narrowed as he watched "fun" approach. He looked up at Dan, who was slamming back mouthfuls of coffee before swallowing his enormous bites of bagel.

"Mac," Cheryl began, "this here is—"

"Meredith Brantley," he stated with an air of stiff formality.

I forced a polite smile as I shook his hand. "Mac, how nice to see you again."

Joshua watched us with a sharp eye, aware of the animosity that existed within the supposedly friendly introductions.

"Roll that back please," I ordered, my face only inches from the monitor.

The technician clicked on a double arrow icon for rewind.

"From there."

Everyone huddled around me, studying the black-and-white images of the Miyakis' apartment building from the previous night. Cheryl had left us to our own devices, for she was needed in a meeting with the Assistant Director. We were in a medium-sized area just off the Operations and Command Center. It was here that the small staff of civilian technicians did video imaging and other technical enhancement procedures. The four of us crowded around a frazzled technician, as we leaned against the long, narrow melamine counter.

Three monitors were playing in timed sync with each other. Monitor A was from the lobby's interior camera. Monitor B was from the main entrance's exterior camera pointing west. Monitor C pointed east. These were the last known live images of Sumi.

In the path of the black-and-white camera Sumi was seen from behind, walking west toward Fifth Avenue. Her clothes: dark slacks, turtleneck and a dark three-quarter-length blazer-type jacket, were clean and undamaged.

"The coat's unaccounted for at the crime scene," I stated, watching the time counter speed through numbers in the lower right corner of the monitor.

Sumi left her apartment at 9:14. If Anthony's time of death was correct, there was approximately one hour and forty-five minutes of Sumi's life left unaccounted for. It was within this window of time that all the answers were hidden.

"Back to the same spot again," I requested of the technician.

Everyone watched for the fifth time as the doors opened on the third of three elevators, and Sumi stepped off and into the camera's path.

I marked the time of 9:12 on a yellow legal pad.

"So," Dan was blunt. "Got a profile?" He aggressively chewed on a wad of gum, staring at the monitors as if the Yankees were playing the final inning in the World Series—again.

"White male, mid-twenties to late-thirties," Joshua rattled off the beginnings of a standard and basic profile; one that he had used many times in the last seven years.

I shot him a look, uncertain if he was serious or merely taking a jab at Dan's impatience. In this instance, there was no basis for these observations, yet.

"Yeah, but how's that gonna help us catch him?" Dan spit his gum toward a trash can a couple of feet away, where it bounced off the rim and onto the floor. "Hey, don't these guys usually hang around the investigations?"

I looked away from the monitor and stared into Dan's dark eyes.

"Well, have you finally accepted that you have a serial killer in New York City?" I said.

Dan shrugged. "I've dealt with a lot of homicides. It's always shoot and get the hell out of there. No one wastes time playing."

I looked away. For someone who looks to abuse his victim, there was always time.

"So, yeah, *maybe* it's a serial killer." He turned to the monitors. "But this could just be victim number one."

Joshua shook his head wearily, and I rolled my eyes. There *had* to be prior victims. "When is Sumi being buried?" he asked.

"Don't know. The body's being released on Monday."

"When you find out when a service is being held, it would be wise to add surveillance around her gravesite."

The counter on the monitors advanced one minute, while Sumi nodded to the doorman standing behind a marble counter—an enormous ledger spread out before him—and exited through the revolving doors of the main entrance. The doorman followed her out to the sidewalk.

It was at this point that everyone focused on monitor B: the exterior camera pointing west toward Central Park.

The doorman said something to Sumi. From his mannerisms and posture, it was clear that he was being nothing but professional. He took a step toward the curb and tried to hail a cab. But Sumi held up her hand and continued to walk across East Sixty-eighth Street toward Central Park. At this hour, the area was moderately trafficked with pedestrians. Sumi did not appear to be in any kind of danger. She paused briefly to adjust the collar on her coat and then continued on her way and disappeared out of the camera's view before reaching Fifth Avenue.

The doorman watched her for a moment and went back inside. In the first monitor, he was seen returning to his desk. Behind him, on the intricately mirrored wall, multiple images of his figure reflected from varying angles like a surrealistic Escher etching. Hundreds of doormen moved in unison as he answered the phone, looked out this way or that way. His head was buried in the ledger for most of the time, except for a moment when he looked up and out toward the front door. At another point, he answered the phone, but the conversation lasted all of six seconds. Twenty minutes passed before anyone else passed by his station.

"It's a pretty clear image," I remarked.

"Yeah, not bad," the technician agreed. "I've seen worse. I guess when you got the money to live in a ritzy building like that, you're hoping that management installed a halfway decent piece of technology." He grunted. "Most of the time people have security cameras, but no tape, or if they do, it's five years old."

"Well, what do you make of it?" Mac asked.

"Sumi doesn't appear to be leaving in any kind of hurried or agitated state," Joshua replied. "She looks confident and comfortable with wherever she's going."

"Has anyone interviewed the doorman?"

"Not yet," Dan replied quickly, trying to maintain his position in the investigation. "It's too early. We'll get him when he comes on duty. Building management said he comes on in an hour. I was going to go over and talk to the parents today."

"I'd like to be a part of those interviews," I said, addressing Dan directly.

He blinked, caught off guard by my suddenly amicable attitude. "Uh, sure."

Perhaps a few hours of sleep had done us all a bit of good. Or more to the point, we were all present in the tiny room filled with gadgets and doohickies on an early Saturday morning for one reason alone: to find a monster.

I watched the monitors. "Why would a wealthy young woman not take a cab? What would make her feel so inclined to walk at that hour?"

"Maybe she got one on Fifth?" Mac offered. "She'd have a better chance there than on a street on the East Side."

"It's a possibility."

"Besides, walking at that hour isn't so out of the ordinary. It was a nice evening. Maybe she just wanted to enjoy it."

The counter now read 9:58. I focused on the exterior camera. "Wait a minute."

I studied the street, the shadows, and the shapes. Black-and-white images, no matter how expensive the camera, were difficult for the human eye to adjust to, especially footage shot within the dark of the night.

Joshua moved in closer. "What is it?"

"Go back to 9:14," I said to the technician.

Because he had indexed it, that part of the footage appeared almost instantaneously.

"Watch the west exterior monitor," I directed of everyone.

It was the same thing as before.

I held up my hand, prone in a signaling position. "Get ready. When I tell you, freeze the image."

Four seconds passed and Sumi was seen walking away from the building as the doorman watched.

"Now!"

The image became slightly blurred when he froze the frame.

I pointed to the lower left corner of the monitor,

where the camera picked up the other side of the street. "Watch here. Okay, go ahead."

Two seconds passed and a dark blobby image appeared, advancing along the sidewalk. As it moved farther into the camera's frame, it became more defined: a figure in a long dark coat, passing through the shadows.

"Go back. All views."

We all watched as the familiar events played out backwards. People moved in and out of the path of the exterior cameras.

I grunted as I watched both exterior cameras' footage. "This figure seems to just pop up into the west camera. He's not in the east's view."

Joshua pointed to the lower part of monitor B. "It's very dark. He might not be seen because of the shadows from the opposite apartment building on the south side of the street."

"Okay, forward."

The technician let the video play out normally.

"Joshua, watch him, I'm checking the clock."

Sumi paused and adjusted her collar. I read the clock, and hadn't realized it before but it was for more than just a moment.

"He stopped," Mac stated in disbelief.

"And then he just picks right back up again when she starts moving," Joshua declared shaking his head. "He's following her."

My stare focused heavily on the monitor. "Sumi paused to adjust her coat for thirteen seconds."

The dark figure had lingered in the shadows for thirteen seconds.

"Unlucky thirteen," Dan quipped.

I watched as the dark figure disappeared out of the frame. "And so the hunt begins."

Chapter Nine

MURDER RATE AT ALL-TIME LOW IN 30 YEARS. I was staring at the front page of *The New York Times* lying on my
lap, a sourdough bagel resting on top of a color photograph of the police commissioner addressing a news conference. I knew that there was irony to be found
somewhere in the headline, but right now I was too edgy
to concentrate on looking for it

"I really hate it when they cake on the cream cheese
like that," Joshua sputtered. As he exhaled, and his lower
lip vibrated.

We were stopped at a red light on Twenty-third and Park
Avenue, both of us desperately trying to spread cream
cheese in equal amounts onto both halves of our bagels.

"I know," I said, taking Joshua's when the light
changed. "There's nothing like a New York bagel, but I
hate that they always spread a pound of cream cheese to
just one side."

"Thanks."

A horn blared behind us, when Joshua failed to step on the gas *exactly* as the light turned green. "Jesus! How can you stand to live in this city?"

"I don't drive," I replied with my lips tightly pressed into a grin.

"So," he tentatively asked, "what do you think?"

"I think that we should go to a different deli next time," I said, struggling to keep most of the cream cheese on the bagels and off my suit.

"Maybe I'll get the Danish next time," he said, focusing once again on driving. "What do you think about the investigation?"

"That was a little risky starting a profile so soon."

"What profile? There was nothing to it."

"Precisely my point."

"It was just basic stuff. The same old workhorse."

I glanced at him sideways. "Don't make light of this—"

"I wasn't."

I rapped my knuckles against my window, because I knew it would irritate him.

There were two schools of thought when creating a criminal profile: Basing your findings by studying the crime scene of the current investigation, or using what has been learned from violent offenders in the past. In a perfect world we could find a happy medium and use both. But with caseloads piling up at an exponential rate and budget cuts mandating a hiring freeze, all that could be afforded was a one- or two-week time investment on site, per investigation, per agent. And oftentimes that kind of commitment was a luxury. Most cases only merited a one-page fax from the sterile surroundings of an agent's office in Virginia. Joshua and I were often at odds on the approach. I liked the happy medium, and he preferred making a dent in the three large stacks of files consuming his desk.

"Sumi was an A student." I paused. "I think."

I really couldn't remember. Ninety-eight students in my lecture hall, I could barely remember half of the names.

A large chunk of cream cheese plopped upon my knee, and Joshua reached over and gently wiped it away with a coarse napkin, three of his fingertips rubbing lightly against my thigh. A chill fell over me and we were suddenly overwhelmed with an uncomfortable silence.

I unconsciously tugged on the hem of my skirt, but there was no extra fabric. I immediately regretted my choice in wardrobe for the day.

"Either way, we need to look at the evidence, know who our victim is," I said.

Joshua stared at me. I was avoiding the situation. Running, as I was so keen on doing. He opened his mouth, but thankfully, caught himself. I was in no mood to have my head analyzed, or to talk about my feelings. And I most certainly did not want to talk about *us*.

We had only driven three blocks and were now stopped in midday traffic gridlock. I looked out my window, observing a group of men on the street corner selling faux designer handbags and sunglasses. Somewhere nearby a police siren blurted out a short squeal, and the unlicensed vendors quickly pulled up the corners of their blankets, ready to gather their wares and flee at a moment's notice.

Nothing was ever what it seemed.

Chapter Ten

The Miyaki residence was in no way modest. The penthouse apartment covered one entire floor of the renovated pre-World War II building. We stepped off the private elevator into an enormous foyer that easily matched the total square footage of my own apartment. A maid greeted us with a polite smile and offered to take our coats, which we graciously declined. She led us down a dimly lit hallway, where the walls were graced with precisely hung abstract paintings. Small, narrow tables displayed sculptures and vases, which I was positive I could never afford. Taekishi Miyaki's love for art was obviously important in his life.

The maid led us into a gargantuan living room where Mac and Dan were already waiting. The furniture, all modern, was imposing so I opted to remain standing. The bright midday sun cut sharply through the vertical blinds like jail bars. The mood in the room was far from dreary, but less than inviting. Taekishi had selected and arranged the décor with precision and purpose. There was no mistaking that this was not a home where one was to feel comfortable or relaxed. It was clear that this was the domain of a precise and commanding person.

"Hello. Excuse me," a quiet voice said.

Everyone's gaze followed the light voice, and we were met by a small, frail-looking woman.

Tae Miyaki was a sweet, middle-aged woman with a soft, high-pitched voice that floated and peaked like meringue. Her delicate features were heightened by her unblemished olive-colored skin, which was offset by thick, shiny jet-black hair streaked with silver.

"I am. Sorry." Her syllables and cadences were broken by her accent.

"Mrs. Miyaki?" I asked, recognizing her from the other night.

"Yes." She bowed graciously, and I thoughtlessly extended my hand. Tae's tiny hand trembled slightly as I held it within my grasp.

My face washed over in a wave of pity. Even Tae's hands seemed sad. "I'm Meredith Brantley. Your husband was expecting us."

"Yes. Sorry. He will be. Soon," Tae said, as she nodded politely. "Please. Sit."

I sat near Joshua on what I considered to be the most inviting chair in the stark room. The cushions of the armchair were firm, and I was surprised to find that I didn't sink into them. The back rose high above my head and arched into a stiff impractical headrest.

"May I offer. Drink?" Tae asked of everyone.

A chorus of, "No, thank you," politely declined the hospitable gesture.

"Please, Mrs. Miyaki, will you sit with us?" Mac asked.

The older woman contemplated her decision as if she were determining whether this would be a socially suitable course of action.

"Thank you," she said, sitting on a dark green couch that looked as if it had never been sat on before.

Her hands were folded gently in her lap and her legs—crossed at the ankles—hung stiffly over the edge of the couch, with her toes far from touching the floor. Even as she sat, Tae seemed refined in the way she presented herself. Only Taekishi's collection of fine statues could compare to his wife's presence.

"Hello," Taekishi said from the archway of the living room.

Tae sprang up from the couch as if the cushions had catapulted her into the air.

Everyone else followed, politely greeting our host.

"Why don't you leave me and our guests, so that we may conduct our business," Taekishi said to his wife, more as an order than a request.

Tae obeyed as she quickly—and quietly—left for another part of the enormous apartment.

Taekishi walked to the large landscape-sized window. The light streaked across his ominous expression in dramatic lines.

"She is a gentle flower, like our daughter is"—he stopped himself—"Was."

I caught Dan's cynical grin, and could practically hear his thoughts. *Just like a fucking karate movie.*

"Mr. Miyaki, we'd like to speak with both of you," Dan said, crossing his arms, his wrinkled suit protesting under the movement.

Taekishi still stared out the window, his voice distant, his words almost scripted. "My wife and I had no idea that our daughter had left. My wife was sleeping, and I was reading in my study. And I have no idea where she was going."

"Could you maybe give us a—"

"I couldn't even begin to speculate. Beverly will show you the room."

Dan threw Mac an irritated look, and I knew what sort of scenarios they were all creating, because I couldn't deny that the thoughts hadn't briefly passed through my mind: an uncooperative parent, a murdered child, who was a self-mutilator, oftentimes in response to sexual abuse. I studied Taekishi's lean silhouette more closely. It was difficult to judge how a parent would react. Some of the guilty are uncooperative, some are very helpful, and it is the same for the innocent. People are different and there are no rules, only instinct. My instincts hadn't marked Taekishi a suspect—yet.

The maid who had met us at the elevator was now standing in the archway of the living room. She stepped aside to allow the train of investigators to pass.

"How come you don't join the others?" Taekishi turned from the window.

"I wanted to speak to you in private." I quietly cleared my throat. "I was one of Sumi's professors."

He sat with a gracefulness reminiscent of an era long forgotten, when the gentlemen who wore three-piece suits carried elegant walking sticks. But his eye traveled the length of my bare calf and thigh. I lowered myself back into the strange chair and crossed my legs. It was hardly a lascivious gaze, but one that made me uneasy. I tugged on the corner of my skirt, unable to discern whether his look was of admiration or disapproval.

"You don't look like a chemist or a mathematician, so you must be the psychologist."

I nodded, but my expression was blank.

"On extended leave of absence from the FBI."

My eyebrows arched.

"I checked out all my daughter's professors before she ever enrolled in a class." He pursed his lips. "I am a very powerful businessman, and security is of utmost importance to me and my family."

"Your wife, her hands shake."

"But today you are a psychologist." He gently rubbed his upper lip as if smoothing out a non-existent mustache. "She is not taking our daughter's death very well."

"And how about you?" I asked, as he unsuccessfully dodged my gaze.

Taekishi thought for a moment. "If I say that I am not doing well, that makes me a weak man. I cannot afford to be a weak man. If I say that I am fine and life goes on, that portrays me as a cold-hearted person. Believe me, I am not a cold-hearted person."

He slowly ran a fingertip down the long edge of his lapel. A gold cufflink weighed down by a raised letter *N* for Noyitsu, his multi-million dollar financial investment company, glistened when it passed through a sliver of light.

"She changed when she went to the university. We tried to get her help, but sometimes there are things that go on inside your child's mind that not even a parent can mend." Taekishi's almost black eyes glistened in the small amount of light that filled the room. "That's a feeling of powerlessness."

I studied him with an intensity that even surprised myself.

And Mr. Miyaki, do you thrive on power and the powerlessness of others?

72

Chapter Eleven

Sumi's large room was noticeably different from the rest of the Miyaki home. The light walnut furniture was polished to perfection against the backdrop of faint rose-colored wallpaper. Pale peach drapes hung voluminously from enormous windows, which in the day offered the natural brilliance of sunlight, and later the romance of moonlight. On the walls hung Sumi's many awards and achievements; her hopes and dreams displayed proudly behind the protective shield of glass. It was the room of a young girl as she approached womanhood with her arms wide open to all that was offered her.

Joshua handed me a pair of gloves, and I played with the Latex, stretching it over my long fingers. Dan and Mac had already gone through most of Sumi's possessions, and they continued with disinterested expressions on their faces. There was nothing to evoke excitement in them, no skeletons rattling in her closet. In the center of the floor, a couple of items had been placed on top of one another. Letters and handwritten notes that they felt might serve as clues when more was known.

I made my way over to Sumi's desk. Paper clips were meticulously placed in a smoke-colored acrylic box. Clean stacks of index cards, blank envelopes and note cards lined the sides of the drawers. Even this motley collection of miscellaneous items was neatly organized. I found myself curious, wondering if this was the true personality of the young woman, or merely her parents' interpretation of how they wished to remember her. As I carefully removed items, I inspected every inch of the underside of the drawers and desk. A good investigator quickly learns that people will hide things in whatever nooks and crannies are available to them. One time I had found a letter—a near confession—taped to the underside of a recently "widowed" woman's kitchen table.

"Did that already," Joshua said, peering up from a spiral notebook, "but you should read this."

He handed me the dog-eared notebook.

I carefully turned the pages and immediately recognized the scribbled notes from the final conversation that I had with Sumi.

So if he didn't actually do the murders, then why does everyone think he's more of a psycho than the people who really did the killing? Sumi had asked. When she spoke, her voice rose into higher pitched squeals. *Why is he in jail?*

Most people like Manson aren't psychotic. In fact they are highly intelligent and quite aware of their actions.

Sumi had difficulty grasping the subtle, yet important difference.

Being diagnosed as having psychotic behavior means that you suffer from a mental disorder. It impairs your contact with reality. It's an actual disease.

Okay.

Now, on the other hand, if you're a psychopath or sociopath, then you have a character disorder. Somewhere during the developmental stage, your mind failed to create a conscience.

So are you saying that people like Manson don't know what they're doing is wrong?

Sociopaths most definitely know right from wrong. They know that they'll get into trouble and they know why; they just don't care. They never learned to love, so they are not capable of responding in that manner.

My reminiscing suddenly stopped short. I had picked up a framed photo of Sumi standing with one of her friends. Sumi was a beautiful young woman. Smooth, flawless complexion like her mother and high cheekbones like her father. The sunlight glistened off her jet-black hair.

"He hated her beauty," I said aloud. "The UNSUB concentrated most of the beating to her face and upper body. He hated her beauty."

Professor Brantley? Sumi said quietly in my thoughts, as she tilted her head sideways. She did do that, didn't she? The more curious she was, the more she tilted her head. *Are you okay?*

I blinked quickly, trying to wash away the intrusive image. "Yeah, I'm okay," I whispered quietly.

"Good."

I looked up with a start.

Joshua was standing next to me looking at the photo. "I think we're done here."

I placed the photograph on the desk where I had found it. "Did you find the coat?"

Mac's eyes narrowed. "The coat?"

"The one that she would've been wearing last night."

He opened the closet door and brushed his hand over

four dark coats that were stuffed within Sumi's mostly black wardrobe. "And how would one tell if one of these was *the* coat?" he remarked smartly.

I went over to him and shoved my hands into the pockets of each coat. "If one of them had her house keys or, let's say," my voice rose, "blood."

He scowled at me.

My hand emerged with a faded plastic orange wristband. It appeared worn, as if it had been to the dry cleaners one time too many.

"That's assuming the killer didn't take it," Joshua commented.

"Or that she came back here before somehow finding her way over to the West Side," Mac added.

I placed the orange wristband back into the pocket and stated with a biting snarl, "Or that the UNSUB didn't return the coat to hide the evidence in plain sight."

There was a gleam in Dan's eyes as he pulled off his gloves. He was beginning to like the way that I was thinking, and that annoyed me to no end.

Sociopaths, Sumi said slowly. Her eyebrows grew closer together in a frown of concern. *How can people be so stupid? How can they fall for—*

When you look at someone like Hitler, what do you see?

A psycho! He killed not just Jews, but anyone he thought was weaker.

But Hitler, like Manson, was intelligent and charming. He was in the right place at the right time. Race wars continue to this day. Turn on the TV and you see religious and racial "cleansing" being exacted.

It's not the same.

How's that?

Hitler killed millions!

Is killing thousands any more justifiable than killing mil-

lions? Just one Jew had to have been murdered before millions could've.

That's not what I meant.

Did Hitler kill the Jews? He was just one man. He only suc-ceeded in convincing highly educated people to commit mass murder.

But he was their leader. If he wasn't dead, then they would've continued on with the genocide.

And that's why Charles Manson is in prison.

I followed everyone out—the tattered notebook tucked beneath my arm—as I quietly and gently closed the door to Sumi's bedroom.

Chapter Twelve

Raoul scanned our four faces as if we were trying to play some sick, morbid prank. "No, Miss Miyaki didn't come back."

He stood proudly behind the gray Italian marble built up into a chest-high counter that swirled into an elegant arch, creating an almost defensive perimeter around the middle-aged man. The guest ledger was open before him, and Raoul managed to keep it beyond striking distance of either Dan or Mac's eye.

"What time you get off work?" Dan asked as he sidled up to the counter.

Raoul cleared his throat in a pretentious manner. "I work until midnight, every night."

"Those are long hours. Even for a doorman."

"I've got a family to support."

Joshua nudged Dan aside, and there was a slight moment of tension as they traded confrontational looks.

I stepped back and withdrew from the scene. I would just be an observer. There were too many stupid male egos involved.

"Mr. Ortiz," Joshua began.

Raoul looked up.

"Did Sumi—Miss Miyaki—appear nervous or excited that evening?"

"No."

"Did she often leave late at night?"

"I'm not her keeper, and nine-thirty doesn't seem very late."

Mac motioned toward the ledger. "Can I have a look at that?"

Raoul hesitated at first, but begrudgingly spun the enormous book to face him. Mac flipped the pages back to a few hours before Sumi left the building.

"Do you keep track of everyone who comes and goes?"

"No, just the guests. They have to sign in."

I watched in the mirrors covering the opposite wall as Dan whipped out a small leather notebook and began scribbling names and times. Mac followed suit, as if not wanting to be outdone by a cop.

"How come Ms. Miyaki didn't want to take a cab last night?" Joshua asked in a kind tone.

Raoul shrugged. "She said something about getting there faster on foot."

"Do you know where *there* was?"

He stiffened protectively. "It's not my place to know their business."

Dan looked at him askance.

"I know that you look after the people living here." Joshua's tone remained friendly and gentle. "But we're only here to figure out what happened to Sumi."

Raoul shook his head. "They don't tell me anything, and I never ask."

Beyond the duties spelled out in his contract, the only relationship that Raoul had with the residents was the occasional "hello," "thank you" and the two hundred dollars in cash he received from each of them, stuffed into fancy linen envelopes at Christmastime.

Joshua nodded and looked around briefly before stepping over to where I was on the opposite side of the lobby, standing next to an enormous tree-like plant.

"Clever." He smiled at me with admiration.

"What?"

"A fly on the wall?"

I grinned impishly. "A fly can learn a lot."

Joshua chortled. "But they have such a brief life span." He looked up toward the cornice. "And all out of the security camera's view."

"This is a beautiful building," I said, tracing the outline of the intricate moulding with my eye. I pointed to the ornamentation framing the mirrors. "Gold leafing. It's very expensive. Kyle's a designer. I've picked up a couple of things here and there."

Joshua scrunched his face into a mock look of contemplation. "Aren't interior decorators supposed to be gay?"

"You're a riot. He's a graphic artist. He does advertising."

"Same thing."

I rolled my eyes and sighed.

"Would you just look at those two," he said as he watched Mac and Dan's reflection in the mirror.

Their pens moved at a fevered pace, each trying to outduel the other.

Joshua lowered his head and watched his feet as he shuffled them against the gray marble floor. "So what's this about a young woman asking you about Charles Manson?"

My mouth dropped. "I never said anything about that."

"You were muttering to yourself upstairs. Don't worry, not loud enough for them to hear," he added, pointing over his shoulder when he caught my look of concern.

"Sumi came to me for some help."

"Kind of a bizarre line of questioning for a young woman studying chemistry or business."

"She was in my class, she was studying criminology as well."

Joshua looked at me. "A basic sociology class. The statistical science of crime and society, not violent killers who slaughter."

I tilted my head back. "Joshua, I can remember when I was ten. I went to the public library and picked up a yellowed paperback of *Helter Skelter*. I hid between two shelves of history books and read the whole thing in one afternoon. It was scary, it seemed dangerous, but it was captivating."

"I know, I read it, too."

I looked him straight in the eye. "Then who are we to brand Sumi because she asked me about Manson?"

"We're not. The only thing that raises concern is that she asked those questions and nine hours later she was dead." His voice began to rise. "She obviously had things going on in her life that she couldn't handle. She left the evidence on her arms."

I frowned and turned slightly from him. The psychologist in me understood the clinical reasons why a young woman would mutilate herself, but the non-professional in me found it difficult to accept that a person could do such a thing. Just as I found it difficult to accept that a person could inflict the same kind of pain on another. From a psychological standpoint, these young women who hurt themselves were driven almost by the same pathological instincts: Pathological Obsessiveness was the clinical term. Similar in the pathological disorder as violent killer, but there was something slightly more sympathetic toward those who abused themselves rather than others.

"There was something going on in her life," I agreed, nodding my head firmly as I stared straight ahead at my own reflection. "But whether it had anything to do with her death, we can't begin to make such assumptions."

The lobby was suddenly overcome with a rush of people coming and going in a steady stream, and Raoul attempted desperately to keep track of who was a resident and who was a guest. I observed in the mirrors as the images of those passing through the lobby quickly became indecipherable, a scene that seemed strikingly familiar. Everyone's image reflected and multiplied. It was difficult to discern who was coming and going. When things finally calmed down, Raoul angrily pulled the ledger away to write in the names of those who were visiting.

"We're not done," Dan said flatly as he spun the ledger back toward himself.

"Joshua?" I said in an empty tone.

"I know what you're thinking," he replied quickly as we stared, unable to move from our position in front of the mirrored wall.

"What if the stranger didn't come from the shadows around the corner?" My eyes were unblinking. "What if he came from inside this building?"

Chapter Thirteen

The thick, corn syrupy filling stretched itself as if it were making a last desperate attempt at keeping the tart intact.

"A pound of sugar for lunch?" I dabbed at my lower lip, indicating to Joshua where specks of white frosting stubbornly clung. "What flavor?"

"Chocolate."

"Frosted?"

"Of course," he answered, as if anything different would be a sacrilege.

I crammed my hand into the box. "Gimme one."

It was well past lunch and the sugary treat appeared to be the closest thing to nourishment we'd be seeing.

Joshua smiled. "They've got a microwave by the coffee if you want."

I shook my head. "They're better straight out of the package." My lower lip extended in a successful attempt at keeping the enormous bite of pastry from escaping my mouth.

It was a different technician from before, and he moved with an almost slow-motion quality that caused me to fidget anxiously. He struggled clumsily with a power button on one of the monitors, and no longer able to restrain myself, I leaned over and impatiently turned on the monitor. The technician threw me an offended look and with his thumbnail scratched away some chocolate residue from the beige exterior of the monitor, before calling up the file of the security footage.

"How far do we need to go back?" Mac asked as he leaned in toward monitor C.

I pushed myself into the huddle. "It depends on whether he was waiting for her, or if he followed her."

The section where the UNSUB was visible played out before us.

"This is some sick shit," Dan said as he leaned back and pulled out three sticks of gum.

I watched as he rolled them into one marble-sized ball and gingerly tossed it into his mouth. I decided right then and there, that one day I would have to find out what was going on inside his odd little mind.

Dan's words were garbled at first as his jaw worked feverishly at softening his little treat. "I mean, I've got my theories about the old guy. And I won't lie about him striking the wrong chord in me. But stalking your kid? That's fucked."

The left side of my mouth puckered. *Yeah, it was fucked.*

Mac cautiously studied everyone. "So are we figuring it's the father?"

Like a Saturday morning cartoon, I could see the arrest warrant reflecting in his eyes.

Joshua confidently leaned back in his chair. "If we determine that he's coming from the building, then anyone living there is a strong possibility. It could be a neighbor. Basically, someone who lives nearby and sees her every day."

"Maybe the missus on stilts." Dan let out a boisterous laugh that filled the room and drowned out the sounds of the electronic equipment humming in the background.

I spun my chair around and faced the monitor. "Start it from 9:10, just before Sumi is exiting the building."

The tapes played and I concentrated on monitor C, the east view. The figure never appeared.

"Again." This time I concentrated on the shadows, but he never appeared in the camera. "And again. This time we'll check monitor A."

Everyone pressed their faces closer to the interior camera monitor. Sumi passed in and out of the frame, where she then appeared outside, but no one cared anymore. Our focus was on the lobby. Raoul followed her out. No one else passed. No one was reflected in the mirrors. The section of tape was played five times more.

"Okay, there's a couple of explanations for this," Mac said with a tone that rang victoriously as he pointed at me with a stiff index finger. "The main one being that *you're* completely off-base with this theory of the spooky man in the dark coat coming from inside the building."

And I thought that he was looking for any excuse to arrest Taekishi.

Undaunted, I wheeled my chair as close to the monitor as I could, the edge of the countertop cutting into my rib cage. "Can you do a frame-by-frame?"

The technician snorted. "Of course."

"Go to 9:10, and advance it one frame at a time."

He raised his eyebrows. Four minutes of footage, one

frame at a time under strict scrutiny would take close to an hour.

At 9:10, Raoul was staring off into space. By 9:12, he had signed in one guest and opened the door for a young woman resident and her infant son returning home for the night. The frames advanced slowly like a cartoon book that children play with, flipping the pages awkwardly to create motion in the characters. Raoul picked up the phone, for the first time, his face buried in some papers other than the guest ledger. In slow motion, his body twisted to the left toward the elevator bank and then back to the papers. And it was there, at that point, once Raoul's attention was focused again on his paperwork, that I yelped out loud.

"Stop!"

Without hesitating the technician smacked two fingers against the button of his mouse, pausing the frame.

"Look, look, look!" Like a child, I bounced up and down in my seat as I poked my finger against the glass of the monitor, leaving more chocolate smudges that the technician, clearly irritated, wiped away.

"What?" Joshua leaned in and shoved his glasses up against his face.

"Look in the mirror. We missed him before because of that stupid plant."

One ear and the upper shoulder of a dark figure passing under the camera, out of its view and out of Raoul's protective eye, moved with a long stride, visible only in the mirror, slowed down in a frame-by-frame advance. Everyone quickly scooted over to monitors B and C. He never reappeared until he was seen stepping out of the shadows, following Sumi.

"Creepy." Mac shivered.

"Can you freeze and enhance one of those images?" I asked the technician.

"I can try."

He replayed the five frames and found one that seemed to be the most likely candidate for successful enhancement.

"I can sharpen, define, or blur," he said to anyone who would listen. "Pretty much anything. I could even add more suspects if you want," he said with a laugh.

We all squinted at him.

I stared at the resulting image of the stranger magnified to three hundred percent and sharpened. "This is worse than the original."

"The guy obviously doesn't want to be seen," the technician said defensively.

"I thought you said you could enhance this."

"Images are made of pixels"—he eyed me—"tiny squares. You can do what you can, but in the end they're still squares."

He exhaled quickly, discarded the altered image, and started from scratch. "I'll magnify it less, and I'll sharpen it a smaller percentage. That will get rid of the blocky quality."

The figure was now more visible. His right arm was raised and slightly covering his face. I focused on the arm covering his face.

"Can you magnify this?" I drew a square on the monitor around his face and right arm.

The technician shrugged and selected the magnification tool from one of the software program's floating palettes. He drew a dotted box around the area and clicked. The face and arm doubled in size and was beginning to become blocky. But I was focused on the square shape on the wrist.

"Magnify this again," I ordered sternly.

"It'll only be worse than—"

"Just do it."

He was right, it was worse, but I was not interested in the face anymore.

"Sharpen it."

He did, but quickly selected "undo."

"Wait a minute," he said with excitement. "I've got a better idea. Let me add some noise."

"Won't that make it worse?" Mac asked.

"Just watch. Sometimes you've got to fill in what's not there." He selected the command from the pull down menu. "Distribution: gaussian," he muttered, clicking the radio button with his mouse. "And monochratic at—let's see—eleven percent should do it."

Surprise, surprise, through the wonders of science and computer technology the program filled in the missing information.

Everyone stared at the screen as the area selected revealed the image of a square cufflink marked with a letter *N*.

Chapter Fourteen

When I finally arrived home, my mind was reeling from the day's events, but I climbed the steps to my second floor apartment with surprising calm. The sun had all but disappeared into the evening, and so had my spirits. I had hoped that the light of suspicion would have quickly dimmed on Taekishi, but it had only brightened. No investigator likes to believe that a parent could be a suspect in the murder of their own child. It was proven fact that the majority of victims are indeed murdered by people they know, but mutilation is not usually in the equation. All my training and instinct was telling me that the scenario was absurd, yet we had no explanation for Taekishi's somewhat suspect behavior.

Kyle wasn't at home, which at the moment, suited me fine. He had left a beautifully printed note next to my growing pile of mail. He had a meeting with a client and needed to spend the rest of the weekend preparing. I could call him at his apartment on the Upper West Side. I read the note again. He had the most anal-retentive lettering I had ever seen. It was precise, clean and machine-like: a style attributed to his art school training.

I slipped out of my skirt and into a baggy sweatshirt and jeans, before ordering dinner from my expansive collection of menus. I hated cooking, and mutilating vegetables didn't count for any kind of culinary expertise. But I loved to eat, and the spicier the better. In twenty minutes my apartment smelled of Lemon Grass Duck, Burmese handmade bread and spiced potatoes. With a glass of White Zinfandel in hand, I headed toward the stereo. I needed something soothing like Gianni Schiccii, but opted for an En Vogue CD I had inherited from my brother. I curled up on the couch with my meal as the Funky Divas sang out in a roaring harmony: *Free your mind and the rest will follow.*

My head fell against the back of the seat cushion. *Free my mind.*

There was something so familiar about the crime scene and the disposition of Sumi's body, and not because it reminded me of another homicide or that I had seen it somewhere it one of my nightmares. The way her arms were displayed struck me as being a lot more precise than I had originally thought. What was the meaning? What did the arms mean to the offender? I closed my eyes and the strange markings on Sumi's body burned themselves onto the inside of my eyelids.

I sprang from the couch and marched double-time back to my bedroom, the corner of a black-and-white eight-by-ten photo clasped between my forefinger and thumb. I dove into the back of my closet, stretching over boxes of shoes I had bought but never wore, until I emerged with a steel lockbox. My arm bounced in the air as I remembered the weight. After dropping the box on top of my bed, I carefully laid the 1:1 scaled photo of one of the markings on Sumi's face beside it. I hesitated a moment, wondering if I could remember the combination to the box, but my fingers instinctively spun the steel rollers to the proper numbers, and the latch clicked inside. I stared at the dark gray polymer with the intense curiosity of a young child. My Sig Sauer 228 hadn't seen the light of day since I turned in my FBI issued model.

These days, the new agents were given the Colt 1911 Government Issue—a custom design manufactured specially for the FBI. Two years ago, Joshua had voluntarily switched to the Glock 23 when the FBI had transferred over its sidearm contract from Sig Sauer. I think he was tired of the constant change and decided to keep the Glock, a sleek weapon that Hollywood always used for its props. But if I was required to have a weapon, I liked my Sig. It was reliable, and very rarely malfunctioned. A 9mm couldn't inflict the same damage as the Glock's .40 caliber or knock a person over like the Colt's .45, but it was never my desire to maim others.

I had never been a huge fan of guns. I had witnessed far too many tragedies that were the result of handguns. A special agent's weapon was unfortunately a necessary evil that accompanied the job description. While working for the Behavioral Sciences Unit, I only had to draw my gun three times, but regulations required that every FBI agent carry a sidearm, and four times a year agents had to prove their skill on the firing range.

Quickly, I loaded one of the two fifteen-round magazines, which hung slightly below the grip designed for thirteen-rounds. A semi-automatic could be a dangerous weapon in many ways. I raised it directly above the photo and slowly lowered it against the strange marking.

"Damn," I muttered. Not a Glock and not a Sig.

It was the right shape; however, the butt of the Sig was about an eighth of an inch too wide. It did not mean that Dan was wrong, though. There was no standard width for a gun's grip, and every manufacturer designed theirs differently. But more troubling to me, was the fact that I still found no explanation for why it had broken the skin along the rounded curve of the "U."

I brought the 9mm and the photo into the kitchen and began rummaging through the cupboards and then the refrigerator. All I had were frozen entrees and jarred condiments. My eye caught sight of what remained of my dinner. I hovered over the duck, Sig Sauer poised before bringing it down with as much hated force as I could. Grease and sauce squirted all over my clothes and pieces of meat shot out across the living room, clinging to the walls and furniture. But I was oblivious to the mess, staring at the familiar shape before me.

Still, no U-shaped cut.

Frustrated that I was now back to square one, I turned the gun over and inspected the juicy mess stuck within the grooves of the grip and up inside the butt. It would take me hours to clean it. My thumb flicked the magazine release and it slid out easily. I stared up into the hollow inside and grimaced at the disaster I had created. But my frown quickly turned to astonishment as I ran my fingertip along the *sharp* edges along the underside of the grip, now empty of the magazine.

I quickly scurried across the living room carpet and reached for what remained of the duck. It was a big enough piece. Taking into account Sumi's position on the pier, I raised the weapon and brought it down upon the unsuspecting food. Carefully, I removed the butt embedded within the mutilated food.

And there it was: the rounded part of the U-shaped cut.

Chapter Fifteen

My fingers banged out the Miyakis' home phone number with such a force that some of the buttons stuck, which only succeeded in making me more impatient. Beverly answered, but said that the Miyakis had retired for the evening.

"Tell them it's Agent"—I caught myself—"Professor Brantley."

She returned shortly thereafter with the same apologetic response. It wasn't until I "advised" her that with the automatic redial button their phone would be ringing incessantly throughout the evening that Mr. Miyaki spoke to me.

He hardly sounded as if he had been dragged out of bed. "This seems like harassment, Agent-Professor Brantley."

I frowned at his little jab. "Where were you Friday night?" My question was more of a demand.

He was silent, tentative at first. "As I said before, I was at home, with my wife. I was in my study."

"The hell you were." I looked at the black-and-white photos of Sumi's beaten face and then at my Sig. He was lying and I'd had just about enough of his evasiveness.

"Excuse me?"

"No, excuse me. We saw the security tapes."

Taekishi began chuckling annoyingly. "And was I in them?"

Son of a bitch! He knew. He knew the path he took through the lobby.

"Yeah, you were."

His chuckling stopped. "How can that be? I was upstairs—"

"No, Mr. Miyaki, you were downstairs." I began swinging the Sig through the air as if I was the one using it as a lethal weapon. "Downstairs with the hired help. Scurrying past the security cameras like a common thief."

He emitted a meek grunt as if being dropped to a lower rung on the social strata was a painful vision.

"And you would've gotten away with it, but we caught it. We caught *you*." I put down the Sig and sat on the couch. "So I want some answers. I want to know why you were following your daughter. I want to know where you went."

After lingering for a moment in a wave of dead air, Taekishi began chuckling again. "Is this a joke?"

"I assure you this is no joke."

"No. It sounds like a joke, because as far as I know, you aren't an active agent. You have no legal cause for badgering me like this."

I closed my eyes, quickly realizing that this phone call had been a strategic mistake and that my behavior was out of line. All the uncertainty I had felt at the crime scene was now creeping back.

95

My tone softened. "Mr. Miyaki, we saw you in the tape following your daughter less than two hours before she was killed. I don't believe that you had anything to do with it, but honestly, the situation doesn't look good."

He allowed for a collective pause before replying. "I was following her. I knew she was sneaking out, and I wanted to know where she was going. I thought I'd finally know and be able to help her." I could hear the pain in his voice. "She hailed a taxi on Fifth before I could reach her."

I shook my head slowly. "Why did you lie?"

"I'm a very private man. I didn't need nosy police officers intruding into my family's life."

That was a crock. "Why did you lie?"

"Because I was afraid." I could hear Taekishi fighting his emotions. "I was afraid of people finding out about my daughter."

I was leaning forward on my elbows, an anxiousness consuming me. "What would people find out?"

"I don't know exactly," he said impatiently. "That's what I was trying to figure out. I thought she was going to her secret apartment."

My eyebrows arched. "Secret apartment?"

Chapter Sixteen

The cab bounced and rattled as it sped up Eighth Avenue, but my stomach was unusually calm, unaware of the jolting movements. I stared out of my partially open window, allowing the cool air to whip across my face as I watched the evening crowd thin and the night come alive. The moment was short-lived when a cloud of dust burst through the opening, filling my eyes with debris.

As I blinked away the dirt and grime scratching my eyes, I called Joshua on my cell phone and told him of my experiment with my Sig and half-eaten duck, and of my conversation with Taekishi. I immediately regretted calling him. He was still downtown at the field office and quickly spouted some textbook rhetoric about not breaking and entering into the "possible crime scene." He lost me somewhere after "Don't." There was no knowledge of it being a crime scene; besides, the most that could be done was the NYPD would send over a sector car, and I was a better deal than two uniforms. After giving him the address, I let him know that the last one there wouldn't get *his* way, just as the cab pulled up in front of the tenement building.

Sumi's apartment was located on West Forty-ninth Street, between Ninth and Tenth avenues—a nice area, but still a far cry from the comforts of the Upper East Side. The front door was secured, but I caught it just as someone was leaving. I suppose I looked trustworthy. I climbed the three flights of stairs to number 4F, and was met by a locked, steel fire door. After rummaging through my bag and then my coat pockets, I found an old breath mint and a paperclip. I popped the mint into my mouth and straightened out the clip. I looked about furtively before inserting it into the lock. Never having picked a lock before in my life, I had no idea what I was doing. The thin paper clip was grasped firmly between my thumb and forefinger and pain ached in my fingers.

Two minutes into my efforts, I gave up. Joshua would be there soon, and he would never let me continue. I ran back downstairs into the vestibule and pulled a business card from a stack that had been shoved into the metal frame of the mailboxes. The locksmith lived two blocks away and was able to make it in record time. Though it was against the law not to, he did not ask for any ID or proof of residency. I was being quite the criminal today. Once inside, I paid him in cash and hurried him on his way.

It was dark inside; a street lamp barely added enough light through the two windows of the studio apartment. I scrunched my nose at the lingering smell of fresh paint hanging heavily in the air. The windows were closed. The smell of paint could've stayed for several days, if she had painted the place before she was killed.

The modest surroundings were in marked contrast to

her luxurious home on the East Side. A small kitchenette, crammed into the entranceway, looked as if it
hadn't been used in months. Typical of New York building owners to cut up and cram as many units as legally
possible, and rent the spaces at an astronomical rate.

I ran my hand over the sparse linoleum countertop. It
was smooth and not sticky. It was then that I realized this
was not a second home to Sumi, it was a hideout: her
clubhouse, someplace to flee to. The cabinets and drawers were empty except for a teapot, some plastic utensils
and a gray box cutter.

I picked it up and stared at it as if it were a criminal.
The blade didn't extend easily, and when it was all the
way open, I saw why: the metal was dulled with dried
blood and tiny scraps of skin. I quickly retracted the
blade and tossed it back in the drawer.

When the phone rang, I jumped and was even more
startled when the answering machine picked up and I
heard Sumi speaking on the outgoing message. Still
clinging to the image of the box cutter, the sound of her
voice was haunting. The caller hung up. I went over to
the phone. No caller ID.

The apartment was on the West Side and only twenty
blocks from where Sumi's body was found. Did she come
here before her death? Things were neat and orderly, no
signs of a struggle or foul play.

I picked up the phone's receiver and hit the redial button. The line rang three times before a young woman's
gravelly voice answered. Stumped for something to say, I
quickly hung up. I barely had time to breathe when the
phone rang. My hand did a little dance through the air
as I struggled with the decision to answer it, but Sumi's
voice called out before I could. The caller hung up.

As I silently cursed the phone company and its *69, I

made my way across the bare and worn hardwood floors, which looked as if they hadn't seen polyurethane in years.

My cell phone rang. It was Joshua. He was ten blocks away, but stuck in traffic and he warned me not to go into the apartment. I hung up on him.

By the windows in front there was a tiny, round table. A pair of scissors rested on top, and I opened them only to find a thin streak of dried blood along the edge. I was suddenly very aware of all the sharp items in the apartment, and it pained me to no end.

The only closet was empty except for a small black nylon bag tucked inconspicuously in the far corner. I suppose that I was hoping to find Sumi's missing coat. I was met with disappointment when I only found a neatly folded gray Champion NYU sweatshirt. My hand groped about the inside along the sides of the bag searching for something—anything. I carefully pulled out the sweatshirt, and as it unfolded itself, the sleeves tumbled through the air revealing small stains of blood. I froze. Someone was standing at the front door.

"Joshua?" I called out. As soon as I had seen the silhouetted figure I knew that it wasn't.

Whoever it was remained still. A lean figure in a long coat and a baseball cap. He was studying me, and I instinctively drew back the right side of my coat and reached for my 9mm, which did not exist.

"Who's there?" I demanded.

He did not stay to answer any questions and sprinted down the stairs, seemingly flying to the next floor.

I raced after him, my head becoming cloudy with the dizzying descent down the stairs that I took two at a time. My knees protested with every pounding step. I could see him as the top of his Orioles cap turned the corners of each landing, moving farther and farther away from me. I picked up the pace and seemed to be gaining on him. In the light of the hallway I made mental notes of his appearance: average height and dressed in black. These were useless, nondescript observations. There was no question in my mind—I had to catch him.

He had just made it through the front door, and it was swinging shut on me when I bolted outside and slammed into Joshua.

"Meredith. What's the rush?"

My breath was labored. "Shit, Josh. Out of my way!"

I threw myself into a sprinter's crouched posture and tore down the sidewalk, dodging people and nearly knocking over a Chinese food deliveryman. I was so close. Cars and tenements were a blur as I raced by them at a speed I had never once achieved on any of the obstacle courses at the Academy.

The cool night air tore through the walls of my lungs, stinging every inch of my body as it demanded that I stop, but I only pushed further. I had him. He had just made it to the corner of Ninth Avenue and the opposing traffic had him trapped. A sense of triumph was short-lived when I watched in horror as he tumbled inside a cab. The door slammed just as I reached the corner.

"No!" was all I could cry out as I slammed my fists against the trunk and kicked the taillights. As the cab careened away from me and was immediately lost in the steady stream of downtown traffic. I could only make out two digits in the license plate.

All at once my body felt heavy. I leaned over and rested my hands against my locked knees, desperately trying to control my breathing. My eyes were watering and my nose was running, as I stared angrily at my breath filling the night air. As I concentrated on controlling my breathing, my attention was drawn to the pavement. A painted, iridescent dotted line formed an outline of a corpse, memorializing Deborah Isley: a victim of a hit-and-run incident. Life, it seemed to me, was continually inundated with victims.

Joshua caught up to me and seemed more winded than I was.

"You'd be in better shape if you'd stop smoking," I snapped.

I was furious with him. If he hadn't gotten in my way, I would've caught the stranger.

"And I told you not to go in that apartment," he huffed.

I shot to an upright position. "Oh, just get over it, will you?" He followed me as we walked quickly back to the apartment. "While you were doing whatever the hell you were doing, somebody showed up at Sumi's apartment and decided not to stay for tea."

"Who was it?"

I stopped in front of Sumi's building and stared at his blank expression. "Now if I knew, do you think I would've risked giving myself a coronary?"

The muscles in his jaw flexed and I could tell that he was seething inside, but I was just as angry and even more frustrated. I tugged on the security door of the building knowing full well that it was locked.

I stomped my feet. "Damn it!"

"Jesus Christ, Meredith. Be a professional and leave the tantrums at home."

I blinked, taken aback and unaccustomed to Joshua scolding me. He reached past me and pressed each of the apartment buzzers. The door buzzed loudly and the tumblers clicked.

He grinned as we stepped inside. "They don't teach you that at the Academy."

As we approached Sumi's apartment, I slowed to a cautious pace. Something wasn't right. The door was closed and the light was off. I searched my brain, trying to conjure up the image of how I had left it. I sure as hell wouldn't have wasted time closing the door and flicking off the light switch. Or had I not turned on the lights when I first came in? I silently cursed myself for not remembering. I was so out of practice. On the witness stand, a defense lawyer would have a field day with me.

"What is it?" Joshua whispered as he searched my expression.

I held up my hand and pointed toward the door several times. He knew instantly what that meant. Joshua stepped around me and entered first. In the dark I could just barely make out his right arm arched back and resting defensively on his sidearm. I searched the shadows trying to define the objects in the apartment. Joshua's left arm slowly crawled up the wall and flicked on the light switch. I squinted as my pupils adjusted to the sudden exposure.

Joshua relaxed as he absorbed the surroundings. "No one's here."

Maybe I had closed the door, or in my haste, I had inadvertently grabbed at it with more force than I had remembered and it shut. I shook my head trying to clear my thoughts of the lingering paint fumes. It didn't matter. Nothing had been touched; no one had been there. But more importantly, I was becoming edgy. I quietly scolded myself. There was no room in the investigation for me to become so easily spooked.

"It really smells in here." Joshua touched his hand to

the wall and rubbed his fingertips together. "It's dry, but this is definitely a fresh coat. Who would paint a dead woman's apartment?"

I stepped back and inspected the walls. They were bumpy with uneven layers of plaster and globs of old paint from maintenance jobs long forgotten.

"Joshua, look at this part of the wall." I pointed to a portion where he was standing, closest to the door. "It's cleaner than the rest."

He scanned the whole apartment. "You're right. It's like someone was just interested in covering up something." Joshua bent down and tapped on the area. "Well, no secret cubby hole," he mused.

I walked over to him and gazed at the worn hardwood floors. "Too bad we don't have any Luminol." I knelt down beside a dark stain that did not win any awards for good housekeeping.

Joshua bounced through the air as he raced out the front door. He returned a couple of minutes later with a small plastic spray bottle.

"Part of the rental package?" I said with raised eyebrows.

"Mac's car," he explained as he unscrewed the top. "The battery in the rental died. I get a new car in the morning." He paused and stared at me with a disapproving eye. "That's why you made it over here before I did."

He mixed up the solution and immediately began covering the area in a heavy mist. Luminol was a chemical liquid that allowed blood proteins to fluoresce: an investigator's magic potion, but if not used quickly, its properties diminish.

I stepped away and covered my mouth with my coat as Joshua sprayed the floor.

When he finished, I hit the light switch. The corner of the floor lit up faintly in small blue-green patches that barely glowed in the darkness. The blood abruptly stopped at the baseboard where the paint was presumably covering it. Joshua sprayed a little along the bottom of the wall, but nothing showed.

He looked up, and what little orange light that seeped through the blinds from the street, highlighted his face like some religious icon. "Time to call in the big guns."

Chapter Seventeen

The FBI's Evidence Response Team was probably one of the most unique units within the agency. Using advanced technology—some old, some tried-and-true—they were able to shed new light into investigations and find hidden evidence that five years ago would have been unimaginable. The New York Field Office's team was one of the most respected—and in my humble opinion—the best the FBI had to offer, often being called in to other cities and agencies to offer their expertise.

This evening we were graced with two of the team's agents: Kelly Gilbert and Moses Meddick, or M-and-M, as he had been nicknamed as a child. We needed to do this at night, when it was darkest.

Kelly immediately set to work, and unzipped the large blue-and-black nylon case she was carrying. For crime scene work out in the field, the FBI had supplied all its

ERTs with the Mini-CrimeScope, a more portable, yet still powerful, version of the CS-16.

Dan watched as the team set up its equipment. He seemed a little annoyed for having been called in after quitting time.

"Thanks for coming after hours," Joshua said.

"Yeah, well you owe us big time," Kelly replied in friendly jest, as she dialed the filter wheel. "I want one of those Academy firearms hats for my kid, and not a generic one that you can get in the commissary."

He grinned sideways. "And M-and-M, what do you want?"

"Peace and lovin' for all mankind," he replied in his husky, soulful voice.

Joshua rolled his eyes. "I think it would be easier to just trade my firstborn for another one of those firearms hats."

Before the lights were switched off, I checked the floor. There were no fresh marks gouging the beaten wood. The dismembering had happened at the pier—or at least not here.

"All set," Kelly said. She handed each of us a pair of reddish-orange tinted goggles.

I slipped mine on and the orange from the streetlights turned to fire.

"Needs to be darker," she said.

Dan fiddled with the blinds as best he could.

"That'll do."

Kelly flipped a toggle switch, and the CrimeScope projected its bluish beam of light. She ran the beam over the floor, and the blood we had seen before under the faint coating of Luminol, now glowed brightly.

Joshua emitted a thin whistle.

Smaller specks that had not been visible with the Luminol appeared before us. The area of blood evidence was even greater than we had originally thought. Kelly slowly moved the light over the wall where the newer paint was, and it glowed toward the bottom. Through my goggles, I could see whitish–blue patches marking blood splatters. Kelly moved the beam away from the area and nothing fluoresced. She brought it back over, and the lower part of the wall and the edge of the floor glowed.

"It never ceases to amaze me," I said like a child at the science museum. "And the UV cuts through the paint."

Kelly nodded.

A siren wailed from somewhere on Ninth Avenue as I scanned the wall. Police. Solid patches of blood fluoresced through my goggles. I listened to the pitch and paid closer attention to the pauses between each squeal. No, it was an ambulance.

A couple of small oblong droplets shot out toward the floor. Long streaks extended from more centralized splotches as if a bottle of ink had been thrown against the floor and wall several times. The beating had been more severe than I could have ever imagined.

In the opposite corner, Dan stood with a pad of graph paper and a stubby, chewed-up No. 2 pencil, drawing out a detailed diagram of each bloodstain and its location in the room. In addition to the color and size, he drew arrows to indicate the direction of the "splash."

"M-and-M, you want to photograph this now?" Kelly said, when Dan finally pocketed his pencil.

"Sure, I'm ready," he said, adjusting the filter over the camera lens. Like the human eye, the camera had to cut through the UV light as well.

"I'll take the overall first, and then the close-ups." He picked up the remote cable release. It was important for him not to create any camera movement during this delicate procedure of using a long exposure. There was only one chance to get it right.

His beat-up tripod was set, and Joshua and I moved out of the way. M-and-M tripped the shutter so it was left open. Kelly slowly moved the beam of the Mini-CrimeScope along the floor and up the wall, capturing all of the evidence in one photograph.

"What do you call this again?" Joshua asked, as he and I watched with unwavering fascination.

"Painting with light," M-and-M replied. "Gives you a nice shot of everything in these dark situations."

"Well," I said dryly to Joshua, "looks like we found the other crime scene."

Chapter Eighteen

Joshua entered the conference room, and without open-ing my eyes I knew instantly who it was. Ralph Lauren's Polo was wearing heavily on him so early in the morning. I had been enjoying the solitude of the empty room and was slumped in one of the dark brown leather chairs with my head resting against the back, a Migraine Ice pad pressed against my temple with two fingers. All of Sunday had been spent grading the worst student essays I had ever read. There would be no grading curve in my class, because the whole group had collectively flatlined the av-erage at a D+. I brought my coffee cup to my nose, hop-ing to mask Joshua's cologne.

"You okay?" he asked, as he slid into the chair next to me.

"Fine," I groaned. Someone really needed to tell him to lay off the cologne.

"What's that?"

My eyes opened. "It's a cooling pad. It's supposed to help with migraines."

"Is it working?"

I peeled away the thin, flexible material shaped like a tiny boomerang and dropped it on the table. "No."

There was an awkward silence before Joshua said, "Meredith."

I sighed deeply. I knew from his tone what that meant.

"I need to talk to you." He wheeled his chair closer to me. "*We* need to talk."

I brought my coffee cup to my lips, but he gently took it from me and placed it upon the table, then turned my chair so we were facing each other.

"I'm not going to let you ignore me."

I couldn't look at him. "Joshua, this isn't the best time to be discuss—"

"No? I think this is the perfect time."

There was anger rising in his tone and it startled me.

"It seems to me that the only people who get your undivided attention are these monsters." He pointed at his case file, then added sarcastically, "Perhaps if I had a character flaw you'd pay more attention to me."

He had left himself wide open to insult, but I held my tongue. My eyes narrowed and I turned from him as I sipped my coffee.

"Meredith, would you for once stop being so goddamned stubborn!"

The pain in my head was banging the walls of my skull and my patience was wearing thin. I sat upright in my chair.

"Fine, Joshua. What do we *have* to talk about right now at"—I checked my watch—"Six fifty-four on a Monday morning?

He shot out of his chair and began pacing around the end of the table, his voice loud enough for any of the other agents down the hall to hear. "About you ignoring me when I ask you to do something. 'Don't go into the apartment,' I said. But you did, and it turns out that some nut shows up and leads you on a foot chase. What if something had happened to you? I'm responsible for you! You are a civilian, and I'm the agent responsible!"

He stood at the head of the table and leaned his fists against the edge, the veins in his neck bulging against the collar of his tan starched shirt. But the corners of his eyes glistened and his thick eyelashes were matted together.

His voice dropped to a soft whisper. "What if something happened to you? I'd never forgive myself."

My expression softened as I looked at him standing there with FBI NEW YORK displayed on the wall behind him. At each of the four corners were service awards. The inscription that ran across the bottom: FIDELITY, BRAVERY, INTEGRITY.

I thought desperately of something sensitive and meaningful to say, but I was unaccustomed to anyone caring so deeply for me.

"I'm a big girl and can take care of myself." I averted my gaze, ashamed by my adolescent response.

Joshua snorted, and the leather chair beside me squeaked when he sat.

I looked up and watched him carefully place a legal pad and ballpoint pen on the table in front of himself. Then he stared off into space and waited for the meeting to begin.

As Mac entered the conference room, I slowly spun my chair toward the enormous window behind me. It faced west and gave a clear panoramic view of the skyline. The sun had just barely crept over the horizon and the buildings were highlighted in a yellow glow.

I watched a pigeon land on the sill, peck at one of its crooked feet and fly away. "Joshua."

"Yeah."

"Thank you."

Chapter Nineteen

Eight-by-ten photos were scattered about the table: black-and-white, color; all of Sumi. It was the usual gang, with Cheryl "visiting." We had been laboring over the details for two hours now and basically getting nowhere. I checked my watch. There was plenty of time before my 1:10 class.

The lab had determined that the tool used for dismembering Sumi had to have been a small ax. Figuring out exactly what kind of ax was a different story and could take weeks, maybe months. Toolmarkings was working diligently to determine which model semi-automatic might've been used—if one had been—to create the U-shaped marks.

"I still think it's a cult," Dan commented as he looked up from a mess of pictures spread out in front of him.

Joshua shook his head confidently. "No."

Dan shot him a look that would've sent even the most ruthless gang member fleeing for his life.

"It's definitely ritualistic, but not in the way a cult operates. The displacement of the body was hardly ritualistic, and her body would've had some symbols marked on it."

"What about the arms?" Dan challenged.

I replied wearily, "Chopping off someone's limbs by no means qualifies their actions as being influenced by a cult."

His dumbfounded expression left me believing that I had used too many words in one sentence.

"Not a cult," I said plainly.

"Then why does someone do this?" Mac's posture was slouched and he appeared to be afraid of hearing the gruesome reason.

"It's a sexual charge." Joshua explained like he did in his basic seminars for the Hollywood directors at L.A.'s finest hotels. "These types never developed an understanding of what a healthy adult relationship is because they grew up in an environment where there was none. So sex and an intimate relationship are foreign to them. They see violence as a means of attaining that sexual stimulation as well as achieving domination and control."

This time Dan smirked. "That's why the fella jacked-off on her after."

I immediately felt dirty being in the same room as him.

"That's psychobabble bull."

We all looked at Dan incredulously, and Joshua's eyes narrowed as he took great offense to the challenge.

"I agree he gets off on the violence. That's nothing new." Dan leaned back in his chair like a veteran sharing old war stories. "I see it every day when some asshole beats his wife or kids. But there's a reason why this guy

115

chose the arms. He could've easily picked her hands and legs. What about just her fingers—"

Mac held up his hand. "Dan has a point. If it's a sexual thing, why not parts of her body that are more representational of this?"

I nodded. "Yes, though it's more common for these types to be fascinated with parts of the body that are more sexual, it's not a requirement."

In silence, we contemplated our exchange. If anyone ever heard us discussing these investigations, they would've thought we were just as pathological as the murderers.

"There is a specific reason for the choice in limbs." With my roller ball pen, I stabbed at the curled corner of a manila folder. "There's a definite reason why he would've taken the time to dismember, pick up the limbs, carry them some twenty feet and drop them."

"What is it?"

"We don't know yet."

Dan smirked, pleased that we didn't have the answer. I knew he hated us. He hated what we did.

I stared back at him. He was being unfair. No one had the answer, and he had an equal responsibility to find the murderer. It wasn't up to Joshua or me to solve his case. We were consultants, to advise as to the *type* of person Dan should be looking for. I wrapped my long, thin fingers around my hands. But I had taken on the challenge of finding this UNSUB, either because Sumi sparked something inside me, or because a large part of me believed that Dan was incompetent and incapable of even finding Waldo drawn on a blank white page.

My light laughter was cut short when I caught everyone's curious stare.

"We don't know, and probably won't know until we catch him." I cleared my throat and leaned my elbows on Anthony's autopsy report. "It's something set deep within their psyche. And even when we do discover the reason, it will probably seem irrational to us."

"It's always irrational," Mac muttered.

"It's rational to them." My gaze was as steely cold as my tone. "A boy is made to continually watch his mother have sex with strange men. Twenty-two years later he's brutalizing and murdering prostitutes. But why did he spread his feces all over them? Because in his own words, 'It was dirty, dirty, dirty.' That may seem like a lame and infantile excuse to us, but it's completely logical to them."

"Pity the child," he muttered disdainfully.

"Want to know my theory?" Dan said, still eyeing me suspiciously. "Let's say that the Miyakis are part of a cult. You know, like the one in—where was it? Texas? They were all Orientals, right?"

Joshua grabbed my knee under the table and squeezed angrily, digging his nails into the fabric of my slacks.

"Well, we all know these cults are into that weird sexual shit," Dan continued, oblivious to everyone's stern expressions. "Partner swapping. Intercourse with minors. I think dutiful daughter couldn't handle it. Cut her arms to deal with it. Daddy was on her case to get a grip. She threatened to rat them out. The cult didn't like it. They convinced brainwashed Daddy to sacrifice his kid in the name of the cult. After all, he admitted following her that night. They took her by surprise in the apartment. She struggled. They beat her senseless. She was offered to the God of the Hudson, or whatever. And the leader got off on all of this control and power."

As backward as his theory was, he actually had the *basics* of cults making sense in this case. However, I was certain, and so was Joshua, that this was not a cult. I looked over at Cheryl and was thoroughly unnerved when I noticed how intent she was with Dan's theory. It was understandable. The FBI was still closely watching cult activity and their prophecies of Armageddon.

In my hand I held a bird's-eye view photo of Sumi's arms. A large crease began to develop where my thumb and forefinger were pinching the edge of the paper. I studied and scrutinized the image, but there was nothing that screamed occult to me.

Dan picked up his blue paper coffee cup with Greek columns drawn on the front from the deli. It left a brownish ring on one of the black-and-whites.

"Well, now it's a real working copy," I muttered just loud enough for Joshua to hear. I picked up a photo that showed the entire length of Sumi's body, and placed it next to the one of her arms.

"Dan," I asked in a friendly tone. "Are you absolutely certain that there haven't been any crime scenes in the area, displaying the same criminal signature?"

I didn't bother to look up when I received no immediate response—I knew what his expression would be.

"Nothing," he finally said. "This is the type of shit you don't forget."

"Well, maybe he's crossing state lines," I said.

I could hear Dan loudly shuffling papers across the table.

I looked up, my face serious. "The crime scene and criminal signature are much too organized and sophisticated to come from a first-time offender. It has to be the result of someone who's had practice. Who's had time to figure out what it is that he wanted to do."

Dan scrunched his face and his neck disappeared into his shoulders. He sputtered his disapproval at what he perceived to be my ludicrous theory. "This is some sicko, who killed a girl. I'd say her father is pretty good suspect."

"I am interested in Miyaki," Cheryl said, and we all turned to her as if we had forgotten that she was in the room.

Dan arched an eyebrow. In his opinion, Taekishi should've already been arrested and strapped to the electric chair.

"How does a college kid afford to pay for an apartment?" Mac asked, leaning back in his chair and adjusting his posture underneath a crisp white Oxford. "It may not be the most expensive, but these days even something like that will run you at least a twelve hundred."

Joshua leaned forward and rested his elbows on the table. "Maybe she got an allowance from Daddy."

A tight frown drew across Mac's face. "A dollar-fifty, that's all I got, and I actually had to do chores."

Joshua smiled. "Fifty cents."

I eyed him through the corner of my eye and had to restrain myself from kicking him under the table. Joshua was very good at playing into the game, and it annoyed me to no end.

"I'm sure that Miyaki found out pretty quickly where his money was going," he continued. "That's probably how he knew in the end. We should look into her banking records, find out whether she paid cash, and ask Miyaki about it."

"Don't worry about that," Mac commented, trading sideways glances with Cheryl.

I caught Joshua's look, and was confident that I wasn't alone in being in the dark. "What's that supposed to mean?"

119

"Let's just say that Mr. Miyaki has some questionable investments and financial dealings."

I eyed Mac warily. "So you think that his daughter's murder has something to do with it?"

He cocked his head to one side. "I don't know. Based on your expert opinion, is that what you think?"

I rolled my eyes and I could hear Joshua chuckling quietly to himself. "Hmm . . . based on my expert opinion?" I tossed my pen onto the table and fell back into my chair. "Look, if this is why you're interested in the murder, you can save yourself some unpaid overtime and concentrate on Miyaki's company and finances. The cult theory makes better sense than this."

Cheryl's expression hardened. "What makes you so positive that the two aren't related?"

My mouth fell slightly and I sighed, tired of all the evasive choice in words and the leading questions. "How can I give you an opinion based on the investigation into Miyaki if you're telling me nothing? But from what I know of violent killers, it's unlikely to be a revenge killing, or some kind of paid hit. People who assassinate don't waste their time with presentation—excuse me, but is there a blank wall I could talk to?"

All eyes were glued on me.

I rubbed my forehead and scanned the table for my cooling pad. I tossed it back down when I felt that it had warmed to room temperature.

"But is Miyaki a likely suspect? Who knows? Is he a possible suspect? Yes. It's easier to eliminate those closer to home than to look for a stranger."

"Precisely," Cheryl said, nodding her head.

"Cults, money laundering, maybe even illegal gambling. How far are we going with these theories, or are we going to start using logic?"

Cheryl's eyes grew wider and rested heavily upon me. "According to information we have, you may not be too far off with some of those suggestions, but if you have some better theories, please share them."

I glowered at the sarcasm oozing through her words.

"Joshua seems to have a pretty good idea of the UN-SUB's character."

My posture stiffened.

"The profile isn't complete just yet," he said meekly, refusing to make eye contact with me.

I leaned over the table and angled my body, forcing my face into his line of sight. "Then I guess you have all the answers and just decided not to tell me so that we'd have something to chat about this morning."

He turned his head toward me. "That's enough."

"So you've got this killer all figured out in just one weekend. I'm glad Sunday was productive for at least one of us."

The muscles in Joshua's jaw flexed rapidly and his eyes widened. When he caught everyone's stare, he awkwardly cleared his throat and readjusted the knot in his tie.

I wasn't going to let it go so easily. "Then you're just going to disregard my little run-in with the darkman?"

"Which leads me to a greater concern." Cheryl stared directly at me. "Last night—"

"The door was open," I protested much too quickly, my attention still focused on Joshua's reddened face.

She scolded me with a silent, yet thunderous look. "Do you have any idea who it was who showed up at the apartment?"

I wished she had just asked me directly if I thought it was Taekishi Miyaki. "No. I didn't get a good look at him."

"How about Miyaki?" Dan asked, without looking up from the notebook he was scribbling on.

"No, he wasn't the right shape."

His pen stopped moving. "Shape?"

"Yes," I said confidently. "He wasn't broad enough and Taekishi's taller."

He chuckled obnoxiously, probably still high from knowing that he was right about the markings on Sumi. "You figured all that from a dark silhouette? You know what we think of the average eyewitness account."

"I'm not your average eyewitness."

"That's for sure," he muttered under this breath.

Cheryl shook her head like a grammar school teacher does when her students are playing unfairly. "The blood on the floor and walls. The lab can run DNA on the samples from the floor. ERT's over there now pulling the place apart." She looked at me with pity in her eyes. "There's a good chance that Sumi was killed in her apartment not long after Miyaki was seen following her."

I forcefully placed my coffee cup upon the table. At the moment, I really didn't know why I was even there. "Again with Miyaki."

Dan squinted at me, but his tone was friendly. "Other than Joshua, he was the only one who knew you were going there."

He was right, and it irritated me even more.

My voice began to rise. "Unless I surprised someone else who was there, looking for Sumi. It's only been a couple of days. Not everyone would know about her death."

He shrugged. "True. But maybe it was Miyaki who didn't want you to find out what had happened in that apartment."

"Then why in God's name would he tell me about the apartment in the first place?"

"From what I know, you had him by the balls. It probably slipped out because he was trying to cover his ass."

My smile was genuine. There was the Dan I had so missed.

"One thing is for certain," I said as my grin dissolved. "There had to be an element of trust, or at least a lack of immediate fear."

"You don't say?" Dan said with sarcasm. "Maybe she knew the killer like her own father."

I ignored him. There had been no need for the offender to secure her with solid ligatures, and there was no sign of forced entry at her apartment. "No matter how he got into the apartment, she didn't feel frightened at first. Not until she was cornered." My voice rose. "Once she realized the threat, he already had her trapped."

"I got Sumi's phone records." Mac was looking at me from across the table in a way that immediately brought me back to our days as New Agent Trainees at the Academy. It was the same way he used to look at me as we ate meatloaf and baked beans in the cafeteria after long hours of studying in the library.

"And?" I asked somewhat unnerved by his familiar expression.

"And most of the calls were made to two numbers." He shuffled through a long printout from Bell Atlantic. "One is a number listed Heather Gross. That was the last number dialed and apparently the one you connected with by hitting redial." He looked up and made eye contact with each of us. "The call was made Thursday night at 9:58."

I caught my breath. "A little more than an hour before she was killed. And the second?"

Mac knitted his brow. "Bellevue Hospital, Psychiatric Ward."

Chapter Twenty

Joshua grabbed my arm out in the hallway and dragged me across the way to where there were no open office doors. When he spoke, heavy lines creased his forehead. "*Don't* ever embarrass me like that *again*."

"Excuse me?"

"Challenging me like that in a meeting with colleagues."

"Joshua, we always challenge each other. That's how we brainstorm." I began walking toward the exit leading into the reception area. "Besides I hardly think that it was a challenge."

He grabbed me again and pulled me over to him.

"Apparently, you're not finished," I said angrily, yanking my arm from his grasp.

"No, I'm not." He leaned in closer to me and our eyes were level with each other. "We shouldn't be surprising each other in meetings."

"Exactly!" I quickly paused and cleared my voice when an agent walked by and nodded at us.

My tone softened. "You never told me about your profile. You asked me to help you. How can I help you if you're holding out on me? You're not playing by the rules."

"I have my profile, and it's right," Joshua stated with tremendous passion.

"Okay, we're not in a meeting. Let's have at it right now. Single, white male, early-twenties to late-thirties," I rattled off in a mocking tone. "Add or subtract five years, accordingly. See, I can make a quick, half-assed profile, too."

Joshua bit into his lower lip.

"A loner," I continued. "A nonsocial, of above-average intelligence. Middle income." I grabbed his upper arm. "How am I doing?"

"It's not as generic. If you'd read it, you'd see that I've outlined specifics—"

"What?" my voice rose, "Like he drives a clean, practical car?"

"Domestic," he stated smartly. "Look at the crime scene. He had to have driven her over there. He was in a car." Joshua reached into his briefcase and handed me a single-spaced, half-page, typed paragraph.

I stared at him blankly. "That's not the point."

"Oh, come on, Meredith, you used to crank out profiles in forty-eight hours."

I leaned against a glass display case filled with nonfiction books whose titles I recognized as painting the FBI in a positive light.

"It's not a race." I turned away from the books.

"Isn't it?"

"It shouldn't be."

"You know how we're supposed to operate," he muttered. "Three more days is all they're giving me, and then I fly to Nashville to deal with a newer and more brutal case. Nashville! That's not even my region. You see? We don't have the luxury of time." His voice grew angry again. "So don't you ever do that to me again."

"We'll talk later, once you've become rational." Before walking to the reception area, I looked at him, my glare piercing his eyes. "But don't ever speak to me like that again. I'm not Kirsten."

Chapter Twenty-one

The smells of the chemical deodorizers were oddly reminiscent of the autopsy suite. Different, yet similar: both covering some kind of stench, both only successful at making the atmosphere even worse. As soon as I heard the click of the ladies' room door behind me, all the muscles in my body relaxed. I wet a paper towel and placed it at the nape of my neck, hoping it would wash away what was left of my migraine. Years ago I had stopped splashing my face with cold water, when I discovered that it gave the illusion I had been crying.

As I stared through the gray film of dust that covered the mirror before me, I suddenly realized that under the harsh green of fluorescent lights, my age was beginning to show. *Screw it.* People were too obsessed with their own vanity, and thirty-five was hardly middle-age.

I smacked on the hot-air dryer and lost myself as the warmth blew over my hands. Joshua's concern for my safety had touched me—reminded me of all that I couldn't have. But his outburst this morning was just a cover. I knew him too well not to realize that something else was bothering him. It was no secret that he and his wife had been having problems for a number of years now. That's probably how we wound up in each other's arms. No, that was just our excuse.

I closed my eyes and inhaled a deep breath, then released it slowly with a measured rhythm. I thought of Joshua's wife and two sons, and how I had betrayed them. Kirsten was my friend, but Joshua was my—

"Feeling okay?" Cheryl asked as she stepped out from one of the two stalls.

I jolted with a start when the door bounced against its metal latch.

"It's almost as bad as being in law school. At least when you're a lawyer, you know you'll be making better money. Did you know that the big corporations are paying first years one hundred thirty, annual? Makes me think that I should've made better use of that law degree."

I should've checked for feet.

"I'll be honest with you." She tucked her blouse into her skirt. "I think there are too many egos working on this one. Things are getting muddy."

"Cheryl?" I asked, moving out of the way as she stepped up to the sinks. "Why did you hold out on us? Joshua and I had a right to know about the investigation into Miyaki."

Her hand rested on the hot water knob. "So you think it may have something to do with his daughter's murder?"

"Absolutely not."

The water began to run, and Cheryl flicked her fingers through the steady stream, testing the temperature. "Have you ever worked with Dan before?"

I shook my head. She was avoiding my inquiries like the plague. Everything was always on a need-to-know basis. If it had nothing to do with Sumi, then I didn't need to know, and it was Mac and Cheryl's job to find out if I did need to know. Little government moles released to infiltrate our investigation and find out if there's a connection. My face reddened with anger.

Cheryl began shaking her head as she washed her hands. "He certainly is a character."

"That's being kind."

"Oh, Meredith, you know how it is in any agency. There are good ones and there are bad ones. I think Dan is a good one, but he's just a bit—"

"Lacking in social grace." I frowned. Funny, I'd heard the same said about me.

"So you never worked with him before?" Then she paused and thought for a moment. "No, I guess he must've come to the NYPD just about the time you left."

I reached into my bag and dabbed some concealer under my eyes. I knew what Cheryl was doing and it wasn't going to work.

"Transferred from New Orleans."

I watched her carefully in the mirror.

"Grew up in New York. Brooklyn—Queens—something like that. Kind of an odd path to take." Cheryl turned to me, her fingers dripping water down the front of her tweed skirt. "Meredith, be honest with me. Why are you back here?"

I stopped with the concealer, leaving thick streaks of liquid makeup across my face. "Joshua asked me."

"I know, but why did you agree?" She pushed on the hand dryer and her voice rose over the noise. "And don't tell me it was because of one of your students. I may be out of the field, but even a desk jockey can put a timeline together. You agreed to help *before* you discovered the victim was your student."

I dabbed gently at my face, blending the makeup into my skin. The tint really didn't match and it did nothing to hide the bags. I wished that I had some Preparation H.

Not heeding Cheryl's words, I continued to lie to myself: *I came back because Joshua asked me.*

The dryer cycled down, and Cheryl's voice became quieter. "Do you mind if I wager a guess?"

I frowned lightly. "Go ahead."

She leaned up against one of the sinks, marking a straight line of water along her backside. "A lot of people, even yourself, would say you left because you were exhausted; tired of fighting a losing battle; drained emotionally from seeing and dealing with people who have been brutalized; tired of the bureaucracy and politics stonewalling your efforts."

I considered this and nodded my head gently in agreement.

"Or you left because you had an affair with a married colleague."

My mouth dropped and my eyes widened.

"Don't worry, I don't think anyone else knows. I could tell because I know you, and women are much more perceptive than men when it comes to reading human behavior, right?

"Yeah, I guess."

"Well, *all* of those excuses are crap."

I flinched.

"You came back because you don't know why you left. You don't have an honest-to-goodness reason. And there are a lot of unanswered questions."

She stepped away from the sink and caught a glimpse

of herself in the mirror. "Oh, damn. This is embarrassing." Cheryl turned on the hand dryer and shoved her backside up as close to the heat as she could.

Try as I might, I couldn't contain my laughter.

"Please, don't let this undermine the validity of my analysis," she said with a grin. She turned and dried the spots on her front. "You didn't come back because you thought you could charm Joshua into a romantic relationship, because every intelligent woman knows that there are two obstacles that can never be hurdled: his kids and his wife."

She flapped air underneath her skirt. "As much as he may be tired of both, he will always love his children unconditionally, and his wife is still his wife. Joshua is a good man, devoted to his family, and he and you slipped up."

The dryer clicked off and Cheryl stepped up to me. Even in heels, the top of her salt-and-pepper hair only came to my collarbone. "So with all the external excuses explained, there's only one place to go." She pointed at my stomach. "You. Think back to why you decided to join the FBI in the first place, not why you left, and then you'll know why you're back now."

"Okay, so you do know me." I studied my tired eyes in the streaky mirror. The concealer had finally faded into my skin.

Cheryl combed her fingers through her short pixie-style hairdo. "After this morning's consultation, I'm going to recommend that Mac not waste his time with finding a connection between Miyaki and his daughter's murder. There's too much at stake with the other investigation."

I bit the inside of my lip. *Too much at stake?* A dead, mutilated young woman seemed pretty important to me. But solving a homicide, even if she was the daughter of a prominent businessman, was not within their jurisdiction, nor did it interest the FBI. Illegal trading, money laundering, or what-have-you: now that's good publicity.

I slathered my hands in some lotion and offered Cheryl some. I held my fingers close to my nose. Joshua had liked the citrus smell of the lotion.

"I guess it could be worse," I said with a sigh. "At least I didn't accidentally fax a subpoena to an unknown recipient."

We both laughed at my reference to an incident that had become something of a joke among government agents. It had been rumored for the past three years that a nameless high-ranking officer of the NYPD drug task force had carelessly faxed a subpoena of a highly sensitive investigation to a city resident. The amused recipient had called to inform the lieutenant of his error, and the response—the punch line—was something of a catchphrase among FBI special agents should they ever find themselves making an ass of themselves.

"Uh, do me a favuh, could you rip dat up real good?" I said in a poorly executed New York accent.

Cheryl began laughing loudly, and then her face tightened into a quizzical expression. "You don't think that was Dan Grissard, do you?"

Chapter Twenty-two

Joshua and Mac were having lunch together at Katz Diner. I was green with envy, staring at my stale plain bagel and cream cheese bought from a street cart vendor. I fantasized about the enormous pastrami on rye with globs of coleslaw that I could have been having. Halfway through Washington Square Park I wound up tossing the bagel into a trash can, where a flock of pigeons immediately descended upon it. The day was chilly, and I drew my coat tighter around me as a gust of wind blew up. I could feel my legs breaking out in goose bumps.

I clutched my briefcase filled with my students' dismal essays. *The government is filled with pre-Madonnas*, one of my students had written, obviously intending to write "prima donna," in a scathing editorial on the current state of the nation's politicians. The future of the planet was doomed.

The image of scantily clad legislators prancing around the Senate floor grabbing their crotches resurfaced as I entered the lecture room. But my grin quickly dissolved when I saw the faces of my students. A dark cloud hung over them, masking their somber faces. Before starting my lecture, I read aloud the form letter that the NYU administration had sent to the faculty and students. A simple one-paragraph statement offering counseling to those who needed it, never explaining the circumstances of the anonymous female student's death. But there was no need to; rumors were already circulating. Suicide, drugs and alcohol were the favorite choices. Murder was never suggested, and I knew that would keep both the FBI and NYPD pleased.

I tried to follow the outline of my syllabus, but like my students, I was in no mood to be participating in the class. I ended the lecture fifteen minutes into the session. As the students filed out, many watched me tentatively, making hesitant gestures, uncertain if they wanted to speak to me about their deceased peer. But they all opted to just pick out their essays from the giant stack. Guilt consumed me when I saw their disappointed, angry and surprised reactions to the low grades. When I thought I was alone in the room, I began wiping the chalkboard clean of what little I had taught.

"Professor Brantley," someone said as I ran the eraser through the words *community structure and crime.*

I turned and was looking into the thin face of a young man.

His blond hair was shaped into flat, choppy bangs that clung to his forehead, resting just above his heavy eyelids. I immediately noted the white collapsible cane dangling loosely in the crook of his arm.

He thrust out his hand. "Hi, Denny Carter."

I shook it gently.

"It's okay, I'm blind, not fragile," he said with a delighted laugh.

My smile was awkward. I wasn't aware that one of my students was blind. There were almost a hundred enrolled in my lecture, but I was surprised that I hadn't noticed him before.

"I don't like to stand out, so people don't make a fuss," he explained, almost as if he were reading my thoughts.

"Oh," was all I could think of to say.

Denny shifted his weight awkwardly between his feet before mustering his courage and blurting out, "Sumi—I don't think they're right."

I was suddenly very interested in this young man, but began slowly gathering my things. "They're not right about what?"

"They're not right about Sumi. She didn't kill herself and she didn't OD on anything."

"Really?" Although he couldn't see me, I pretended to be disinterested by occupying myself with packing up my briefcase.

"She was my friend. I know she was screwed up, but she would never have killed herself. And she was clean. She didn't drink or do drugs, ever."

"Why are you discussing this with me? Shouldn't you be telling this to the police?"

He was silent, and listened to make sure no one else was near. "You used to work for the FBI."

I paused while slipping some folders into a stiff compartment of my briefcase.

"It's no secret," he continued. "It's probably the only reason why everyone's taking this course."

My right eyebrow arched and I sucked in my cheeks, mildly irritated with his graceless approach.

"And we know you used to be a profiler. Right?"

I nodded. "Yes."

"Cool." But it came out sounding like *kewl.* A mischievous grin enveloped his mouth. "Hey, can I ask you something? Is it just like on that TV show? I like that show. My little brother describes what's happening when we watch it."

I smiled with amusement, trying not to burst out into raucous laughter. "I've only seen the show once, but it plays well for a TV series."

Denny seemed disappointed with my diplomatic response, but his face fell back to its serious expression. "I know you're working with them on this."

I eyed him warily. He was beginning to sound like he was spouting dialogue from that TV show. "Who's them?"

"The FBI and the NYPD," he said, as if I had forgotten how *Hollywood* made this all work. His eyebrows drew closer together. "Aren't you? I mean, that's how they do it on the show."

My briefcase felt unusually heavy this afternoon, and I heaved it up onto my shoulder and adjusted the thick leather strap. The elevators in NYU's main building always operated slowly, especially between classes. But they were empty now, and I fidgeted as I waited for one to arrive. Part of me really wanted to get away from Denny. He had followed me to the elevator bank, and I watched as he awkwardly slipped on his coat while still holding on to his backpack. Denny moved well for a blind person, and he always directed his expression in the general vicinity of my voice. If not for the tinted glasses he wore, it would have been difficult to realize he was visually impaired.

Denny stepped over to where I stood and adjusted his glasses. "Hey, um, I was wondering." He began nervously scratching the back of his neck. "I was wondering—can you get FBI shirts?"

I smiled politely and pressed the "down" button repeatedly.

"Or a sweatshirt. That would be *kewl*."

"Probably not," I replied in a kind tone.

He seemed only mildly disappointed.

Much to my relief, the elevator arrived. The buttons were on Denny's side of the elevator. He slid his hands down the braille numbers on the panel and pressed the lobby button.

"Tell me something, Denny." I approached the question with a slight hint of hesitation. "Are you friends with Heather Gross?"

His lips puckered and confusion spread across his face.

"Isn't she one of your friends?"

Denny's voice rose in a smooth curve as if I was mad as a hatter. "No."

"There was a picture of Sumi and another girl—"

"Oh!" His head bobbed up and down with excitement. "You probably mean Becca. Yeah, we hang out sometimes. She's more Sumi's friend than mine."

"Were you good friends with Sumi?"

His face darkened, and I immediately felt guilty for asking him such a direct question in a setting that was definitely claustrophobic, but hardly intimate.

"Yeah. We were really close. We did everything together."

With his left hand Denny reached for the buttons on his coat, but faltered slightly when he realized the button eyelets were on the other side. If it had been anyone else, it would have meant nothing to me. But I shamefully acknowledged to myself that because he was blind, I watched him more closely. There was something very familiar about that coat. My gaze ran up and down the front of it. The eyelets were on the right side, the buttons on the left: a woman's coat. Denny had reached for the buttons instinctively, as if he were wearing a man's. This was a new and unfamiliar garment to him.

"Nice coat," I said, eyeing the snug fit.

He seemed a bit thrown. "Thanks." He paused awkwardly. "It was Sumi's."

The elevator doors opened, but I could not move. Denny unfolded his cane and stepped off into the lobby.

"Are you coming?" he asked, turning back toward the elevator when he realized I wasn't with him.

I stepped off, still in mild shock. "Sumi's? Where did you get it?"

We slowly headed to the doors facing Waverly Place.

"She gave it to me the other night." His expression drained of all life. "You know, that night she—"

"You were with her Thursday night!" My voice rose and echoed off the thick walls.

The security guard eyed us—probably thinking we were involved in some kind of December-May romance.

I cleared my throat and gently hurried Denny outside.

My tone was softer, but I sped through my words. "You and Sumi were together?"

He nodded his head. Now it was he who wanted to get away from me.

I grabbed his upper arms like a frenzied mother who wants to shake information from her child. "When?"

Denny shook his head, his face blanketed in pain. "I don't know. I've got to go."

He quickly pulled from me and raced down the sidewalk toward Washington Square Park, leaving me with nothing but the sound of his white cane tapping against the pavement.

Chapter Twenty-three

There was something extremely troubling about the situation. I stared at the edge of the sandwich, wondering just how I was going to wrap my mouth around the four inches of pastrami and coleslaw. It was a gift—a peace offering from Joshua. I squashed a corner of the bread and shoved as much of the sandwich as I could into my mouth. Watery mayonnaise dribbled across my lips. It was better than an orgasm—I looked over at Joshua—better than ice cream.

I struggled through another bite. "You know, I feel really stupid being driven four blocks."

"Well, you could get out and walk," he said, steering the car uptown. "So who's this blind kid?"

"Apparently, a friend of Sumi's," I said, wiping my mouth and choking on the pieces of pastrami I hadn't chewed well. "He's a fan."

"What?"

"He enjoys our work."

"Oh."

"He wanted a shirt."

Joshua laughed, his mouth wide open and revealing perfectly lined teeth. "Tell him to buy a fake one some-one's selling on one of those online auction sites. One dollar plus a ten-dollar shipping fee," he cried out, his laughter reaching near hysterics.

"I'd like to know how he got Sumi's coat." My tongue worked its way around another enormous bite.

"Me too." Joshua squinted when the orange sunset shot a bright reflection off a nearby office building. "How could you just let him split after saying something like that?"

"Excuse me?"

"His behavior, if not his words, were very odd. Not to mention, he took off with what may amount to possible evidence."

"I couldn't just take off after him and harass him." I winced and swallowed hard. It felt like there was a golf ball in my throat and the top of my mouth felt itchy.

"The old Meredith I once knew, would have."

"I'm not the same." No longer interested in my sand-wich, I stared at it mournfully. "Besides, I'm just a civilian now, as you so like to constantly remind me these days. If I had confiscated the coat, right now we'd be having an argument about evidence and chain of custody."

Joshua pulled up alongside the curb in front of my apartment. The light on the front stoop switched on. Mrs. Polencek, who lived just below me, was incredibly nosy, but she had a good heart.

"I can talk to him tomorrow," I said undoing my seat-belt. "He's scheduled for an appointment during my of-fice hours."

"You shouldn't do this by yourself."

"And why shouldn't I do this myself?"

"Because I want someone involved who has a badge. You're not an agent."

"And you're not a professor," I argued, surprised at how protective I was for one of my students. "This isn't an interrogation."

"I'm coming."

"The hell you are. You asked me to get involved, and now I am. You can't just pull this FBI crap and bulldoze your way into other people's territory—"

"No. You disobeyed—"

My body jolted with a start. "Disobeyed? If you keep this up, you're going to owe me a hell of a lot more sandwiches."

"Ignored. You ignored me about the apartment. You're not getting your way on this one." Joshua leaned his left elbow against his door and began scratching his chin. "It will be a good place to interview him. Someplace where he's comfortable."

I wrapped up the remaining half of my sandwich in the white deli paper and squashed it into a messy wadded ball.

"How long ago did you graduate from college?" My words were heated. "Were you ever comfortable in your professor's office?"

He smiled mischievously. "Depended on the professor, Mrs. Robinson."

I frowned at him. It was something I didn't want to know about.

"But then again, if he has this admiration for law enforcement, bringing him in and sitting him down in front of Dan might be just what we need to set him babbling."

"No," I said firmly. "My office."

"I was only joking about brining him in."

I looked up at him through half closed eyelids. "Next time I want Genoa and provolone on a hard roll."

Chapter Twenty-four

The full moon was barely visible, hanging against the backdrop of a dusky sky. Joshua drove off, as I waved and wrapped my coat tightly around myself like a security blanket. My throat was dry and my eyes were watering, but I opted to sit on the front stoop, the cold of the cement seeping through my wool coat and cutting through my body. I watched as students passed by me, joking and carrying on like they owned the world. At that age, they did. The world was theirs—for the time being.

My gaze drifted off to something my mind couldn't focus upon.

Empowerment, that's what he felt. He felt empowered by the pain he could inflict upon someone who was weaker, just as he had been subjected to when he was younger and weaker. Sheer hatred for his victim and ultimate power over her. Just your standard run-of-the-mill pathological violent offender, committing murders that appeared random and unprovoked. That's why society never understood why they happened. The victim was a stranger to the killer—a matter of convenience. But there was always a reason, whether it was the perfume she was wearing, the way she parted her hair or how she let her head fall back when she laughed. It only took one thing to set him off. She was the cure to an emotionally debilitating anomie giving way to an uncontrollable rage.

I shuddered and my body tingled. I still refused to believe that Taekishi would have killed her, or hired someone to kill her. He was a difficult personality, but I believed that he loved his child. Parents couldn't hate their child—or could they? Mine did.

I climbed the stairs to my second-floor apartment and fell into the cozy warmth of my couch and a fleece blanket. The phone rang.

Dan took great pleasure in telling me that the strange U-shaped marks did not come from the butt of a gun whose magazine had been removed. The lab had tested sixty-two different models of semi-automatics, and not one fit.

I abruptly hung up.

The U-shaped marks were created by something unique. And that's what this sociopath wanted—to be unique. But right now, I didn't care about the unknown marks. For the next twenty minutes I slipped in and out of a light sleep. Images of Sumi's scarred arms flashed before me in stark contrast to her smiling face from the photograph on her desk. The bloodied blades cut through the photograph and sliced those two smiling faces into shards that floated to the floor.

"Weaker," I muttered in a half conscious state. "He preyed on her because she was weaker. He lashed out at her because she was weaker."

Again, Sumi's scarred arms flashed before me: evidence of the turmoil within. All her successes were merely overcompensation for her helplessness.

"She cut because she was weaker." My mind began racing in a cloud of incoherent and fragmented thoughts. "*He* cut her because she was cutting."

I sprang to an upright position. My heart was racing and my forehead beaded with sweat. I patted my face. I was warm, but I shivered and pulled the fleece up around me.

The phone rang. It was Joshua.

"You sound terrible," he said. "You coming down with something?"

"I think I already have," I groaned, sucking on a thermometer.

"I was calling to let you know that Heather Gross is actually one of Becca Randall's roommates."

My body felt disconnected from my brain. "Becca, the one from the photograph."

"Yeah, I know. It makes more sense now. And I just heard from Toolmarkings." He chuckled. "Bad news is—"

"I know. Dan called me a while ago."

"He has your number?"

"Apparently."

"Sorry."

"The cuts were a little too deep, anyway." My eyes narrowed as I read the mercury resting unmercifully at 101°. "I think it was just wishful thinking. We need to get on their case and find out what the hell made them."

"The good news is, Dan can't walk around like some cocky piece of shit."

"Joshua!" I managed to croak.

"What's it read?"

"One-oh-one."

There was concern in his voice. "You haven't been taking care of yourself. Want me to come over?"

I fell back into the sofa cushions. "No, thanks, that's okay. I'm expecting Kyle later."

"Oh."

"Joshua. I think I know why he chose the arms."

"Yeah?"

The walls in my apartment began to close in on me and I saw sharp flashes of light shooting through my line of vision. Great: a migraine and a fever. Give me cramps and we could call this a party.

I coughed violently. "Pull together all of what we know of the typical generalizations: weaker, a sense of power, yadda, yadda. Well, this guy is obviously smart, and even more intelligent than we'd normally perceive this type of offender as being. In fact he's downright self-absorbed."

"It was a well-planned crime."

"Right." I wiped my nose with the backside of my sleeve. "He obviously stalked his victim: learned her routine, knew her inside and out."

"That's standard."

"No, I mean, he *really* got to know her. Not just watching her for a few hours one night at a club. He followed her very intensely over a period of time. Whatever it took."

"The killing was perfectly timed in a location that was easily accessible, but conveniently hidden from sight," Joshua said.

"And he presumably cleaned up the apartment. Everything was virtually undetected. He's very organized."

"So what about the limbs?" he asked with genuine interest.

I shot to an upright position and my ears popped loudly. "Because he's an arrogant fuck!"

"I don't think that will hold much merit in the medical journals."

"The choice of the arms has nothing to do with being ridiculed as a child for having boney elbows, or whatever the hell," I explained eloquently, clearing phlegm from the back of my throat. "It has to do with us hunting a very intelligent and self-infatuated personality."

There was skepticism in his voice. "The UNSUB is a narcissistic egomaniac, who kills for the hell of it?"

"No, he definitely kills because he hates." My eyes were watering, and Joshua's voice was becoming distant as a wall of congestion filled my head. I could hear my own words echoing against the inside of my skull. "He feels inferior. He's lashing out."

Joshua snorted. "Thanks for the trip back to Profiling 101."

I cringed at the mention of my body temperature. "But specifically why the arms? Because he's on some kind of goddamned mission. Sumi was a weaker person, and to anyone who knew, her arms were proof of this. He specifically targeted this area. He was removing her weakness."

"And this guy was doing her a favor? How do we know he knew about her cutting?"

My nose was running endlessly, and I wadded up a corner of a tissue and shoved it up my left nostril. "We found Sumi with her sleeves rolled up to just a few inches below her elbows with some of her scars visible. A woman who cuts makes damned certain that her scars are covered. In fact, keeping them hidden becomes an obsession."

"They could've ridden up her arms during the struggle."

"No," I said firmly, falling back into the sofa cushions and staring at a photo of Sumi's arms. "They were definitely rolled. He was letting *us* know." My voice became flat. "His criminal signature: it's all kind of godlike."

"Then he must be a doctor," Joshua chortled.

My laughter hurt my teeth. "It's also about power and control, and his sheer anger toward women."

He grunted with slight approval. "He's just a grab bag of psychological analysis."

I frowned into the phone.

Joshua was silent, and I feared that if he didn't say something soon, I'd be unconscious before the conversation went any further.

"You know, you think better when you're ill."

A hacking cough attacked my chest, forcing me to spit into a tissue. "I'm sexier, too."

He laughed, but his tone quickly became serious. "He has to be very manipulative and conniving in order to get close to his victims."

"A good performer, with a talent for appearing . . . harmless." I rested my head against a pile of throw pillows. "The mind is a complicated minefield."

"I thought it was a terrible thing to waste."

I pulled an Imitrex from my purse and wondered how it would mix with NyQuil. "In some instances, I think that it would be better if minds were wasted."

Joshua's tone became sullen. "Hey, Meredith, I'm sorry about the way I've been treating you lately. I guess I've been really moody. Kirsten had called in the morning. . . ."

His voice trailed off and I woke to hear him asking, "So would it be okay if I sat in on your meeting tomorrow?"

I couldn't open my eyes. They were glued together with gunk. "Yeah, sure. Why the hell not? The kid likes the FBI. It would be really *kewl*."

"Thanks. I'm going to have Dan track down who Sumi

was calling at Bellevue. That's a good place to start with the psychological dysfunction, and maybe where we'll find him."

"Seems logical," I mumbled. "Anyone there could've acquired a list of potential victims. Welcome to the Big Apple. There are plenty of people in therapy he can prey upon."

Joshua's nervous laughter quickly faded, and I awoke an hour later to find Kyle looming over me, kindly taking the buzzing phone from my ear.

Chapter Twenty-five

The NYPD had finally given its official news conference on the matter. Actually, it was part of a bigger news conference. A little footnote to a discussion on the mayor's budget plan for the next fiscal quarter. *The Times'* surprisingly brief article was accompanied by a small picture of the mayor captured in midsentence. It was the same on page eight of the *Daily News*. In the picture, half of Dan's body was seen poking into the left side of the frame. He seemed alienated and uncomfortable surrounded by the dark stiff suits of the mayor's aides standing around him. I studied the mayor's expression. He was probably in the midst of explaining how his heart went out to the victim and her family, and how he had personally gone to their home to comfort them, spending a good few hours out of his day. I folded up the paper. I really disliked the mayor as a person, but respected him as a politician. He was good at being just that, and that's what makes a successful mayor.

I dialed Noyitsu's number, and the receptionist directed my call to Mr. Miyaki's office, where I was instantly placed in the responsible hands of his assistant.

"I'm sorry, ma'am, but I can barely hear you."

I drew the receiver closer to my mouth. My head was still cloudy from cold medication, and I was feeling worse than I had the night before. To me, my voice was loud and ringing in my ears when I spoke. Everything else was barely audible. Everyday sounds were buffered against a thick wall of congestion. I raised my voice and repeated my request for Taekishi's attention. He was at lunch—I checked my watch—at 11:00 AM.

I rolled my eyes, and Joshua shrugged. "Tell him it's about his daughter," I ordered.

"I'm sorry, but he's at lu—"

"Just tell him." I leaned back in my office chair. My first appointment would be banging on my door in half an hour.

One minute later I had Taekishi on the line.

"I need to know what kind of help you were getting for her."

He didn't respond.

"Mr. Miyaki, enough of the games." I wiped my nose, and the edges of my nostrils protested with a burning sensation that seemed to spread throughout my body like a parasite. "I need you to be up front with me. Who was she seeing? What was her therapy for?"

Taekishi sighed deeply. "Her arms."

"Yes, I know, but—"

"Then isn't it obvious?" his tone was heated. "She was sick. She had no regard for her safety."

My eyelids fell. "The cutting isn't the reason, it's just

the end result of something deeper. I need to know what was destroying her."

"Why? She didn't kill herself, someone else did. Why aren't you looking for my daughter's murderer?"

"I am," I replied firmly. "If I knew more about Sumi—"

There was disdain in Taekishi's voice. "I wasn't privy to that information. I have a meeting now, Ms. Brantley."

As I considered my strategy, I crossed my legs and leaned back in my chair so it rolled until it hit the wall behind me.

"I wish you hadn't run from me the other night at your daughter's apartment."

Joshua looked up from the floor.

Taekishi was silent at first, but then he replied with a cracking voice, "I don't know what you're talking about."

I nodded cynically at his predictable response, but couldn't be certain if he was being honest. Taekishi always sounded untrustworthy.

"Good day, Ms. Brantley. I have a meeting now."

Chapter Twenty-six

When Denny arrived, Joshua guided him to an empty chair across from me on the opposite side of the desk. He didn't seem to mind that a "colleague of mine researching professor-student relationships" wanted to sit in on our meeting.

Denny ran his fingers through his hair, as if he were being interviewed on television. He was very peculiar, and seemed to be thriving on the attention.

"So, Denny, what did you want to talk to me about?" I sipped on some tea with honey. My body relaxed as the caffeine dripped through my veins.

"Well, when I originally signed the appointment sheet, I was going to ask you about crime rate versus social structure. From last week's lecture."

I nodded the boulder on my shoulders called my head, but added for Denny's benefit, "Yes."

"Now I think I've got a bigger concern." He fidgeted

awkwardly and shifted his body's angle so that it symboli-
cally shut Joshua out from the conversation.

"You know," Joshua said graciously, "I could really use a
cigare—"

He caught my look.

"A soda. You want anything, Denny?" he offered.

Denny nodded and put in an order for an orange
juice. He waited a few minutes after the door closed as if
he had been fooled before into believing that someone
had left the room when they really hadn't.

"He's gone," I assured him.

"Yeah, I know. His stinky cologne isn't as strong
anymore."

When I smiled my face began to tingle.

Denny licked his lips and tipped his head up. I heard
small bones cracking in his neck. The fluorescent lights
hanging from the ceiling reflected off his tinted glasses,
making him look like some overgrown mutant bug from
an old sci-fi movie.

"I'm kind of worried about my grade on the essay." He
pushed himself farther up in his seat. "If my GPA drops
below 2.5, they'll put me on academic probation and I
could lose my scholarship."

I wiped my nose again and caught myself shoving the
used tissue up the sleeve of my sweater. As a teenager, I
had always vowed that I would never grow old and do
that. The tissue landed squarely in the trashcan where I
tossed it.

"Denny, you shouldn't worry. There are still two more
essays and a final exam."

He cringed. The thought of more essays merely sent
an agonizing shock through his body. "Can I get a redo?"

My watering eyes widened. A redo? This was college;
there were no second chances. "Why do you think I

should offer you a chance to rewrite your essay?" After all, he was the one who had written *Pre-Madonnas*.

Denny shrugged. "I dunno, because."

Because he was blind?

"I can't let you do that. You'll just have to work harder on the next one." I softened my approach. "Take my comments and apply them to the other essays. You have good ideas, you just need to organize them better."

Joshua returned and passed out a brown bag full of goodies. As Denny sucked on a straw, I slowly ate a chocolate Pop Tart. The sounds of orange juice riding up the inside of Denny's straw filled the awkward silence that had fallen between us.

I carefully placed the Pop Tart on my desk when Joshua cleared his throat.

"Denny," I said.

He withdrew his lips from the straw.

"How well did you know Sumi?"

His expression hardened with tight creases and he suddenly looked much older. "We were really good friends," his soft voice in stark contrast to his face. "We did everything together."

My right eyebrow arched. So he had said before.

"Everything?"

"Yeah." A large smile spread from his lips. "We'd go places like the museums, and we'd see movies. Romantic comedies were her favorite. We'd even go clothes shopping. She was very comfortable around me."

I smiled, and took a sip of my lukewarm tea. It tasted like crap. "Yesterday you mentioned something about her problem—"

He began shaking his head solemnly. "I wish I could've helped her. Her dad was such an ass to her."

Both Joshua and I traded quick glances.

"How?" Joshua asked with intensity.

A large, knowing grin spread across Denny's face and his mouth puckered with amusement.

"Nice job," I scolded dryly.

Joshua pressed a finger to his sinuses.

"I knew it!" Denny declared gleefully. "I knew he was a Fed, and you're helping him. You know, you could've just asked me. I would've helped. You didn't have to do all this acting, because honestly, you guys suck."

"I'm still your professor," I reminded him through a narrow stare.

"Right, sorry." He pulled himself together and sat up straight in his chair, again combing his hair with his fingers. "Ask me whatever you need. This is so cool."

Joshua's eyes were like saucers when he looked at me.

"Okay." I blew my nose and it made an embarrassing honking sound. "How did you wind up with Sumi's coat?"

Denny's face dropped. "Anything but that."

"Really?" Joshua pulled his chair closer to Denny.

"You said she gave it to you Thursday," I reminded him. "Sumi was killed that night."

"I know," Denny whined.

"Then how did you wind up with it?" Though my questions were direct, my tone was gentle and almost motherly.

He remained surprisingly calm and collected—maybe too calm. "I saw her earlier that night. We were going to check out a store on 115th and Amsterdam. It was cold, and I didn't wear a jacket because it was warm earlier, so she gave me her coat."

Joshua leaned back in his chair, and I rolled my eyes as we both considered the validity of Denny's claim.

"I'm going to have to take the coat," Joshua said kindly.

Denny's head bobbed from side-to-side like a child who was trying to avoid his chores. "It's kind of cold outside."

"It's evidence, Denny. I'm required to."

The idea seemed to intrigue him, and Denny slipped his arms from the sleeves and handed Joshua the coat.

"I need everything that was in it," Joshua said, inconspicuously eyeing a small dark stain on the edge of the right sleeve. "We can go back to your home if—"

"There was nothing in the pockets." He paused. "And there's nothing in them now."

Nevertheless, Joshua dipped his hands inside all of them anyway.

I casually took another bite of my Pop Tart. "You know, Denny, this does raise some interesting questions."

He cocked his head to one side and crossed his legs. "Like what?"

"Well, why you kept Sumi's coat once you found out about her."

His expression hardened. "What difference does it make? Was giving you the coat going to bring her back?"

"No, it wouldn't have."

But he knew that it would've been important to us. That we would've been searching for it. I didn't believe for a moment that Sumi had given him the coat, if it was even hers, but how and when, in the timeline of events Denny acquired it was important. He wasn't telling us everything.

I studied him and absorbed all that was Denny: a very clever young man who knew more than he was allowing himself to reveal, or a broken-hearted friend who was revealing more than he knew.

Joshua's voice fell to a deep rumble: his Fed voice. "It could've been potential evidence."

There was a mild look of fear on Denny's face.

"Sumi's father." I finished off the last of the Pop Tart. "You said he was mean to her—"

"An ass."

"Okay."

As he pointed, Denny began waving a finger through the air. "Now there's someone you should be arresting."

Joshua's eyes narrowed. "Did you ever witness him mistreating her?" he asked.

"Well, I never *saw* him. But I'd go over to their apartment and he'd be there, railing on her like she was the maid." Deep wrinkles cut across his forehead. "She wasn't good enough for this or that, her grades were bad, he didn't like the guys she dated."

A stern expression enveloped Joshua's face. "And that's why she was cutting?"

"Cutting? Class?"

"No—"

I held up my hand. "Yeah, cutting class."

Chapter Twenty-seven

As much as it pains me to do so, I can probably attribute my first lesson in deceit and the importance of observant investigative skills to—of all people—my mother. In the very early seventies she was the envy of all her God-fearing lady friends. For she possessed the supernatural ability to fold fitted sheets with perfectly square corners.

On laundry day I would stand in front of the linen closet, the crown of my head barely reaching the shelf with the sheets. One could not discern which were the fitted and which were the flat. It had caused me great angst in the early years of my education, casting upon me an unspoken pressure to measure up to the same perfection and quality that to a young daughter epitomizes her mother.

But just as a child begins to question the existence of Santa Claus, I too began to question the ability to fold fitted sheets square. What was my mother's black magic?

One afternoon as she made molt cider while singing a roaring rendition of "Mack the Knife," on my tippy toes I quietly removed her stacks of sheets. To intrude upon her domain was an open invitation for the back of her hand against the side of my head, or anywhere else that it could reach, but I was determined and filled with reckless abandon.

My heart was racing and my palms sweaty as I unfolded the enormous piece of fabric on the floor of the upstairs hall. Large creases had pressed themselves into an equilateral grid. Fine perfection. As I breathed in deeply and pulled back the last of the remaining folds, I hadn't noticed that my mother's singing had stopped. It was then that I made the discovery—the fitted corners were messy and bunched up, surreptitiously hidden and wadded beneath the outer layer of the sheet. On that bitterly cold afternoon my six-year-old brain realized two things: My mother was not infallible; and one must look beyond what was cosmetically obvious. The real answers lie deeper, and I had to be willing to delve a little further regardless of the risk.

I also learned that the inside of my mother's hand was just as painful as the backside of it—but I guess I had already known that.

The Brittany dorm was not as I had remembered it. It seemed like a lifetime since I first set foot in the lobby as a nervous and wide-eyed freshman. The very overweight security guard seemed less than interested with the comings and goings of the students, failing to check most for college IDs like he was required to. However, Joshua and I were obviously out of our element, and the guard made us wait for Becca to come down and sign us in. Wearing his large Maglite flashlight like the sidearm he wished he could've had attached to his belt, the security guard pointed to the guest sign-in book and asked for photo IDs. Joshua and I both handed him our Virginia driver's licenses.

Through a sea of tight-fitting black clothing and over-sized college sweatshirts, I caught a glimpse of a tall, thin young woman weaving her way through the crowd. With her flowing auburn hair and pouty lips, she could have just as easily have been a supermodel strutting down the catwalk, for the snapshot in Sumi's room did not do her justice.

She paused and studied me curiously before extending her hand. "Hi, you're Professor Brantley?"

I nodded my head and introduced Joshua. Now that we were closer, I could see that she wore a lot of makeup, though she probably didn't need to. When Becca leaned over to sign the guest book, she tossed her head to the side, sending a mass of long, thick curls over her shoulder. The guard inconspicuously inhaled a whiff of her shampoo, but quickly turned away when he caught my biting stare.

As we rode the elevator to the fourteenth floor, Becca spoke nervously of her classes, college life and the stupidity of the university's meal plan. We all watched the numbers above our heads light up as we passed each floor. The missing number thirteen was proof of the building's age.

On the east side of the building, Room 1408 was one of the larger suites, divided into two rooms with a private bath. With its stocky, modular furniture and wooden bunk beds, it was a long way from being the Park Plaza. A thick cloud of hazy smoke lingered in the air, and I could immediately feel the pressure against my sinuses. One of the upperclassmen living in the second room nodded as she rushed past us, apparently late for a class. Becca welcomed us inside and immediately lit up. Joshua eyed me tentatively and did the same.

"You don't mind, do you?" she asked me, her cigarette glowing like an inviting bull's-eye.

"No, that's fine," I said impatiently, keeping a steady eye on Joshua's guilty expression.

Becca sat on her bed cross-legged and offered us old wooden desk chairs. When she pulled up the sleeves of her sweatshirt, I was quick to search them for any scars, but I found none.

"So what does the FBI want with me?" she asked, her pretty face disappearing in a cloud of smoke. "This doesn't have anything to do with what happened at Berkeley, does it?"

"No," Joshua replied curiously.

Becca looked away, hoping that he wouldn't pursue the matter.

"Becca," I began gently. "This is about Sumi."

She squinted at me, her eyes watery and red from the cigarette she held close to her chin. About a half-inch of ash dangled dangerously from the end, and I nervously watched it, expecting to have to catch it before it landed in the folds of her bed sheets.

"What about her?"

"She called you the other night."

Becca snorted. "Well, talk about not wasting words. She called me a lot of nights—and days, and afternoons."

I offered her one of my penetrating gazes and was unnerved when she gave one right back.

"She called you the night she was killed."

"Maybe. I was hanging out with some friends, just down the hall. The music was kind of loud, so the phone could've been ringing but I wouldn't have heard it."

"And she wouldn't have left a message," I mumbled to myself.

She stared at me. "What was she going to say? Hi, Becca. I've got a box cutter and I'm just about to use it. Call me when you get in." Becca shook her head angrily, her luxurious curls bouncing like springs. "She was in a lot of trouble. I couldn't understand the stuff with her arms." She shuddered. "It was sick."

"Yes, it was," I said softly. "She was sick and was getting help."

"Yeah, whatever," she replied with the wave of her hand and a long drag on her cigarette. "Those idiots at the Medical Center weren't helping any."

I sniffled ungracefully. "NYU's Medical Center?"

Becca reached over to the windowsill and tossed me a box of tissues, which landed squarely in my lap.

"Thanks," I said dryly.

She nodded. "Sumi just began hurting herself more. Christ, I had to stop her one night from practically tearing up her arteries in one arm."

Joshua winced at the image and his cigarette dropped, nearly hitting him in the chin.

Becca looked over at him and finally flicked her ash through the narrow neck of a half-empty bottle of Heineken. "So are you going to ask me anything?"

"What happened at Berkeley?" he shot back.

Becca looked away and I followed her gaze to a duplicate copy of the photo of her and Sumi. But my eyes quickly fell upon the Orioles baseball cap slung over one of the bedposts.

"Are you from Baltimore?" I asked her as casually as possible.

"No, San Diego." She looked over at the cap. "My boyfriend is from Baltimore."

I pulled my chair closer to the bed. "Becca, did you go to Sumi's apartment Saturday night?"

Her face was filled with alarm. "How did you know about the apartment?"

"Her father."

"Bastard."

Joshua looked at me quickly before asking, "You were there. Did you see someone?"

She took another long drag off her cigarette, squinting as the smoke filled her eyes, and flipping her hair from her face as she exhaled. Becca was flirting.

I looked over at Joshua's stupid grin. And he was enjoying it.

"I went over because Sumi called." Becca tossed the remaining butt into the Heineken bottle. "I mean, I thought it was her. I didn't know about what happened until Sunday, when I called her home. Sumi used to call me all the time and hang up without saying anything when she was going through one of her cutting spells."

"She was reaching out," I explained.

Becca lit up again. She didn't seem to care either way. "There was someone there. I don't know who it was, but I didn't wait to find out."

Her eyes narrowed on me. It was the same look she had given me when we first spotted each other downstairs in the lobby, and I instinctively stiffened my posture.

"It was you, wasn't it?" Her tone was accusatory.

As I casually took off my coat, without looking at her I said, "I bet you want to be a lawyer."

"Yeah," she said in bewilderment. "If the acting thing doesn't work. How did you know that?"

I looked up at her with a gentle smirk. "Why did you run?"

"Why did you chase me?"

I nodded. She did have a point. "Because you ran."

Becca shoved her cigarette into her mouth and when she sucked on it her cheeks disappeared only to accentuate her already angular face.

"You had a gun," she said in a lawyerly tone.

Joshua quickly looked over at me.

"No, I didn't," I said much too defensively.

"You reached for one."

That I had. I stared at Becca, and I was beginning to hate everything about her: her stinking cigarette, her pretty face, her perfect hair, her roving eye . . .

"Well, I run for the track team, so it wasn't so bad," she said, tugging at the front of her baggy sweatshirt. "Looks like our little misunderstanding at least gave one of us a workout."

I smiled with mock politeness. She was a cocky little bitch on wheels, and the idea of her and Sumi being friends seemed unbelievable. My only satisfaction was in knowing that twenty years from now, at the rate she was sucking through those cigarettes, she'd look like a piece of crumpled parchment.

"You got there rather quickly," I said in a not-so-friendly tone. "Only five minutes to get from Tenth Street? Oh, I forgot, you run for the track team."

Her eyes were like slits and her lower lip was pushed out so far it looked swollen. "Heather and I were on Forty-second Street rehearsing on Theatre Row. We have our calls forwarded to my cell phone when we're out together."

Cell phones. The times had definitely changed. I remembered living on hot dogs and baked beans while I was at NYU.

"Look, for real, my phone went off a couple of times that night. I knew it was her, but I just ignored it." Becca's face softened and she looked apologetic. "I was having a good time."

I wanted to tell her that she should not blame herself, that if she had gone to Sumi's apartment, she might have been murdered, too. But my conscience failed me, and petty jealousy got in the way.

Joshua held what was left of his cigarette between two fingers and searched the room. Becca reached over and handed him the Heineken bottle, where he extinguished the butt.

"Do you know Denny Carter?" he asked. He lit up another, the flame from his chrome Zippo extending high above the color FBI seal that was printed on its side.

Her eyes scanned him and landed heavily upon his wedding ring. "Who?"

"Denny Carter. He's one of Sumi's friends."

Becca's stare was unblinking.

"He was in my Criminology lecture, along with Sumi," I explained. When her befuddled expression remained, I added, "He's blind."

Becca threw her head back, and it clunked against the wall. Her laughter was loud and almost wild. "Oh, him! That little nerd."

Joshua stared at her with disapproval.

"He's so bizarre," she said once she had calmed down and began sucking on her cigarette again. "He's creepy. He actually thought that he and Sumi were friends."

My body straightened. "They weren't?"

"No. She loaned him a notebook one time in class when he forgot his. But he was always hanging around in the same places. Sumi barely knew who he was. I think he was obsessed."

Deep concern blanketed my face. "Didn't Sumi ask for any help from NYU? Stalking is a serious issue."

"Stalking?" Becca casually waved her hand, dismissing the situation. "He was harmless." She stared at me and her voice trailed off into a meek string of excuses. "He was a geek. Just a big joke to us."

I remained focused on Becca's awkward posture, and I wasn't laughing.

We waited for an elevator going down that was empty.

"Okay," I said with a heavy sigh. "An admirer who's just one step removed from being obsessed with a woman who winds up dead. And he's wearing something that he *claims* is her coat." I stepped into the elevator. "Plus, he has a more than average interest in the investigation."

"All the makings of a prime suspect," Joshua said, staring off into space. He did not believe it either.

"But he's blind."

"That's his alibi?" He shoved a breath mint into his mouth. "Harmless, isn't that what you predicted the UN-SUB would be?"

I looked up at him from underneath my heavy eyelids. "A blind man manages to keep physical control over a young woman, who would be struggling on some level—no matter how small—for survival, kills her and *drives* her to the banks of the Hudson where he dismembers her? And we don't even know if that's really Sumi's coat."

"If it is, then he's got some 'splainin' to do, Lucy."

"Yeah, some 'splainin' would probably be some big thrill for him. They can give him a *kewl* shirt." I leaned up against the wall of the elevator.

Joshua closed his eyes. He looked so peaceful.

"There's nothing wrong with creating a fantasy if that's what gets you through the day." He began bobbing his head up and down. "Millions of people do it and don't wind up murdering. I wonder what the UNSUB took for a souvenir."

"Perhaps the sheer thrill of knowing that he brutally took the life of a young woman," I said with only mild sarcasm as I buttoned my coat.

Joshua grunted. "Well, nerd-boy is at least an interesting character."

My mouth fell agape. "Nerd-boy?"

He shrugged and smiled. "Becca was right, he is a nerd."

"Great," I frowned. "I really don't buy the bit about Sumi giving up her coat to him, especially now, with that little bitch telling us that he was basically the butt of all their juvenile jokes."

He gave me one of those indecipherable frowns.

"I can't imagine Sumi being friends with her," I said.

"Why?" He looked genuinely surprised. "We don't know what Sumi was like in person."

"Well, the little Sharon Stone-wannabe has an attitude problem."

Joshua grinned. "She's probably confused. Her friend's dead."

He was right.

I wiped my nose on an old tissue. "I guess she's stuck in the second stage of mourning. I hope it's not a chronic trait."

The elevator chimed above us as it passed by each floor, finally stopping at the second. No one got on.

"We almost made it," I mused.

"Sharon Stone-wannabe?"

"You weren't helping."

"Jealous?" He stepped closer to me and began poking me in the shoulder.

"Quit it," I said angrily, moving to the opposite corner and then adding in jest, "I thought I was being traded in for a younger model."

Joshua's expression fell. "Interesting."

The elevator bounced before coming to a halt, and the doors opened.

"That's what Kirsten said to me yesterday morning."

Chapter Twenty-eight

For years the NYPD's Forensic Investigative Unit had been housed at the Police Academy in the 13th Precinct on East Twentieth Street, between Second and First avenues, but a new building had recently been erected.

Dan met me in front of the new facility in Jamaica, Queens, while Joshua parked the car.

In silence, Dan brought us to the Blood Analysis Division. His taciturn demeanor was a result of the idiotic competition growing between the two agencies. As far as anyone was concerned, our retrieval of the coat had been a point for the FBI. But what angered Dan even more was the fact that I had contacted Joshua instead of him when I learned of the coat.

He was right. I should've called him first. It was his case and his evidence. But the less I had to deal with him, the better.

"Have you interviewed Denny?" I asked cautiously.

Dan didn't look at me.

"Don't you think it's odd that he was running around with what might be a murdered girl's coat?"

His tone was firm. "No. What I find odd is that"—he paused and shook his head—"Never mind. I want to see what this coat's about. First."

We followed Dan into the lab.

"Elliot," Dan shouted out jovially, as he lumbered over to him: a quick about-face in his mood.

Joshua and I approached cautiously, not wanting to disturb any delicate procedure that Dr. Elliot Thomas might be conducting.

An agarose gel was resting on the counter before him. At the moment, Elliot was just about to apply an electric current to DNA fragments and perform the procedure of electrophoresis.

He looked up. "Hey, Grissard. You got something for me?"

Dan nodded and performed the cursory introductions.

Elliot laid out the coat on another counter top covered with white paper. He dimmed the lights, and an assistant helped him with the ALS. Through my goggles, small specks and hairs of varying lengths cut through the darkness like glowing embers. Elliot began filling paper envelopes with different pieces of evidence that he picked out from the folds of the coat. When he was finished, he turned the right sleeve toward the ALS, and the suspicious stain Joshua had noticed earlier glowed like a beacon. Elliot scraped a sample of the dried substance onto the tip of a cotton swab. The assistant flicked on the lights, and we all blinked in response to the sudden shift in the environment.

"I need to determine whether this is blood and if it's human," Elliot explained, as he placed a drop of distilled water onto the substance and it turned dark brown. "You wouldn't believe how many things get sent here and they turn out to be paint, ketchup or very expensive marinara sauce."

Quietly, he applied a drop of the reagent, phenolphthalein, and the tip of the cotton swab turned a muted greenish color. He then added a drop of hydrogen peroxide and the cotton swab turned pink.

"It passed the first test," he declared. "It's *probably* blood." He spun around on his stool. "So, Grissard, how're your kids?"

"Eh, what can I say. The oldest boy tells me he wants to be a cop. Just like his old man."

Elliot released a hearty laugh, as he placed more of a sample of the brown substance on a glass slide. "Mine tells me he wants to be a ballerina."

Dan's eyes grew wide with sympathy. "Hey, man, I'm sorry."

Elliot added a few drops of a chemical and smiled. "He's only two."

He stepped aside and allowed each of us to take a peek through the microscope. Tiny red crystals of hemochromagen were magnified to the size of winter icicles.

"This means it's blood," Elliot explained. "We'll test it with a human anti-agent and that will tell us whether it came from a person."

"Dr. Thomas?" I asked quizzically, as I held one of the envelopes and peered inside. "These are the only hairs that you pulled from the coat?"

He nodded.

"No others?"

I caught Dan shooting him a look, but Elliot replied diplomatically by shaking his head.

"All the hairs are blond," I muttered to myself. "If this

coat was in someone's possession up until a few days ago, wouldn't there still be some of her hairs on it, as well?"

Elliot stood from his stool. "Probably. After all, a person can shed a lot of hair in a twenty-four-hour period. Of course, it varies from person to person, and is dependent on variables such as individual grooming habits. But I'm not a hair expert."

Dan looked as if he was about to fall asleep.

"So if this coat belonged to a young woman and then had been worn around by a second person for the past," I counted back in my head, "five days, and assuming it hadn't been cleaned, then there *should've* been some of her hairs present. Don't you think?"

Elliot nodded his head ferociously. "Absolutely! But a barrage of comparison tests would have to be run. You can't just look at these hairs and say who they belong to. However, I can say this: They're from two different people."

I brought my face closer to the evidence. "How?"

After all, he was not an expert.

He leaned in. "The color appears very close, but there are much longer hairs and then some are cut shorter." Elliot sighed, as he straightened his posture. "Used to be that one could say if it belonged to a man or a woman, but these days, there are no rules about hairstyles."

"The woman whose hair should be on the coat had long dark hair."

"You can see that with the longer hairs, the whole hair is blond." He pointed to one of the samples that still had the root attached. "Well, these are definitely not dyed," he explained as he eyed the darkish color making its way from my scalp.

I uncomfortably massaged my roots with my fingertips.

He looked through the other envelopes spread out on the counter. "There aren't any other hairs, but these."

I stared at the coat like it was a bitter enemy. There was nothing unique about it. It was just like three million other coats that people owned in this city. Tracing it would be nearly impossible.

Dan eyed me accusingly, as if I had wasted his time. Through a massive wad of bubble gum, he murmured the question that was on everyone's mind:

"Then whose fucking coat is this?"

Chapter Twenty-nine

Dan had waited after one of my classes in order to ask Denny some questions. Nerd-boy seemed all too thrilled with the notion. If he had been a sighted person, he probably would've been reeling with excitement when Dan—by force of habit—displayed his shiny gold detective shield. They waited in the far rear corner until the room cleared and held a seemingly cordial conversation that I was not invited to. Based on their body language, the fifteen-minute conversation was relaxed and more like two guys eating pizza and drinking beer than a member of New York's Finest trying to acquire information about a murder investigation. They were finished when I heard them break out into roaring laughter. Dan stood and smacked Denny between the shoulder blades in a friendly gesture. He reached inside his coat and handed him a navy blue cap that had NYPD in white letters across the front. Denny nearly squealed with delight as he ran his pale fingers across the embroidery.

I watched this exchange with an undeniable admiration for the sergeant. Dan left Denny with his hat, and shrugged and rolled his eyes as he walked past me on his way out of the lecture hall. I wasn't certain if Denny was aware of my presence, but I packed my things quickly and quietly, and bolted out of there without saying a word.

Clutching my briefcase in one hand, I searched sections A and B of *The Times*. There were no more articles on Sumi. There were bigger things happening in the world, and the public wouldn't hear another word about the dead college student until there was an arrest, or . . . another victim.

"Professor Brantley!"

I shoved the paper into my briefcase as I walked briskly along Waverly Place. My expression fell to an unenthusiastic frown when I saw Denny walking alongside me.

He was wearing a new coat today. It was black wool and very similar to the one he had given up as being Sumi's. Except this one buttoned on the opposite side.

"I tried getting to you after meeting with Sergeant Grissard," he said with rushed words. "But too many people got in the way. I thought I was going to lose you on the way out of Main Building, but I was able to still smell your perfume."

My eyes widened curiously and I stared at his gleeful expression—I didn't wear perfume—perhaps it was my shampoo. I was usually very accepting of people's individual quirkiness, but I was beginning to believe that Becca was correct—Denny was a nerd.

"Wasn't that the coolest?" he hollered. Denny put on

the navy blue cap with a firm and confident tug. "Wait 'til my little brother hears about this. He'll be so jealous about the cap."

I struggled with a smile, but only managed to grimace. "Well, I hope Sergeant Grissard wasn't too hard on you."

Denny's face drooped. "No, not at all. He was really nice. Look, I'm sorry about Sumi's coat," he said with sincerity. "I should've given it to you before, when it came up, but I was kind of edgy. I mean, I only want to help."

We were stopped, waiting for traffic on the corner of Waverly and Broadway.

"Which way are you headed, Denny?"

Hopefully, in the opposite direction.

"Eighth Street. I need to get the N."

I sighed quietly. "Well, I'm headed that way, too."

The light changed and along with the rest of the hordes, I stormed across the street. I slowed my pace when I realized that Denny was trailing behind me.

"You know, I really hope you can find out what happened to Sumi." Denny's demeanor had become somber.

I rolled my eyes, but replied: "Yes, I can understand. It must be very difficult to lose a close friend."

"Sgt. Grissard said that you guys are making headway."

"Did he, now?"

He shook his head sadly, as we crossed to the other side of Broadway and reached the entrance for the uptown N train.

"Sometimes I just wish that I had stayed with her a little longer that night. That I hadn't let her go off on her own."

"Oh, right, the store," My tone successfully feigned interest in his delusional fantasy. "On 100-and—"

"On 115th and Amsterdam." Denny placed his hand

on the handrail and took the first step down into the subway.

"Looks like this is where we part," I said kindly. "Start working on your paper."

He cringed.

"I'm sure you'll do fine." I stood at the top of the steps waiting for Denny to descend, but he remained stationary. "Was there something else?"

He lowered his head and shifted his weight awkwardly between his feet. "Well, I was wondering if you looked into Sumi's dad, yet?"

I stepped closer to him as a steady stream of people climbed up out of the subway and the sounds of a train leaving the station faded into the bowels of the city.

"Why are you so interested in Sumi's father?" There was an accusatory tone in my voice that I was almost successful in smothering. "Do you think he mistreated her?"

"Think?" Denny cried incredulously. "I know it!"

"How? You didn't see it."

He flinched, and I immediately felt guilty at the unintentional harshness of my words.

"But I know it." Denny's voice was soft. "I heard the things he said. 'You won't amount to anything; you're not good enough for this-or-that.' There was a change in her."

I put a hand to my throbbing temple. Whatever make-believe relationship he thought that he had with Sumi was his own, but it was wasting my time and giving me a migraine.

"Denny," I said as gently as possible. "We're doing what we can with this investigation, but please, for your own sake"—and mine—"would you please concentrate on your class work?"

He was silent, his deadened gaze focused on the mannequins displayed in the Gap's window. He turned to me. "You think I'm crazy."

I inhaled. "No, I—"

"Yes, you do." He came back up the first step, but on equal ground I still towered over him. "You think I'm a liar." His body began to shake, and he anxiously banged the end of his cane against the pavement. "Well, I think you suck! I think this whole thing sucks! And I think the rest of you suck!"

I remained stiff, but my words were firm. "Denny, keep your voice down."

"No," he yelled, and people turned and stared as they walked by. "Hey, everyone, she works for the FB—"

I quickly thrust my hand over his mouth. People still gawked, but no one broke their stride to find out why the tall lady was stifling the blind boy.

Anger quickly grew inside of me, and my blood boiled. "Listen, you little pathological liar. We know that everything you've told us is untrue." I tentatively removed my hand from his mouth, and felt assured that he wouldn't yell out. "We know the coat wasn't Sumi's. We know she wasn't your friend."

He shook his head in disbelief.

I grabbed him gently by the arm, but hurried him down the stairs into the subway station.

"What do you want," he whined.

We stopped in front of a large laminated billboard of a New York subway map, mounted to the dirty white tiles of the station. My index finger drifted slowly along the Upper West Side as it followed Broadway uptown. Columbus first, then Amsterdam; or vise versa? *Columbus crossed Amsterdam on his way to Central Park,* rang through my head. I

178

quickly followed Amsterdam until my finger stopped at the top of the park.

"110th Street," I shouted over a nearby musician's tempo-free rendition of a "Brahm's Lullabye."

A quizzical look spread across his face.

"Amsterdam stops at 110th Street," I declared, stabbing my forefinger into the map. "You said several times that you had gone with Sumi to Amsterdam and 115th."

The wheels of the approaching train screeched along the rails as it neared the station, and it slowed to 30 mph as it traveled down the final 100 feet of track. A swift breeze filled the station with a stale smell of urine.

"That address doesn't exist," I said with a tone that rang of pity. "Denny, where did you get that coat? Did you buy it somewhere and pretend?"

"We were close," his querulous voice rose to a grating pitch. "We looked out for each other."

"Denny," I said impatiently, "she barely even knew who you were."

He broke free of my hold and clumsily raced through the turnstiles onto the train that just pulled alongside the platform.

"Denny!" But he ignored me.

I sighed deeply and turned, bumping into a man in a leather jacket.

"Nice job, lady," he said sarcastically. "Next time you can go pick on a cripple."

Chapter Thirty

"Not human," was the message that played through my answering machine.

I hit the *repeat* button and listened to Joshua's voice again.

So the blood on Sumi's—Denny's—coat was from an animal, not a human. The technology did not exist yet for Elliot to determine what type of animal. Not Sumi's blood, but then again, the coat wasn't hers either. It was my opinion that Dan had been too easy on Denny the other day. He should've brought him in and given him the real interview that he wanted, and not just an interview—an interrogation, like the movies: stark white light and detective badgering him until he cried for his mommy.

I looked over at the crime-scene photos that I had begun to tape up along the living room wall by the kitchen. The small round table was no longer being used for entertaining guests; it had become my investigative office. Yellow legal pads were piled in neat, precisely square stacks of even heights. Photos of the crime scenes and the autopsy were taped along the wall, their edges parallel and evenly spaced to one another. I studied my setup like a queen on the first day of ruling her kingdom: I was just as meticulous as the killer.

I did not hear Kyle creep up from behind, and I jumped slightly when he wrapped his arms around me.

"You're a little edgy tonight," he said softly, brushing my hair aside as he began laying light kisses along the nape of my neck.

I fell back against his chest. "This thing Joshua's got me working on just gets more interesting by the day, and more frustrating."

"So what's not human?" he asked, as he gently ran his hand across my stomach.

"Just some evidence we found that we thought was pertinent. Turned out it wasn't from a human like we thought."

"Like an alien autopsy?" His face was buried somewhere in my blouse, and his words were garbled as he brushed his soft lips against my back. He purred like a lion. "I love it when you do police talk."

My soft chuckles quickly dissolved into light groans.

"Let's go to bed early," he whispered. He turned me in his arms and lightly caressed my neck with his lips. "We can get up for a late dinner." His kisses fell between my breasts. "Or an early breakfast."

"It's so tempting."

He lowered me onto the sofa and ran his hands up under my blouse.

"I thought you said bed," I said coyly.

Kyle shrugged and brought another one of his tender

181

kisses upon my lips. "It's a long way to the bedroom. I can't wait that long."

I sighed sadly. I needed to talk to Joshua and get confirmation on the status of the coat. "No, really, I've got to make some phone calls."

He pulled my blouse up under my arms and began running the tip of his tongue over my breasts.

I rubbed him gently on his shoulders. "Come on, Joshua—"

Kyle froze. "What?"

I closed my eyes and pulled my blouse back down and secured two of the top buttons. "Shit," I whispered.

I swung my legs over the edge of the sofa, and he dropped against the cushions in a mass of defeated male pride.

Kyle was staring at me, anguish filling every inch of his face.

"I'm sorry," I said.

"Me, too."

Chapter Thirty-one

The fragrant smell of oranges and lemons reached my nostrils and calmed me. It always reminded me of the night we had spent in Cliffside. Joshua had rubbed the lotion all over my body. Spreading it seductively in an even layer of oil and perfume that had bathed my skin. That night the coarse sheets covering the bed smelled like an orange grove: a lovely, sensual orange grove in the middle of—New Jersey. I quickly shook the memory out of my head and squeezed another large bead of lotion into my palm. It stung the small scratches on my hand as I rubbed it across my chapped skin.

Kyle had forgiven my Freudian slip, but I had not forgiven myself. However, what had troubled me more was whose name I had inadvertently blurted out. Perhaps I said Joshua's name after just having listened to his message, or because I had the business with the coat on my mind. I could have just as easily said anyone else's name involved with the investigation. I shuddered at the thought of calling out Dan's name.

My face hovered over the legal pad, leaving a canary yellow glow against my skin and a yellow tint in my eye. I reread my chronological outline of the events as they were now known to us, and was surprised to discover that one week had passed since I received Joshua's initial call. It seemed like months had gone by.

I flipped over the page, leaving a greasy fingerprint on the corner from the lotion. Now, it too smelled like that night.

Sumi left her apartment after 9:14 PM. At about 9:25 she hailed a cab on Fifth Avenue and presumably went directly to her apartment. With crosstown traffic, it probably took her twenty minutes. By the time she opened the front door to her apartment, it was about 9:45 or 9:50. Her final call to Becca was 9:58, but Becca did not visit her. That left a little more than an hour for someone to surprise her, beat her and kill her. Not much time. The offender definitely drove.

What happened to Sumi's coat? Her ID was intact, along with her money and jewelry. What we thought might've been the missing coat actually belonged to someone else. A dead end. Maybe the UNSUB did take her coat.

From my chair, the black-and-white photos taped to the wall were a blur to me. Just as my involvement—the FBI's involvement—in this case was a blur. Our job was to create a profile, which we did. Why was I trying to hunt down the offender? That was Dan's job. What was my obsession?

It was because I knew. We all knew that there was going to be another victim. But all we could do was wait. I was disgusted with myself. How many young women would be killed before the path became straighter and led us to this vile piece of human garbage? How many women would *I* allow to be killed?

Ockham's Razor.

I stared down at the words I had just scribbled. William Ockham: a fourteenth-century English philosopher whose words rang with so much truth and wisdom. My roller ball pen scratched through the paper as I began scribbling a figure eight in the upper corner of the page.

The simplest of competing theories be preferred to the more complex.

Maybe I had been wrong. I put on my coat and went outside.

Chapter Thirty-two

The cab left me off on the far corner of Lexington and Eighty-sixth. With my bag slung over my shoulder, I ignored the DON'T WALK light and briskly crossed to the other side when there was a break in the traffic. Both sides of Eighty-sixth Street were lined with cars, just as it had been on the night when Sumi left her building for the last time.

The Metropolitan Museum of Art loomed majestically at the end of the block, Central Park serving as its glorious backdrop. Powerful incandescent lights illuminated the façade, and large rectangular banners announcing the current exhibits flapped rapidly in the intensifying wind.

My pace slowed as I approached Sumi's building, glancing into the ornate lobby as I passed under the green awning covering the entryway.

It seemed possible that Denny had deluded himself

into believing that in his own little world, he and Sumi had some sort of relationship. And even after her death, he continued to cling to his fantasy even if he needed to fabricate evidence in a murder investigation.

To get inside the mind of a killer, you must first get inside the mind of his victim.

Those were the first words I had heard Ken Wallis utter, fourteen years ago in the small lecture at John Jay College. For a moment, I was Sumi standing at the curb, considering whether or not to take a cab and deciding that for some reason it was not in my best interest. Was the walk to her apartment time spent searching deep within herself after a confrontation with her father? She fled to her hideaway in order to escape the problems at home.

Inside the mind of his victim.

A woman whose father demanded nothing less than perfection, who demanded nothing less than his own wishes. With all her successes, Sumi still felt that she could never attain perfection. No one could. She could not control her life. But in the solitude of her safe haven, she controlled her pain. Only Sumi possessed the control over her arms. I stared at my outstretched arm. The blade searing through her skin didn't hurt her, life did. That sharp edge did not bring her tears; it nullified them. It brought her satisfaction.

I stopped where Sumi had and adjusted my collar just as she had done. An edgy wave of alarm consumed me and I looked around with a careful eye. I was being watched. It was the same feeling I had at Sumi's apartment. There was no one I could see. Perhaps it was the presence of the security cameras. Did Sumi pause because she knew that she was being followed? Had she inconspicuously checked her surroundings and then laughed and shrugged off the innate instincts serving her the warning?

In the shadows, someone was watching. I searched the block again, my eyes darting back and forth with careful precision. But things were blurred. My refusal to get prescription glasses was now coming back and biting me in the ass.

I stepped away from the glow being emitted from the light hanging beneath the awning. Someone was creeping up from behind. My heart began to race and I swung around just in time to find a dark figure almost pressed up against me. My body reacted solely on instinct and I took a step back. When the figure came toward me, all I saw was the arm that reached for me, and I grabbed it, twisting it under and pulling it behind the stranger's back. I pushed the tall figure up against the wall of 29 East Eighty-sixth Street, demanding information before I got answers to the previous questions.

"Would you mind releasing me?" a voice calmly asked from the dark.

"Mr. Miyaki?" But I didn't loosen my grip.

"Yes," he said in a forced and controlled tone.

I let go, but only after studying the outline of his figure a little longer. "You shouldn't sneak up on people, you could get hurt."

He adjusted his wardrobe and combed his hair with his fingers. "You mean, I shouldn't sneak up on you."

Raoul came racing through the glass revolving doors. "What's going on? Mr. Miyaki, is everything okay?"

"Fine, Raoul," Taekishi replied. "It's my fault. I just startled Ms. Brantley. Go back inside."

Raoul was like stone.

"Please."

He hesitated before returning to his desk.

Taekishi looked me directly in the eye. "Why are you standing outside my building?"

I returned the stare. "Why are you?"

Taekishi chuckled. "I'm just returning home."

"From where?"

"This doesn't have anything to do with this morning's phone call?"

"No, it has to do with your daughter's death."

His smile made me uneasy. "Good night, Agent-Professor Brantley."

Taekishi walked briskly away from me, but I easily matched his long stride.

"You're very persistent," he commented without allowing me eye contact.

I studied his hardened expression and was unable to discern if he was grieving or hiding behind his stoic mask.

"Walk with me," he demanded in a cordial voice. It was the gentlest tone I'd heard flow from his lips so far, and it caught me by surprise.

He turned back and headed toward Fifth Avenue, not bothering to wait for me to catch up to him when the DON'T WALK light changed to WALK, and he bolted across the street to the Met.

"Son-of-a-bitch," I muttered.

Even when he was being friendly he was an asshole.

The Met had late hours on Thursdays, and it was still open. I climbed the front staircase, and followed him through the main entrance and over to the Admissions area. He had already entered and was ascending the Grand Staircase, so I quickly reached into my coat pocket and pulled out whatever dollar bills were within reach.

"Only one?" the man at the register asked facetiously, staring at the crumpled two dollars that I had tossed at him.

I hurriedly pointed to the sign above him. "It says twelve dollars *suggested donation.*"

His eyes grew wide and he handed me a receipt and an admissions pin, which I attached to my coat by bending the tab through the buttonhole of my lapel. Today's color was maroon.

I always hated museums. They were too dark and they smelled funny. Kyle dragged me to a museum only once. MoMA—The Museum of Modern Art. We were a couple of weeks into the relationship, and he thought that it would be good for me and for us. I spent the whole afternoon trailing behind him and wishing that we were strolling through Central Park instead. After that experience, Kyle never invited me again.

I could see Taekishi just ahead of me passing through one of the smaller galleries. As I raced to catch up with him, I stole cursory glances at the boring paintings of pudgy, rosy-cheeked women in petticoats that left me unaffected and longing for images that were more bold and brash. At least MoMA had that.

I stopped, and realized that I had lost Taekishi. I turned the corner and stepped into another gallery. The Met was a confusing place.

Taekishi was standing a few feet from a painting, his left arm wrapped around his stomach and his right hand pressed underneath his chin in a pensive gesture. Not wanting to disturb him, I slowly walked over to stand by his side. It didn't surprise me that he ignored my presence. I looked over at the dark painting consisting of mostly browns. The paint was cracking from age, and I found that there was something rather fascinating about the image.

My gaze scanned the painting, which depicted a table with some kind of bubble or transparent globe and cut flowers. A human skull rested below it, with coins scattered underneath the macabre image. Two unrecognizable male faces adorned the bottom of the canvas. It was moving in a somewhat analytical way. I looked at the curator's card. Gheyn was making a very depressing statement about life in general.

Taekishi stepped aside and gently nudged me so that I was centered to the painting.

"All the images that appear here," he said, waving his hand through the air, "remind the viewer and the artist of all that has corrupted mankind. Fame, wealth and vanity, have all contaminated the naive minds of the people of the modern age. Sometimes it is not enough for a mere painting to shock us into the reality of our vulnerability." He looked at me. "Sometimes it takes a tragedy to do so. You can understand then, why this painting affects me."

I nodded gently.

Without a word we made our way back toward the Great Hall, and Taekishi stopped just before reaching the main staircase.

"The death of my daughter is a tragedy, but do you know what the greater tragedy is, Ms. Brantley?"

I shook my head, since I could not fathom what could possibly be more tragic than a young woman so brutally murdered.

"The greatest tragedy of all is a parent who outlives his child."

Pain tore through his face as if he had been robbed of a lifetime of joy and left only with memories. For the first time, I think I finally understood the true anguish, rage, despair and emptiness that many of the victims' families—the parents—felt when they learned of their child's death. Or maybe I could never truly know until I had a child of my own.

Taekishi turned, and I followed him through the main entrance after dropping my admission tag in a Plexiglas bin for recycling. The museum was closing, and the security guards in their gray polyester uniforms were anxious to see us leave. As we stepped out into the cold late night, my gaze lingered on Taekishi as I watched him cross Fifth Avenue without expressing any farewells.

Four hours later, as I suffered through a spell of insomnia and watched an old rerun of *I Love Lucy*, the phone rang. The stark images in Gheyn's painting haunted me as a male voice sounded firmly through the receiver of my phone.

"Agent Brantley?"

I rolled my eyes. "Joshua, this is getting to be old really fast."

"This is Agent Ransome, the Duty Agent in New York. Agent Luker asked me to call you. He said to meet him ASAP at the Miyaki crime scene."

My breath caught in my chest.

"There's been another."

Chapter Thirty-three

One would think that as human beings we could learn from our past experiences.

"Nicely done," Dan smirked, as Joshua reached out his hand and pulled me to my feet.

I ignored him and brushed myself off, all the while staring at the embankment as if it had been guilty of contributing to my second ungraceful entrance. The fishy-smelling salt air was just what my sinuses needed. My ears popped, clearing my head. When the stench of rotting sea life finally hit me, I wished that my sinuses hadn't drained.

The late hour worked to our benefit in terms of keeping the public away, but the bright floodlights that had been set up only served as a beacon announcing the police activity.

I peeked up into the dark, overcast sky. The clouds

were thick, and visibility was low, but I did not see any helicopters.

Even with the added lights, I still stumbled along the riverbank as we headed for the pier. Just as I reached the ladder, someone grabbed my elbow, and expecting that it was Joshua I was surprised to see Dan chewing up a fresh piece of gum.

I looked above at the pier, where Joshua had already begun studying the victim's body.

"We've got a problem," Dan stated.

"Oh, what kind of problem? PR?" I scanned the crime scene, half expecting to see the reporters being carted away in handcuffs.

I noticed the blond reporter standing at the guardrail, trying desperately to find a way down to the crime scene.

Dan's fingers tightened, and I stared at him with piercing eyes.

"Not that kind of problem," he said under his breath.

A cloud of white fog blew out from his mouth and brushed against my face. Through the sweet cover of peppermint, I caught a slight hint of beer lingering on his breath.

My voice was firm as my words seeped through my clenched teeth. "I think you'd better release me, Sergeant."

His grip loosened, but he still held on. "Don't ever go and interview my witnesses before me."

The muscles in my arms tensed, my stare exploding through him like shotgun pellets. The confrontation that we had been building to since day one was finally upon us.

"Which witnesses?" I calmly asked.

Dan let go, but his words were still filled with anger

and resentment. "That blind kid and the college girl. Sumi's friend."

I cocked my head to one side. "Tell me something, Sergeant. Did you know about Denny before? And Becca, did you know about her before tonight?"

His face fell and he shook his head.

"Then I guess at the time she wasn't your witness."

A wind touched off the Hudson, and I drew the collar of my coat around my neck. I should have called Dan immediately, as soon as I had known about either of them. But I refused to be kicked around by him or anyone else.

"Tell you what," I said, heading for the pier. "You show up to a crime scene sober, and I'll start sharing information with you."

"It was only one," he shouted after me as I joined Joshua where the victim's body lay. "And I was off duty."

I looked back at Dan with half a smile. I knew he was sober, but it didn't matter; now he was unnerved.

The night was like some bad recurring nightmare, filled with harsh reminders of a killer who was meticulous and intelligent.

I stared down at the new victim; it was her nightmare.

My eyes traveled along the wave of her flowing corn-silk hair, the ends now matted and swimming in her still warm blood. Approximately three hours was all that Anthony had allotted since the time of death. I looked at the digital numbers on my Casio Pathfinder watch. It was 2:21 AM. She had been killed just as the nightly news was wrapping up. A little less than an hour and a half since the body was first discovered. It was barely enough time for the killer to flee, but I knew he was nearby taking great pleasure in the excitement of the scene. He was out in that thin crowd of anonymous onlookers corralled just east of the West Side Highway, watching and laughing at us.

Though it may seem macabre, I was thankful not to recognize the victim as being one of my students. She was young, but definitely older than Sumi. That bothered me. The staging of the crime scene was very close to being the same. The disposition of the body was almost a carbon copy. If not for the blond hair, I could've sworn I was looking at Sumi. I was careful to note that, again, the killer had left her eyes open. It had been exactly one week since Sumi had been killed.

Joshua grunted.

I moved closer to him and drew my face close to the victim's neck.

"More brutal," he commented.

The offender was no longer cutting his victim; he was plunging the tool, driving it deep into her body. Two wounds placed side-by-side in her neck had very nearly gone through to the other side.

"Same crap with the arms," Dan said careful to address everyone but me.

He grimaced at the crime scene, knowing that he could no longer deny that a serial killer was finding a home in his precinct.

I pulled a Sure Fire flashlight from my coat pocket and depressed the button on the end cap. With methodical motions, I moved the laserlike beam side-to-side along the rotted wood to help guide me toward the end of the pier. Even with the bright incandescent lights that CSU had set up, I refused to become known for being clumsy at a crime scene.

The arms were tied with the same basic double knot and dropped at the end of the pier. The victim had what appeared to be the same type of self-inflicted cuts.

Under the white light four detectives began laying out measuring tapes around the body. Though he huffed in protest, I looked over Dan's shoulder while he sketched out the area on a pad of graph paper. His artistic abilities could have used some coaching from Kyle, but his attention to detail was remarkable.

A uniform held a tape at the near end of the pier and a detective ran it to the victim's foot.

Another detective looked up. "Four feet, three inches."

Dan drew a dimension arrow and marked it. This went on for another thirty minutes, and by the time they were finished, the drawing looked more like some alien instructions on how to build a warp drive conduit—whatever the hell that was—than a crime scene sketch.

Dan pulled out a photocopy of the sketch he had made of Sumi's crime scene. The drawings were in marked contrast with the first crime scene diagram having very little dimensioning, but there was enough information to confirm our worst fears.

"Oh, shit." As if all that had transpired earlier was forgotten, Dan looked at me, his face ashen. "It's almost exactly the same."

I turned the sketches so that Joshua and I could have a better look. The layout between the two crime scenes was close to being the same, within six inches either way. My expression was tight as I gently pushed the drawings back toward Dan.

"ID?" Joshua asked, kneeling down beside the victim.

"Yeah," Dan replied in a slightly quizzical tone. "Rita Schaeffer. Found the coat a couple of feet from her. Got her wallet."

I curiously listened to him. It was puzzling that, again, the offender found it unnecessary to take anything.

"Everything's intact." And then Dan added sarcastically, "Guess we can rule out robbery as a motive." He knelt beside Joshua. "It's the only thing that's different. Everything else is practically the same."

I remained standing, and looked up toward the highway. The area had been blocked off—the same streets were closed to traffic and the public. Now I was baffled. Why did the UNSUB take Sumi's coat, but not Rita's? Or maybe he *didn't* take Sumi's, and somehow in the time leading up to her death she had been parted from it.

I looked down at Rita's broken body. "For this victim, the the body was found sooner—a factor beyond the offender's control. The disposition of the body and limbs is the same." I pointed toward the Hudson, down at the far end of the pier. "Even the disposition of the arms, which we originally thought had been dropped arbitrarily, has been duplicated."

Dan rubbed his forehead just above his eyebrows. "Arrogant son-of-a-bitch."

"He probably took pictures," Joshua said as his eyes lit up. "That was his souvenir."

I lowered myself, and we all hovered over Rita Schaeffer like we were taking some oath in a secret society.

"Probably, but there's more to it than that," I said.

Dan eyed me, and I accepted his light challenge.

"For one, even with pictures it's too dark for anyone to be able to work at duplicating a scene like this. Also, there wouldn't have been enough time for him to measure out and space everything." With my index finger, I began tapping my temple methodically. "It's all up here."

"Oh, yeah, right!" Dan broke out into cackles of violent laughter, but I remained stony with seriousness.

"He probably had the photos and he studied them endlessly. Learned them by heart and relived the moment. But when it came down to doing it again—for real—he had it all internalized so he could act quickly and on instinct.

"This victim's belongings are intact," I continued, as I stared out toward New Jersey, where twinkling lights were barely visible along the riverbank. "He didn't take anything. His trophy is all stored in his memory and his photographs."

"A photographic memory." Joshua ran his hands through his short black hair. "They need something tangible. Something to feel."

I shook my head, and my hair swung about my face. "Yes, but even with the pictures, recreating the crime scene is his tangible experience. Which is why his cooling-off period is so brief. He has very little to relive the fantasy."

I looked up to the highway and the flashing lights of the police cruisers.

"I got someone taking pictures of the crowd," Dan said as he spit his chewed gum into a piece of scrap paper. When he caught my surprised look he added, "I figured they could come in handy. I figure that bastard's up there. Copycatting his own handiwork. Now I seen it all."

Joshua stood and stretched out his hand, pulling me to my feet when I took it.

"He has to be a very visual person," he said, squinting into the hotspot of one of the floodlights. "A very intelligent, visual person, who not only recreated his *own* crime scene, but brazenly did so in exactly the same damned place!"

My eyebrows arched, and Dan cleared his throat awkwardly.

"We can set up surveillance," Dan explained. "But this guy's no dummy. He won't do it here again, right?"

Maura Sheridan

I looked down at Rita's mutilated body. Blood was seeping through the rotting planks of the pier. Common knowledge would dictate that, no, he wouldn't risk putting another body in the same place, but the risk was obviously a part of this offender's signature.

Joshua and I climbed the embankment to the highway, and I stared down Twenty-sixth Street at the crowd of onlookers in the distance. The blond reporter was approaching us, but we quickly jumped into Joshua's rental, so she accosted Dan instead.

The man we were looking for just might put his next victim in the same exact place to taunt us, to tell New York City that he was smarter than the rest of them. Maybe he was. And that's what scared me more than any of my nightmares.

GET UP TO
4 FREE BOOKS!

You can have the best fiction delivered to your door for less than what you'd pay in a bookstore or online—only $4.25 a book! Sign up for our book clubs today, and we'll send you **FREE* BOOKS** just for trying it out...**with no obligation to buy, ever!**

LEISURE HORROR BOOK CLUB

With more award-winning horror authors than any other publisher, it's easy to see why CNN.com says "Leisure Books has been leading the way in paperback horror novels." Your shipments will include authors such as RICHARD LAYMON, DOUGLAS CLEGG, JACK KETCHUM, MARY ANN MITCHELL, and many more.

LEISURE THRILLER BOOK CLUB

If you love fast-paced page-turners, you won't want to miss any of the books in Leisure's thriller line. Filled with gripping tension and edge-of-your-seat excitement, these titles feature everything from psychological suspense to legal thrillers to police procedurals and more!

As a book club member you also receive the following special benefits:

- **30% OFF all orders through our website & telecenter!**
- **Exclusive access to special discounts!**
- **Convenient home delivery and 10 days to return any books you don't want to keep.**

There is no minimum number of books to buy, and you may cancel membership at any time. See back to sign up!

*Please include $2.00 for shipping and handling.

YES! ☐

Sign me up for the Leisure Horror Book Club and send my TWO FREE BOOKS! If I choose to stay in the club, I will pay only $8.50* each month, a savings of $5.48!

YES! ☐

Sign me up for the Leisure Thriller Book Club and send my TWO FREE BOOKS! If I choose to stay in the club, I will pay only $8.50* each month, a savings of $5.48!

NAME: _____

ADDRESS: _____

_____

TELEPHONE: _____

E-MAIL: _____

☐ **I WANT TO PAY BY CREDIT CARD.**

☐ VISA   ☐ MasterCard   ☐ DISCOVER

ACCOUNT #: _____

EXPIRATION DATE: _____

SIGNATURE: _____

Send this card along with $2.00 shipping & handling for each club you wish to join, to:

Horror/Thriller Book Clubs
20 Academy Street
Norwalk, CT 06850-4032

Or fax (must include credit card information!) to: 610.995.9274.
You can also sign up online at www.dorchesterpub.com.

*Plus $2.00 for shipping. Offer open to residents of the U.S. and Canada only.
Canadian residents please call 1.800.481.9191 for pricing information.

If under 18, a parent or guardian must sign. Terms, prices and conditions subject to change. Subscription subject to acceptance. Dorchester Publishing reserves the right to reject any order or cancel any subscription.

JOIN NOW!

Chapter Thirty-four

The shadows on the ceiling flickered and moved in a dance that mocked my insomnia. When a car drove by, the shadows shifted as the headlights moved from one end of my bedroom to the other. I rolled over onto my side and stared at Kyle as his body rose and fell with every breath. I always liked watching him while he slept, just as I had liked watching Joshua. There was something vulnerable about a man while he was sleeping that I found sexy.

The red numbers from the alarm clock glowed against the white sheets—5:49 blazed across the room like a beacon. I'd have to get up in twenty-one minutes.

To hell with it.

I swung my legs out from under the covers and made my way to the kitchen, where the coffeepot, running on automatic timer, had begun to perk and gurgle in protest at having to work so early in the morning.

"I hear ya, buddy," I mumbled with half-closed eyes.

The first cup tasted like nuclear waste, as did the second. I checked the roasting date on the coffee bag and tossed the remaining beans. As much as my taste buds rejected the foul liquid, I didn't hesitate in the happy pursuit of polishing off the entire carafe.

With my final cup in tow, I dressed in one of my dreary gray pantsuits, finely pressed and fresh from the dry cleaners. Then I went downstairs and grabbed *The New York Times* from the front stoop. Back in my apartment I tore through sections A and B—nothing on the discovery of Rita's body. I checked the early morning news. The local CBS affiliate was airing archival footage from Sumi's crime scene of the blond reporter practically shoving her microphone down Dan's throat. His eyes were wide and he looked like roadkill caught in the oncoming traffic, and the eighteen-wheeler that was fast approaching was named Lynn McDonald. Irish and stubborn like me, and harassing Dan—I liked her already.

In one hour Anthony would be carving into Rita Schaeffer while Joshua and I ignored Dan and his intrusive comments.

I watched myself in the hall mirror, the bristles of the thick brush trapped within the strands of my limp hair. As I studied the bags under my eyes, I could not help but wonder if Taekishi's visit to the museum was merely a performance for my benefit to generate some kind of sympathy.

I tossed the brush someplace where I would never find it again.

Chapter Thirty-five

In front of the Medical Examiner's Office, Joshua managed to squeeze out the other contestants for the only remaining parking space, and his gloating smile only meant that I'd be singing his praises at lunchtime.

Dan was waiting for us by the curb, downing a large coffee and chocolate donut from Dunkin' Donuts.

A smallish man by the front entrance was trying to watch us inconspicuously. He wore faded jeans and a brown leather bomber jacket. The beak of a navy blue baseball cap with the logo for the New York Knicks was pulled down over the top half of his face. I kept an eye on him, carefully noting everything. Could he be the offender watching the progress on his prey? But then I caught sight of the upper corner of a yellow press ID hanging around his neck and poking through the collar of his coat.

Two victims brutally murdered. There would be a bigger story in tomorrow's papers, and if the NYPD chose to acknowledge a serial killer, then all hell was going to break loose.

I motioned with careful hand signals to both Joshua and Dan, and we expertly avoided any confrontation with the reporter. We rushed by and didn't make eye contact. How's that for expert?

Anthony's autopsy of Rita Schaeffer proceeded normally, and this time, much to Dan's chagrin, I didn't flee from the room when it was time to remove a sample of her brain.

Hairs were picked off her coat and clothes. Most of them were long and blond, presumably Rita's. On the coat there were a few shorter blond ones, and Anthony found some darker ones, mostly short but of varying lengths that had been broken. Like Sumi, Rita had been beaten, cut—stabbed mercilessly—with this odd U-shaped tool, her arms had been tied and severed—chopped away with the small ax; and when he was finished, the offender found it necessary to masturbate upon her lifeless corpse. The lab would compare the two semen samples and through science could "officially" link the two crimes. Everything about the condition of Rita's body was the same as Sumi's except for—

"Bruising," Anthony said, slipping along the bloody floor, as Roth began sewing up the incision running down Rita's abdomen. "The first victim had much more extensive bruising, and this victim's were all fresh."

"How fresh would you say they were?" Dan asked.

Water ran in the background and pattered along a stainless-steel surface.

"Within twenty-four hours."

I suddenly felt terribly depressed. "Maybe Taekishi did beat Sumi."

"Or maybe he beat *both* of them," Dan said, still insisting that Taekishi was a suspect.

Joshua looked at me with interest. "You're not beginning to believe Denny the pathological liar?"

"It has nothing to do with him. Sumi's bruises were older and the second victim wasn't subject to as much of a heavy bruising. Sumi's abuse could be an explanation for her cutting."

I stared at Rita's beaten face.

"The U-shaped cuts are deeper, too," Anthony reminded us.

As much as they had appeared violent and brutal, Sumi's shallow wounds had been kind in comparison to the two- to three-inch cuts inflicted upon Rita. I stared at the two wounds that had nearly gone all the way through the thickness of her neck. Ligaments and tendons stared back at me. The soft flesh shaped itself into a gaping mock expression of horror. The offender's purpose with the mysterious weapon seemed different between the two victims, as if Sumi's had been placed and Rita's had resulted from a lashing out. There was an escalating hatred brewing within the offender, and what concerned us was that his cooling off period was decidedly brief.

Anthony pulled off his bloodied gloves and apron. "Sergeant, have the wizards in your lab figured out what kind of weapon is being used to create these stab wounds?"

"No," he replied, making certain that his back was turned from Rita's corpse.

"Well, from the deeper wounds this time around, I could see more of what the blade is doing."

We all moved in closer to him, and Anthony's eyebrows twitched.

"The top edge of this tool is obviously sharp, but what's curious is that the sides are blunt," he explained. "There's also a slight scooping quality to the blade."

My right eyebrow arched. "Scooping?"

"Yep. Which makes sense since the tip is shaped like a U."

"So what is it?" Dan asked impatiently.

Anthony smiled. "If I had the answer, I'd be working in Toolmarkings. All I can tell you is, it isn't a knife. And it certainly isn't a conventional tool."

"Something related to the offender's occupation," I muttered. My mind began racing through all the professions that I could think of that would require the use of oddly shaped tools: mechanic, carpenter, engineer—all blue-collar jobs, which I was certain the offender did not have.

We watched Roth wheel Rita's body out of the autopsy room. Her belongings were secured in a large brown bag and positioned at her knees between her legs.

"It don't matter what Sumi's wacko father was doing," Dan said, tearing off his gown. "There's a connection with the cutting between these two. And I found out this morning that they were both treated by the same doc."

I traded a quick glance with Joshua. "At Bellevue?"

"Yep." Dan put on his coat. "Want to take a trip next door? I hear the coffee's really good over there."

Chapter Thirty-six

The reporter was gone by the time we left Anthony's office. Late-morning sun glinted off the glass-covered awning that ran the length of the walkway leading to the main entrance of Bellevue Hospital. The long, stringy ivy creeping along the infamous red brick façade gave me an eerie sense of nostalgia; reminding me of the old New England charm of my childhood. I frowned. Something I'd rather forget.

The guard at the security desk in front of the elevator bank of the New Psych building appeared to be only half conscious and oblivious to our approach as we easily passed through a supposedly secure section.

Suddenly, an agonizing fear gripped my insides and refused to let go. If ever I had a phobia, it was hospitals. I hated them, and they hated me. The city morgues I could stomach because the people there were already dead, but in a hospital the living could still cry out and voice their pain and discomfort.

Joshua pressed the button for the nineteenth floor and fell back against the smooth wall of the elevator.

"Long night?" I asked.

His eyelids were heavy when he looked over at me, as if I had forgotten all about the latest crime scene.

"Yeah, one long night." He shoved his hands into the pockets of his coat.

I wished that Dan wasn't in the elevator with us.

As we stepped out of the elevator onto the Juvenile Ward, I nearly tripped over a messy toolbox full of thin brushes. Just across from the elevator bank, a painter was busy filling in a puffy cloud with white paint on a colorful mural. It was a scene depicting children from all races and age groups, playing happily along a flat, two-dimensional green landscape. Kyle would've called it "Kindergarten modern art."

"It's still in its working stage," a lanky man explained.

His gray T-shirt and ripped jeans were covered in dried paint, evidence of past work. He sketched out another child with a fat piece of a charcoal stick that crumbled, leaving a film of a fine black dust upon his long effeminate fingers.

"Sorry, about the mess."

When he bent over to move the box of brushes, a large tear in the backside of his jeans spread open to reveal that he wore no underwear.

I quickly turned away and followed everyone to the secured entryway. The nurse there paged Dr. Davidson, and after letting us wait for fifteen minutes, a corpulent woman with a short crop of silver hair greeted us warmly and insisted that we call her Sarah. She was in the middle of making her rounds through the floor and kindly extended the offer for us to tag along. After Dan unsuccessfully argued that we meet with her immediately, Sarah reminded him that our unannounced visit didn't follow standard protocol and should have been set up with his own NYPD liaison to the hospital. We graciously accepted her invitation for a tour of the ward.

Sarah led us down a long fluorescent-lit hallway. We slowly followed her into the Recreation Room, where children calmly played. The day seemed to be relatively sedate and uneventful, but the vigilant nurses still kept a watchful eye, prepared to enlist the aid of any necessary force should one of their charges become violent or disruptive.

When Sarah entered, the room was filled with the children's gleeful cheers of laughter. Her care and concern for each child and her attentiveness to call each by their name, moved me and brought a smile to my own face. Even the teenagers allowed themselves to have the tops of their heads patted or to accept a warm hug with open arms. I immediately lost myself and forgot that I was in a hospital.

"They need that kind of attention," she said, as she waved her good-byes and we returned to the hallway.

My gaze lingered on the room for a moment longer as the children returned to their activities. It was just that kind of attention from an authority figure, for a brief moment in their difficult young lives, that would make all the difference as they approached adulthood.

Sarah led us back through the secured entry and down a hall just before the elevator bank. I stole a quick glance at the mural and noticed that little progress was being made.

"So," Sarah said, making sweeping motions with her arm as we entered a small shoebox of a room. "What do you think of the doctor's office? I used to have a pictur-esque view of the East River. Then in '85 they turned the old Psych building into the men's homeless shelter. The heating works, but I now have an office the size of a bread box," she joked.

Dan and I took the only two chairs, while Joshua opted to hang back, and found a spot along a large bookcase where he leaned up against a cushion of thick psychol-ogy textbooks.

"All they have to do is install a toilet and a kitchenette; call it a cozy studio with charm, and you can put it on the market for twelve hundred a month," I said wryly.

Sarah threw her head back and laughed, but her face quickly became serious. "So what brings both the NYPD and FBI to my humble realm?"

"You were treating a young woman," Dan started di-rectly.

"I treat a lot of young women."

He glanced at me quickly, and I got the feeling that he saw Sarah as an older version of myself.

"Sumi Miyaki," he continued.

Sarah's face darkened and she shook her head solemnly. "I heard the other day. Her parents have been speaking to me about it."

Surprise spread across my face. "In therapy?"

She smiled, but refused to answer.

"She was mutilating herself," Dan declared.

Sarah's eyes narrowed and she weaved her stubby fin-gers together. "We prefer to say that she was a self-harmer."

"The patients you treat for this disorder," I said gently, "they're admitted through Bellevue?"

She looked at me with a soft expression of surprise. "Not many people are astute enough to recognize this as a disorder." Sarah leaned forward. "They're an extension of my private practice. But I often hold sessions here in this office."

Sarah looked over at Dan as he began unwrapping a piece of gum.

"And they call you," he stated, chewing with his mouth open.

"Yes," she replied in an antagonistic tone. "I'm available to all my patients twenty-four hours a day."

"And the last time Sumi called you?"

Sarah directed her answer to me. "Wednesday. I suppose the night before she was killed." She shook her head sadly. "It's painfully ironic. Those who cut themselves never intend to kill themselves."

I allowed for the moment to settle before asking, "Did anything seem different during that call?"

"Different?"

I shrugged. "Like she was preoccupied with something else."

Sarah shook her head. "No." But then her posture tensed. "However, she did seem better."

"Better?"

"Yes, like she was making a turn. That things were improving." Sarah slumped back into her chair. "I guess that's what makes it all the more heartbreaking." She began shaking her head. "I just can't believe that it happened again."

We all froze and quickly traded furtive glances.

Again?

It wasn't possible for Sarah, or anyone for that matter, to have learned about the second victim already. Even a nosy reporter standing in front of the ME's office couldn't have spread the news that quickly. My mother

211

on a hot summer day with the heavy receiver of the old pale green rotary phone pressed to her ear—yes, she *might* have been able to do it. But even the best investigative reporter could only dream of developing my mother's special gift for "enlightening the people."

That familiar fear gripped my stomach again, and I could feel my insides twisting and knotting themselves within each other.

"Ah-gain?" Dan questioned in two long, drawn out syllables.

Sarah eyed him as if he were a pesky house fly. "Well, of course. It's not like it just happened this morning."

Both Dan and Joshua's faces became pasty white, and I could feel all of the blood draining from my head.

"The other victim was only found early this morning," Dan said with intensity. "How did you know?"

Sarah's expression fell to a quizzical stare. "This morning?"

"Yes, Rita Schaeffer."

Her face became a sheet of white. "Rita? Rita Schaeffer? Why, what's happened to her?"

I spoke slowly. "She was found this morning."

Sarah stared back at us, and a frightful look flashed across her face that sent a chill up my spine. "You mean there's been a third?"

Chapter Thirty-seven

Anthony collapsed into a high-backed leather chair behind his cluttered yet organized desk. The décor in his office was that of city-issued furniture. Dark, practical, and along with cockroaches, indestructible in the event of a nuclear holocaust.

"I like my coffee bitter, just like my women," he declared, as he licked his lips and longingly eyed the mug in my hand.

I rolled my eyes and handed him the large white mug with bold red letters that read: HE SLICES, HE DICES.

Anthony smiled, then proceeded to spill half of it onto his lap.

"Oh, shit!" He sprang into the air, and both Joshua and Dan winced, doubling over slightly as if they felt his pain through some secret telekinetic male force.

"Well, do you think I could at least sue myself for three million dollars?" Anthony quipped, frantically wiping his trousers with a napkin. The brownish stain would stay with him for the rest of the day.

"Okay," he said like a cheerleader, once he had cleaned himself up as best he could. "Trina Williams, you say?"

"Yeah." Dan leaned in close to the computer monitor between Joshua and me.

I moved away as far as I could, while still keeping the monitor in view. There was a fire within me, and I wanted nothing more to do with Daniel Grissard. Even his presence enraged me.

Anthony tapped out the name on the keyboard and within a matter of seconds her case file jumped to the screen.

"Mm-hmm," Anthony said with self-assurance. "That's why I didn't make the connection, it wasn't one of my posts."

"Doctor Gilbert Rowland," I read from the text.

"He's the new guy, and quite frankly, I don't think he'll be around here for much longer."

Dan was chewing like a horse, and his gum cracked and popped through the air.

"You know, Sergeant," Anthony remarked without looking away from the monitor. "You'll grind your teeth down with all the chewing you do."

The room quickly became silent.

Trina Williams was ten years older than Sumi. Her body with its arms tied behind her but still intact, had been found bumping along the banks of the East River. The location, though of a similar environment, was different. Location and condition: two differences between the crime scenes. What had me more concerned were the similarities. No signs of sexual assault. Her arms had the same cuts and scars and her face was covered with the same U-shaped marks, but this time—at a depth of an eighth- to a quarter-inch—they merely scratched the surface. The offender's use of the tool was becoming more aggressive with each victim. He was evolving and coming into his own. But what was most alarming was the fact that all three women were receiving treatment for the same condition by Sarah Davidson.

"Trina Williams was African-American," I said gruffly.

"Yeah, she's black. What's your point?" Dan huffed.

I stared at him accusingly. I had my theories as to why the connection hadn't been made between Trina and Sumi.

"This is fascinating," Joshua whispered. "Race obviously isn't an issue with him."

"No, it's not," Dan said, never taking his eyes from mine.

"I mean with the offender."

"Oh." He finally turned away from me. "Huh?"

Joshua stood and began pacing around Anthony's desk. "Most of the time, these repeat offenders strike out at victims who are similar, very rarely deviating from their own race, let alone mixing up the nationalities of their victims and the age group."

"I guess he's just a PC kind of guy," Dan said with an annoying chuckle.

Joshua waved him off. "It only strengthens the theory that it's the self-mutilation, the self-destructive characteristic of these victims that's attractive to him."

My eyelids fell heavily, and my body begged for sleep. "Only a fraction of the idealized characteristics will ultimately fit the killer's actual victim." My voice was groggy. "Being female is the only requirement. Age and race mean very little."

"There has to be something significant with all the victims being found near a body of water."

My eyes popped open. "I think we can conclude that he's from the area, at least the city." I looked at Dan askance. "He's not moving around—that we know of."

With his back to me, he was oblivious to my visual attack. "And the water?"

"The connection among the victims is Bellevue."

Everyone looked at me.

"If the first *known* victim was found in the East River," I continued, "It's possible that he chose that as a dump site because of the close proximity to the place where he would've made contact with her."

Dan grunted at me like a Neanderthal. "Yeah, but you forgot. She was found almost seventy blocks away."

I paused, surprised that he was able to do the math so quickly.

"How long was she in the water?" My questions were rhetorical. "Probably four days?"

Anthony nodded after checking the computer monitor.

"What were the currents like at the time? What about passing boats and ferries? She could've been moved in any direction."

Dan considered this briefly and surprisingly, nodded his head in agreement.

"He switched over to the Hudson, because Sumi's apartment was closer in that direction."

"And he chose the Hudson with Rita," Joshua said, "because now he's becoming more sophisticated."

He was pacing back and forth across the office. I really hated it when he did that.

"By duplicating the crime scene in the exact same place," Joshua continued, as he burned a hole in Anthony's rug, "he thinks he's being funny, and oh so smart."

Anthony looked up at us. "Both charming and practical."

"Just like your women," I teased.

Anthony's mouth fell, but quickly developed into a toothy smile.

"Now this is interesting," he said, as the glow of the monitor reflected off his glasses. "It appears that the U-shaped injuries were inflicted postmortem."

"Really?" Joshua stepped over and read the information for himself.

"He was playing and testing out his weapon." I could feel everyone's eyes resting upon me. "Trina was already dead, so he was testing the boundaries of the tool. Sumi was alive; he was testing the victim's boundaries. Rita was alive; her wounds were the deepest. Now he's just inflicting pain."

"*Just* inflicting pain." Joshua sat back down in his chair. "The first victim was found three weeks ago. Sumi was killed five days ago. It's too quick."

Dan fell into a padded leather chair. "He's not on some kind of murdering spree, is he?"

"No. There needs to be *no* cooling off period for us to classify it as a spree murder, but the downtime here is unusually brief."

"He'll kill again, *very* soon," I said in a muffled tone. "And next time it will require less planning. Murder is now an addiction for him. He harbors a need to kill."

Silence had befallen us, and the clanking of the radiator moved into the foreground.

"Next time will be more brutal," Joshua said, easily topping the morbidity of my previous comment.

I rested my cheeks within the cupped palms of my hands. "That's his *raison d'être.*"

Chapter Thirty-eight

It was the heart of the evening rush hour and all the cabs had their not-in-service lights turned on. Those trying to hail a ride found themselves stuck in the shift turnover.

I stormed out through the main entrance of the Medical Examiner's Building and followed Dan to where he was unlocking the driver's side door of his car.

He looked up and his face fell. "Aw, shit."

"Sergeant Grissard. Why didn't you tell us about Trina Williams?"

Joshua quickly left us and climbed into his rental where he waited for me.

Dan stared at me like I had four heads. "What?"

I glowered at him, annoyed that he was making me repeat my question. It was the oldest trick in the book: when put on the defense, make the offense repeat themselves so you have time to regroup.

"Trina Williams," I said through gritted teeth. "All the similarities—"

"All the differences."

"The same self-inflicted wounds, the same unexplained U-shaped markings."

Dan shoved two sticks of gum into his mouth. "Jesus, shit. That's not in my precinct."

"Don't give me that bull, Sergeant. It's not like the East Side is another country." I stretched my posture, taking full advantage of my height. "You know what I think? I think that East Harlem isn't as important to your agency as other more glamorous areas." My words were heated. "I think that the detectives in this city didn't give a crap about another black woman who was killed because they assumed she was a heroin addict or a prostitute."

"And he probably looked at her arms and thought it was drug related."

My tone was low and growling. "Track marks look a hell of a lot different than slices or gouges."

Dan's face turned beet red, and for the first time I realized that he was actually taller than he looked. His voice roared like the engines of an airplane.

"Never tell me how to do my job." He spat his gum, and it bounced off the tip of my shoe before landing on the ground. "The Twenty-fifth deals with lots of heroin addicts. And they just happen to be black. Just like the Nineteenth deals with a lot of white heroin addicts. Cokeheads, too. You name it; it's everywhere. But don't start accusing us of playing favorites. A dead body is a dead body. They're all the same. They all have someone who's trying to get away with a crime."

Dan stood before me in silence, his shoulders rising and falling and his chest heaving.

My eyes narrowed and I shook my head incredulously. "What the hell do I look like? Some nitwit with press credentials slung around my neck? Wealth and skin color take precedence. The fact is, we should've known about her murder when we were called in to investigate Sumi Miyaki."

Dan's face was still flushed. "Hey, it's up to the detective in charge of that case. Three weeks? He probably didn't have time to put all the paperwork through. It's his choice to put it into VICAP. And even if he did, how fast do you think your guys down south would've processed it?"

He was right. There was a backlog in every aspect of the FBI's information cataloging, just as there was in every agency all across the country.

I stepped close to him and could see every hairy pore on his face. "I specifically asked you in the first consultation whether any similar crime was under investigation. This seems pretty damned similar to me."

"Look." He shrugged and his posture was more relaxed. "When the floater was discovered, the detective probably figured it was a drug case. If I had known about it and figured there was a connection, I would've said something."

"There are three dead women," I said through clenched teeth.

Dan quickly looked up at the NYU Medical Center, and then back at the ivy winding its way up Bellevue's façade.

"Hey, I'm not going to pretend that I don't think that what you do is bullshit."

I flinched and my head drew back upon my shoulders. He shook his head violently. "Yeah, what kind of success rate do you guys really have? This profiling shit. It's crap. And you're wrong a lot more times than your PR agents will ever admit. I think we have better luck with the psychics," he added with thick sarcasm.

He began wagging his finger at me, and I had to fight the urge of wanting to snap it from his hand.

"So if you want to disrespect me or this department, I don't give a crap. We sure as hell have no respect for you."

There was a tempest brewing inside of me, and although the wind chill was making the air feel almost frigid, sweat began to bead along my hairline. I scowled at him as he reached for the car door.

"It's not like I enjoy making things difficult." Dan smiled calmly and unbuttoned his coat. When he climbed into his car it bounced in response to his unforgiving weight. "They just are."

As he pulled out of his parking space, I looked down and turned my shoe toward my instep only to see Dan's gum sticking to the sole.

Chapter Thirty-nine

Normally, I'm not a sentimental person, but seeing Sarah with all her young patients had stirred something inside of me.

Sitting tensely on the edge of my bed I stared at the phone on the night table. With a hesitant motion I picked up the receiver and held it a moment before quickly resting it back in its cradle. Five minutes of this little game ensued before I finally began to dial numbers. At this late hour, I was hoping that there would be someone there.

The phone rang five or six times, and I was about to hang up when the sounds of the other receiver being fumbled with crackled through the line.

"Hell-lo," a groggy male voice answered.

"Um, hi. It's um, Meredith."

His voice jumped to a perky awareness. "Meredith? Merry is that you?"

"Yes, hi."

"Where are you?"

"In New York. I'm at home."

"Well." He began to whisper. "Have you adjusted okay to the city?"

"Yes," I replied as emotion began to grip at my throat.

"What are you doing these days?"

"I'm, uh, working on a case," I barely managed to say.

"Oh, good, good for you."

"Can I talk to—?"

"Oh, no, sleeping. Not a good idea."

"I'm sorry, I didn't mean to call so late."

"Well, that's all right. It's always nice to hear your voice."

I hesitated before mustering the courage for my next question. "I was wondering if I could come visit, it's been so long."

"Merry, honey, I don't know. I don't think that's such a good idea right now. Why don't you call in a couple of days, after I've had a chance to test the waters?"

"Okay."

I allowed the tears to roll down my chin, but I angrily wiped them away. My shirtsleeve left a hot stinging sensation along my skin.

"Good night," he said.

I could hear her moving around in the background.

His words were rushed. "I'll talk to you later."

"Good night."

I heard the click of the other receiver as I choked on my final words, "Good night, Daddy."

"Yes?"

"It's Joshua."

I quickly dried my eyes before hitting the buzzer to release the front door.

"How about a late dinner?" he asked, stepping into my foyer.

Joshua had never been to my apartment, not even when I lived in Virginia. We had always met someplace else. He looked around and bobbed his head in subtle approval.

It wasn't a palace, but it was home. My furniture was sparse and the plants were dying. I had enthusiastically spent one Saturday afternoon combing Sixth Avenue between Twenty-fifth and Thirtieth streets, searching for the enormous plants, but now the leafy jungle was brittle and dry. The yellow and brown leaves drooped somberly toward the hardwood floors, unable to continue their struggle for survival without water.

Joshua glanced curiously at my botanical cemetery.

Silk plants next time, I decided.

"Thanks." I shook my head and easily became dizzy. "But I'm not very hungry."

Joshua's expression grew heavy with concern. "Are you all right? Everything okay?"

"Yeah, I'm all right. Just a misguided phone call." I paused for a moment. Joshua was suddenly acting very peculiar, standing before me stiff as a board and saluting.

"What are you doing?"

"Half mast," he said, as if a parrot were sitting on his shoulder.

"What?"

"Yer eyes are at half mast, maytee."

I began to chuckle, finally understanding the joke.

"How about some coffee then?" he asked.

"No, I'm too tired to go out," I replied lethargically as

I walked into the kitchen where the coffeepot was already perking its fourth pot for the day.

"What do you do?" Joshua joked as he followed me. "Just turn that thing on in the morning and then shut down before you go to bed?"

"We all have our vices." A light smile drew across my face, and I filled two mugs and handed him one.

I had already poured into his the one-third of half-and-half and three sugars. Mine was always black.

"You're sounding better these days," Joshua commented.

"Yeah, I guess it was just a twenty-four-hour bug."

I knew he was dying to ask me about the phone call. I never spoke of my family or the rift that had kept my parents and me apart for so many years, and I was grateful that Joshua never pushed the issue.

"So, is *Kyle* around?" he asked before blowing on his steaming coffee.

I didn't like the mocking emphasis he had placed on Kyle's name. "No," I replied casually. "He's tied up with clients."

Joshua smirked.

"Busy," I quickly amended. "He's busy in some new ad campaign."

We let silence fall between us, and I stared at the front of the lower cabinets.

He placed his hand on my shoulder, and I quickly slid to the opposite end of the counter and began rummaging through the cupboards for some biscuits.

"Meredith."

"I think I've got ladyfingers if you don't want crackers."

"Meredith, we can't keep avoiding things."

I stood straight up, a package of Stella Dora Breakfast

Treats in one hand, my coffee in the other. "Why not?" I was good at avoiding many things.

He moved closer to me. "Because it's there, and we have to resolve it."

The plastic wrapping crinkled under the pressure of my grasp, and I hurried away from him, placing the broken pieces of cookie onto a plate.

"Resolve," I muttered with a chortle. "It's such a human trait. Everything must have an ending."

"Not an ending."

I frowned. "What? A beginning, oh sage one?"

"Smart ass."

I turned and shoved the plate of cookies into Joshua's chest. "Okay, how about resolving who killed Sumi Miyaki."

"Jesus Christ, Meredith!" He tossed the plate back on the counter, and it spun with a clatter. "Would you just take a break for one minute? For just one minute concentrate on something else."

He grabbed my wrist, and droplets of coffee jumped into the air and stained my sleeve. "On *someone* else."

His face was close to mine and I could taste his nicotine-tainted breath, but it didn't bother me.

"I can't," I replied shamefully, and it took all of my concentration to keep my eyes dry.

"You can't, or you won't?" Joshua's dark stare was penetrating.

I yanked myself free from his hold, and he nodded with disappointment.

"Okay, then. Resolve Sumi's murder," he said almost as a challenge. "But did you forget about the two other victims? What about Trina Williams? What about Rita Schaeffer?"

My voice was quiet. "Yes, them, too."

In a daze I absentmindedly caressed my left wrist, the clasp on my watchband digging into my skin.

"No. It's all about Sumi for you. Why?"

I shook my head and stared into my mug. "I don't know. Because I knew her."

"Barely."

"I can't explain it. Please, just leave it alone for now," I begged.

I looked up from under my eyelids and caught him studying me curiously. I had never been so pleading before—not since . . .

"Meredith." He reached out to me, but I moved aside. "What's happened? What are you not telling me? Please, just open up, for your own sake. I—"

We both froze.

"You what, Joshua?"

He didn't reply, and I stared back into my mug. I could never tell him. As much as I was dying inside, I could never open up to him like he wanted me to.

I concentrated on my reflection in the swaying of the dark coffee as I gently swirled my mug. Then my expression fell to a serious stare. "Some people when they encounter violence, they either run away from it or they embrace it—to learn all they can about why something . . . like . . . that . . . could . . . happen."

My final words trailed off like a distant memory. I was too surprised that I had revealed as much as I had, to even be concerned with the fact that I did. I avoided Joshua's eyes and hurried back into the living room.

He followed me, and I felt his hand on the small of my back, guiding me to the sofa. But I ignored him and purposely sat in the armchair facing him.

227

"I'm sorry," he said gently.

"Never mind. Someday I'll be ready."

I watched him over the rim of my mug as he sat across from me on the sofa. There was something horribly attractive about him, and not just physical beauty. He was a married man. There was always something safe about a married man. Cheryl was right. There was never any danger of commitment or of falling in love. And if you did fall victim to either circumstance, you could easily return him to *his* commitment: his wife. Our interludes had been more like college romps. Something that occurred—circumstances beyond our control. My feelings for Joshua were nothing earth-shattering. My world did not spin off of its axis.

I shook my head and hid behind my enormous mug of coffee as I tipped it back for another mouthful. That was bullshit, and I think that's what scared me the most. *Absence makes the heart fonder.* Or in my experience, prevented me from making regretful mistakes.

Joshua easily fell back against the cushions and his face scrunched in disapproval. He reached behind his back and emerged with my hairbrush.

"Hey, I was looking for that." I stretched out my arm and grabbed it from him, tossing the brush someplace where it would be lost to me for a few more days.

Joshua leaned forward, resting his elbows on his knees. "Tell me something."

"Okay," I replied smartly. "The Yankees aren't the 'team of the century' and global warming is a lie, concocted by a weak liberal front."

He grimaced, but then his expression grew tense. "Tell me you don't miss it."

I pursed my lips. "What?"

"The challenge." His voice grew more and more hollow. "Getting into people's heads and seeing how they think. Re-creating the thought process that goes into committing these acts."

I stared at him curiously.

"But you do, don't you?"

I looked at him thoughtfully. "Yeah, I miss it."

Chapter Forty

The hairs on Rita's clothes were identified as belonging to her. The hairs on the coat could not be identified. Four medium-length blond hairs that had all been broken, with no root or follicle attached, making it difficult to determine the actual length. The only thing we were certain of was that they didn't belong to Rita Schaeffer. The short darker ones could not be identified either. Perhaps a second suspect? A murdering duo? No, that was ridiculous. This was the work of one person. The hair found on Sumi's body couldn't be identified either.

Joshua and I were seated in stiff, uncomfortable wooden chairs, at a plain wooden table in an all-purpose interview-conference room at the Tenth Precinct. The small, poorly lit room with black fingerprinting ink smeared along the walls was hardly on par with the FBI's, but it did have a coffeepot.

It was early Saturday, and when I had left my apartment the sun hadn't even begun to make an appearance. I was surprised to see that Dan was now willing to come in on the weekends. He paced about and sauntered with the confidence of a man working on his own turf.

"Three victims," he declared, making another turn around the table. His voice was loud and boisterous, as if he were performing Shakespeare on stage.

Victims wronged thricely, I heard in my head, accompanied by the horrific image of Dan wearing an NYPD uniform and codpiece. I chuckled quietly.

"Victim number one: thirty, husband and child, worked as a low-wage receptionist," he continued in that annoying thespian voice. "Never showed up at her mother's house in Jersey City. Reported missing by her husband. Self-mutilator."

Self-harmer, you asshole.

It was not even eight yet, and I was in no mood for melodramatics. I scribbled on my yellow legal pad, hoping to feign interest in facts we already knew.

"Victim two: twenty, wealthy, college student. Self-mutilator." Dan leaned his fat hairy knuckles upon the table. "Victim three: thirty-one, no family, worked at a supermarket. Self-mutilator."

I stopped writing and looked up at him, the rim of my eyes red from another sleepless night. "And?"

He looked at me like he was putting us through an interrogation. "And I want to know how he picked these victims."

I blew air through my nose and chuckled softly. "The link is obvious enough, however unorthodox. Most serial killers will choose something a bit more"—I tapped my fingers upon the table, searching for the appropriate word—"basic, to be one of their qualifiers in choosing a victim."

"In English, please," Dan said, slamming back what remained of his coffee.

Leaning my elbow against the armrest, I slouched and said, "Hair color, perfume, a style of dress, the way she walks, the sound of her voice—"

He held up his hand. "Yeah, yeah, yeah. Got it."

Dan lumbered toward the coffeepot, the rubber soles of his heavy work shoes thudding loudly against the linoleum with each step.

"What I don't get is this cutting business. It's freaky."

Joshua gazed at me pensively: He didn't get it either. No one ever did. Not even the young women who enacted such things.

"It's all about control," I said with a focused determination, as if trying to convince myself.

"Ironic," Joshua commented, as Dan fell heavily into his chair. "That's precisely what a violent offender exacts on his victims: total control. It's almost pathological in a way."

"Great," Dan said with as much disinterest he could muster. "Now, how about finding out what psychopath attacks another psychopath?"

I looked up at him disdainfully. "The question is: What about the cutting attracts the offender to his victims? Is it the idea of their weakness, or is it the hatred he feels toward a young woman destroying her body?"

Joshua nodded in agreement. "The removal of the victims' arms, indicates to me he wanted that part of her life to be no part of her death."

"Then why attack her with a sharp implement? Why remove the evidence of cutting only to do exactly the same thing himself?"

"Because that's exactly it!" Joshua cried, slamming the flat of his hand against the table.

Dan and I both jolted with a start.

"*He* controls the cutting."

Dan cocked his head to one side and was looking at us like he had just eaten some rotten meat. "That's great. But it doesn't tell me *who* is removing their arms."

"Someone who knows their secret."

"Yeah, so you said before."

In one swift motion, Dan ripped a piece of paper from my legal pad and took a pen from his shirt pocket. He began listing names as he said them.

"Dr. Davidson knew about all of them. Trina Williams's husband knew about her cutting. Sumi's friend Becca; Denny, that weird blind kid; her father—"

"Denny didn't know," I corrected.

Dan grumbled something and put a little mark next to Denny's name. "Rita Schaeffer." He looked up from his paper.

Joshua spun his pen between his fingers. "The only common bond they all had was Bellevue and Dr. Davidson. Maybe he's an employee there."

"You keep saying 'he.'" Dan eyed me knowingly. "The good Dr. Davidson is the only one who had total knowledge of her patients."

I ran the tip of my pen through the letter *P* someone had carved into the tabletop, as the theme song from *The Crying Game* began racing through my head.

"Yes, but unless the good doctor is hiding a deep dark secret she wouldn't account for the semen found on the two victims." I leaned forward and very nearly sprawled myself across the table. "And if Trina Williams hadn't been found in the East River, there probably would've been semen on her, too."

Dan stood and leaned all his weight upon his white knuckles. "The first murder wasn't the same."

Joshua said in a low tone. "The first was similar—"

Dan ignored him. "What if the second and third is a copycat?"

"It is a copycat," I declared, my patience wearing thin. "We've determined that it's the same offender repeating his—"

"No."

I slumped into my chair and felt all of the muscles in my face tighten. I was tiring of Dan interrupting us.

"What if someone else is copying his work?"

"They're not," I said with confidence.

"How can you be sure?"

"The general public barely knew of Sumi, and they sure as hell didn't know about the arms, her cutting and the U-shaped marks." I stared directly into his beady little eyes. "Unless, of course, you're suggesting that someone within your own investigation is suspect, or is leaking information."

Dan chewed his gum slowly but with more determination. "What about those dark hairs on Rita's coat? Could be another player."

Anything was possible at this point.

Joshua shook his head exhaustively, tiring of our contentious behavior. "When the DNA results come back, the semen will match the two crime scenes."

"Who would have access to the patient files?" I said.

"Dr. Davidson," Dan said. His theory had already become old, but at least he had moved away from Taekishi.

"Nurses," Joshua added. "Cleaning staff. It could be anyone. We don't know how Bellevue works. We don't know how Dr. Davidson works."

The door stirred, and a robust woman with long dark hair pulled into a tight bun, poked her head inside.

"Sgt. Grissard," she said, handing him a pink message slip.

He took it from her outstretched arm without getting up from his chair.

"Lynn McDonald," he said with disdain, as the door closed. "That damn reporter wants a quote. On or off the record." He crumpled it up with one hand and threw it across the room, where it landed on the floor.

Dan swung his feet up on the table and tipped his chair back on two legs. "Oh, hey, I almost forgot."

He pulled a folded piece of white paper from his shirt pocket, and handed it to Joshua. It was a photocopy of a plainly sketched hand tool with a knifelike handle and a curved tip blade. It looked as if Dan had used it as a napkin during lunch. Smears of ketchup and encrusted sauerkraut indicated that he'd been to the vending cart on the corner.

"This is what the guys in Toolmarkings think this thing looks like," Dan explained.

I studied the unfamiliar image. The blade was an inch and a half wide at the curve, and then narrowed as the neck came and met the handle.

"They said it's gotta have some weight to it."

Even in its sketchy form it looked horrible.

Chapter Forty-one

The painter had been up early working on his mural, as was evidenced by the fresh streaks of paint that covered him from head to toe. His expression sang out gleefully behind splotches of primary colors. Not much had changed since I last saw the mural. It had to make one wonder if he was actually working on it. A few more faces of happy children had been added to the collage, but that was about it.

The painter was bent over, mixing up some ecru color. But he took a moment to wave a brush soaked in yellow, and voice a "good morning" to me.

Without breaking my stride, I smiled lightly and gave his painting a superficial once-over before following Joshua into Sarah's office.

Sarah was jovial and obviously a morning person. I detested morning people—especially on Saturdays—and their ability to be so alive at a time of the day that nature had intended for sleep. How did that nursery school song go?

Good morning to you, good morning to you.
We're all in our places with sunshiny faces.
Is this not the way to start a new day?

But at the age of five I had changed the last line to:

This is NOT the way to start a new day!

Sarah warmly welcomed Joshua, me and my venti cappuccino into her office. I offered her a biscotti from the bag I had bought at a nearby Starbucks, and she accepted graciously. If I had known that it was so easy to win people over with a stale cookie, I would've started the practice a long time ago.

I sat in the same chair as my previous visit to Sarah's office. Surprisingly, with only the three of us occupying the tiny space, it seemed even more cramped.

Sarah smiled pleasantly enough, but there was something slightly different in her expression. I studied her carefully, following her every move closely.

"What can I do for you two?" she asked as she sat down behind her desk. Sarah folded her hands gracefully and placed them gently upon some neatly scattered papers that covered her desk.

Sad. Sarah looked—seemed—sad.

Joshua pressed the palms of his hands against his legs. "We're here about—"

She nodded her head quickly and fell back into her chair. "I know, my patients. It doesn't look good for me, does it?"

237

My eyebrows arched curiously. "I'm sure that your practice won't suffer too much."

"Too much?" Sarah smirked. "Actually, I thought that this doesn't look good for me because it makes me look suspect."

I glanced at her sideways and said slowly, "You're not a suspect."

"I should be," she replied matter-of-factly, taking a dignified nibble from her biscotti.

I dipped mine into my coffee and took a bite of the now softened cookie. "You should?"

"If not in reality, then in theory," she said, pulling a tissue from a square box and wiping the corner of her mouth. "I created the environment that set my patients up to be vulnerable to someone who is unforgiving and. . . ."—Sarah stared at me with penetrating blue eyes—"and vicious."

A tingling sensation crept up my spine, but I quickly shook it off.

"Are all your patients referred through NYU?" Joshua said.

"Sumi came to me because the help she was receiving at the Medical Center wasn't working. It's not that my colleagues over there aren't capable, but this sort of disorder needs specialized care. The others were referrals from elsewhere."

With my index finger, I traced the rim of my coffee cup. "How many patients are you treating for this disorder?"

"Seven, total—"

She caught herself and grimaced. "Five." Pain shot through her expression. "Before all this started, I had eight."

Joshua and I gazed at her sympathetically.

"It's unsafe for them. Can you protect them?" she asked.

"Sure," he said, attempting to assuage her concerns.

There wasn't the manpower or the finances to set up twenty-four-hour protection for five potential victims, and Sarah knew he was lying.

She smiled somberly. "It doesn't matter, he's probably already picked his next victim."

"But I'm sure the NYPD could have sector cars drive by a couple of times a day to check on them," I quickly added, as I pressed crumbs of biscotti into fine cookie dust with my thumb.

"How do you maintain your patient files?" Joshua's untouched biscotti was balanced on his knee.

"I have everything in spreadsheets on my computer."

"Do you keep paper files?"

She nodded.

"Then that would make it easy for someone to look through your patient files."

Guilt blanketed Sarah's face.

I began flicking field goals with pieces of biscotti, but immediately halted my activities when one landed squarely on the end of one of Sarah's silver hairs.

"But this is a big hospital," I pointed out. "I'm sure that several different copies of the same form need to be submitted to many different departments. The paper trail could be endless."

Sarah picked up a form that had eight different colored pages attached at the gummed header. "This is a submittal form to request a box of pens."

We all smiled, welcoming the moment of comic relief.

"Six weeks later, I still haven't seen those pens."

Joshua looked out through the office doorway and

down the hall. "The offices aren't beyond the secured door."

"That security door exists for the protection of the juvenile patients, not the doctors."

"It had to be someone who knew you were giving this sort of treatment, and someone who could watch these women."

"The staff and doctors undergo a very strict security background check," Sarah said in defense.

"Could we take a peek at your files for these patients?"

"I can't let you do that," she said. "Patient-doctor confidentiality."

My eyes rested heavily upon her. Nobility was getting in the way of catching a killer.

"We could subpoena you for them," I said in an exaggerated tone of politeness.

She hesitated then rose from behind her desk, where she stepped over to the five-drawer file cabinets against the wall. She opened one and began flicking through the tabs protruding from the hanging files.

"There has to be some sort of methodology behind his victim selection," Joshua said to me.

"Williams, Miyaki, Schaeffer." I gulped the last of my cappuccino. "It's not alphabetical."

"And it's not based on age."

Sarah returned to her desk with a stack of folders. "Here's all of them."

I stretched and grabbed the first two on the top of the pile. It was for someone named Allison Beauchamp. The next was Catherine Eckert. I flipped through the rest to confirm that Sarah had filed her patients alphabetically. He wasn't choosing them based on how her files were arranged.

"Should I hide my files?" Sarah asked.

Joshua was flipping through Trina Williams's file and shook his head. "No, not just yet."

I looked over at him and could hear the wheels turning.

"We don't want to chase him off to find another resource for his killing."

Sarah's expression was incredulous and filled with compassion. "But my patients are in jeopardy."

I pointed to the PC sitting on Sarah's desk. "Do you have everything backed up?"

She nodded her head in bewilderment.

"Could we get a copy of your hardrive?"

A light laugh rose through the air, and I was uncertain of where it was originating from.

"I can't do that," Sarah said through a pleasant smile.

"Why not?"

"Patient-doctor confidentiality."

Joshua began to chortle lightly, and I did too.

"I thought we settled that. Anyway, we're already looking at them right now," he said.

Her expression never changed. "Which is fine. But once they leave this office there is a threat of potentially placing my patients under public scrutiny."

"Look, you *don't* want to make us get that subpoena, trust me," I said.

Joshua quickly looked over at me, his mouth slightly agape.

"I see." Her tone was brusque, her eyes never moving from me. "Well, I'll have one of the nurses put it onto a Zip disk for you."

"Thank you," I said with forced politeness.

She returned the favor. "PC or Mac?"

"PC."

Joshua began making clucking noise with his tongue.

I watched as Sarah tossed a broken half of her biscotti into the trash can. The symbolism did not escape me.

"When do you meet with your patients?" Joshua asked, as his eye followed Sarah's perfectly arched toss of the other half of the biscotti, where it too, landed in the trash can.

"It varies. Once a week, every other or as many times as needed." Her tone was filled with irritation—I had fallen from her graces. "I was available to them twenty-four hours a day, and they knew that."

A thought crossed my mind. "Do you have a record of their appointments?"

She eyed me warily, but I acted oblivious.

"A list of both their standard scheduled appointments and their actual visits."

Joshua's face lit up. "Of course, chronological."

I leaned on the edge of my seat and firmly grabbed the armrest. "It makes sense if he's observing these women, he needs to be present when they're here at Bellevue. We can cross-check them with the employee time records."

Sarah handed Joshua the pages.

He smiled sympathetically at me and began reading. "Trina Williams, Sumi Miyaki, Allison Beauchamp, and Rita Schaeffer." Joshua looked up. "That was the order of their regular appointments on Tuesdays."

"Damn," I muttered.

I caught Sarah studying me, as I began spinning my watch back and forth around my wrist.

"Allison Beauchamp was a bi-weekly patient," she said, carefully watching my nervous habit.

I immediately stopped with the watch. "When was her last visit?"

Joshua scanned the calendar, but Sarah was quick to respond.

"It would've been last week—"

"Damn," I said again. I wasn't making a good impression with my vocabulary. "Which means she would've had an appointment the week Sumi was killed, which would've been when the offender had gone through his selection process. Allison Beauchamp should've been his next victim, not Rita Schaeffer."

Sarah sat stiffly in her chair, hands folded before her on top of her desk. "But she missed it and rescheduled for this week."

Joshua's face lit up. "He missed her last week. That's why he skipped to Rita Schaeffer."

I spun around in my chair and faced him. We were like kids figuring out the physics behind a Slinky. "As simple as that?"

"As simple as that!"

"Well, based on this theory, then Allison Beauchamp should be next."

Sarah slammed her fist down on her desk. "Enough!"

Joshua and I nearly jumped out of our skins. My eyes were wide and filled with guilt as I stared at the woman who had played such an important role in the lives of these young people, who were suffering inside. And we had unintentionally discussed them without compassion or empathy like they were statistics in one of our FBI case studies.

Sarah cleared her throat and calmly pressed out the front of her white lab coat with her hands. Her words were smooth and flowed gently from her lips. "If you think you've figured out this disgusting person's MO and know who his next victim will be, then you can capture him." She spun her chair away from her desk and walked down the hall. "I'll have Jan make the copies of my files," she called back to us.

We sat awkwardly in silence, and I watched light wisps of snowflakes flutter through the air and cling to the window before disappearing in the warmth of the late morning sun. There was hardly enough falling on the entire city to make a snowball, but it was the first snow of the season and it was unusually early.

I stood and angrily put on my coat.

Joshua rose. "We didn't mean it."

"It was heartless." I stared at the biscotti lying at the top of the trash can. "I was heartless."

Chapter Forty-two

"I don't like it." Dan's beady eyes were like black marbles in a bowl of cream, as he stared at me with all the distrust of someone who had been lied to on far too many occasions.

We were huddled around his cluttered desk. Old fast-food wrappers covered in hardened orange cheese and Styrofoam cups stuck out from under enormous stacks of papers that had fallen in a cataclysmic hurricane of disorganization. It took all my self-control to restrain from tidying up the mess.

"Well, I can say with all confidence that I finally agree with you on something," I said, picking up a wad of napkins with grease smeared all over them, and tossing them into the trash.

"Why not?" Joshua shook his head. "This is perfect. We know where the victims are coming from."

Dan eyed me as I began shuffling arrest reports into a neat pile.

"Can you say that you know positively this woman is the next victim?" he asked.

"We're pretty certain," I said, shoving my hands into the pockets of my slacks.

"That's not enough."

Joshua began rocking back and forth on his feet. "We can be fairly certain, but nothing is one hundred percent."

I don't know why, but Dan began pointing at me as if he were jabbing me with a knife. "It has to be. She's a civilian. We'd be placing a civilian in jeopardy."

I stared at him with a confused expression. What was the deal? I was in agreement with him.

"She'd have twenty-four-hour surveillance, and you can assign some plainclothes to tag along," Joshua argued.

I pressed my fingers to my temples. "As soon as we warn the patients they're going to want to split for the far corners of the Earth, and I don't blame them."

Dan sank into his chair, and ran the palm of his hand across what remained of his hair. "If something happened—"

"If."

He studied Joshua carefully. "Then we'd be in such deep shit."

With one arm I leaned against the corner of his desk, a bit annoyed that all Allison Beauchamp was to the NYPD was a potential PR nightmare.

"Is anyone hearing me?" I felt like I was talking to the blank wall again.

"How old is she?"

Joshua scratched the back of neck and mumbled.

"What?" Dan asked melodramatically, cupping his ear. "I'm sorry. I didn't hear that."

Joshua lifted his head and repeated himself more loudly. "She's legal."

"How old?"

"Nineteen," I said with intensity, throwing Dan one of my penetrating stares in the hopes that he would back down from this foolish idea.

"Nineteen," he muttered, kicking his feet up onto his desk and knocking down the neat piles of paperwork I had arranged for him. "All right."

I shot to an upright position. "What?"

"All right," Dan repeated, staring deeply into my eyes; too deep for my liking. "If you get her to agree, then we'll go ahead with it. But we do it my way. This is my game now."

Joshua and I walked at a moderate pace out of the Tenth Precinct.

"I don't think it's wise to ask a young woman who's obviously insecure and has emotional problems to place herself in jeopardy." I quickly shut my mouth when I noticed someone on a nearby pay phone. It was the reporter who had been standing in front of the Medical Examiner's building yesterday morning.

We hurried over to the main entrance.

"We're not asking her to place herself in jeopardy," he said, holding the door open. "We would never do that. She's going to have twenty-four-hour protection. All the patients will, if they decide to stay."

"But we're not giving Allison the option of leaving."

"We can't make her stay."

I buttoned my coat and angrily pulled on my leather gloves. "And you don't think that a team of police officers and FBI agents 'asking' her to stay put while her life is in jeopardy, isn't going to intimidate a child into doing what you want?"

He studied my pained expression. "Nineteen is hardly a child."

"And it's hardly an adult."

"Hey!" the desk sergeant yelled at us. "To the uninitiated, it's almost winter. Close the damn door!"

We stepped outside and I turned to Joshua, my breath blowing clouds of thin white smoke, the noise from Twentieth Street pounding against the inside of my skull.

"There has to be another way," I said with determination.

Joshua pushed his thumb and forefinger together. "We're this close."

My head was still throbbing, and I squeezed my eyes shut. "We can't be playing with her life like this."

He smacked me on the upper arm, and my eyes popped open.

"We do this all the time," he argued.

"But not with someone who has this disorder!"

Joshua tapped me gently this time, and I followed his gaze to the main door. The reporter who had been using the pay phone was now lingering inside the entranceway on the other side of the door. I turned and used my back to shield our conversation.

"If she finds out," I continued in a hoarse whisper, "that the cutting is what's attracting a murdering sociopath to her, Allison will without a doubt lash out at herself. Potentially causing severe physical harm to herself. She's a human being, and we're putting her in danger."

"What danger?" he asked rhetorically. "She's already at risk. She just doesn't know it. She's better off because now she's got protection."

"Yeah, so much better," I mumbled, while clumsily stepping out of the way as two uniforms squeezed by us.

We were blocking the front steps, but at the moment I didn't care who we inconvenienced.

"We won't tell her," he reassured me. Then he grinned like a Cheshire cat. "I want you to come with me and meet with Dr. Davidson and the Beauchamps."

"Shit, Joshua."

"You're starting to sound like Dan."

"Bite me."

"Nice." He frowned. "I need you there to convince them to go along."

I began ferociously shaking my head. "No way. This is your dumbass idea, you two boys do it by yourselves."

Joshua stopped me as I headed down the steps. "Look, it's going to happen either way. You can convince them yourself in that compassionate way you have—"

My narrowed eyes penetrated his, searching for evidence of any sarcasm.

"Or someone else will do it. Either way, it will happen."

He put his hand on my shoulder, and I fell into the depths of his puppy dog eyes.

"And I'd rather you talk with her," he continued.

I hated myself for falling for that look—again. I dug my nails into my palms as hard as I could. Not this time.

"No way," I shouted, taking the steps two at a time. "It's bad news."

"We do it all the time, so does the NYPD, so does every agency in the world."

I could feel all of the muscles in my face contract in response to the biting wind that was whipping through the streets like a wind tunnel.

"Does that make it right?" My nose began running. "It's no good this time."

"Premonition?" he asked jokingly as he followed me to the curb.

"Intuition," I fired back.

Joshua bit into his lower lip, not out of anger, but to contain the laughter pushing its way from some deep place within himself that I could only assume was evil. It only infuriated me further. Maybe if I made him stifle it more, it would kill him.

"Come on, Meredith." He was dying inside.

His shoulders trembled and then began moving up and down, as short cackles broke free with every other syllable.

"You've got some of that Irish blood in you." His words were broken and barely distinguishable between his cackles. "I've seen you put up a bigger and better fight when a cashier packs the bread at the bottom of your shopping bag."

"They squash it that way," I said through gritted teeth.

Joshua could no longer contain himself and he doubled over in hysterical laughter.

I was not amused and stepped beyond the curb with my arm thrust in the air to hail a cab.

"Meredith," he whined, "just say, 'Okay, Joshua, I'll do it,' and save me the hassle of having to squabble with you for another twenty minutes."

A taxi pulled up, nearly running its front tire onto the sidewalk and flattening my new suede loafers.

"We need to keep her here. So he doesn't think anything's different." Joshua moved around me and opened the back door. "It's the only way we're going to find him, and you know it."

Our faces were inches from each other. In flats I was eye level with him. "Fine, then we'd better be damn sure that she's the next one."

Joshua smiled.

"But you owe me, remember?" I said.

He eyed me quizzically.

As I climbed into the cab I shouted back to him, "Genoa and provolone on a hard roll."

Chapter Forty-three

A baby wailed from somewhere inside, colicky and agitated, in desperate need of food or a diaper change. Dan had wanted to meet with the Beauchamps at Sarah's office, but it was necessary to keep the family comfortable and in a familiar surrounding.

I rang the doorbell. The button was cold, and it rang a low gonglike tremor through the house that reverberated in my bones. As I waited for someone to answer, I began reviewing my notes.

Jim and Sandy Beauchamp: upper-middle class. He was an algebra teacher at a private school, and she was a poet. Likely that his job was providing for the family. Okay, I was being cynical, but art doesn't pay. Their combined incomes could just barely afford the small three-bedroom house they owned on Thirty-third Street in Queens, so it was not surprising to learn that they had inherited it from his grandmother, who had owned it since the late '40s. They had three daughters; Allison was the eldest.

Allison had been treated by Sarah for five months, and was making very little progress. She had cut herself with everything from scissors and kitchen knives to the rough edge of a piece of splintered wood. In one of the session transcripts, her mother was quoted as saying, "Our home is childproof. It needs to be. But not for the little one, for Allison."

I checked my watch. I was intentionally twenty minutes late.

We were desperate. I was desperate. Sure, there were many occasions in the past when we had been able to predict where and how a killer would strike next. But how many times were we so close that we actually knew the identity of his next victim while she was alive and not floating in some murky waters or lying sprawled out in some dusty roadside ditch? This was almost unprecedented.

I shook my head. No, this was disgusting. We were disgusting. This was just the sort of thing I hated. But Joshua was right. She was a target either way, because unfortunately, she was the next name on the list.

There was movement inside. I watched as the light shifted gently, like two lovers secretly meeting behind closed doors. But the fantasy quickly became ugly in my head. Why was I standing here? If such common tactics sickened me, why had I allowed myself to be sucked into this by Joshua? And it sure as hell wasn't the puppy-dog eyes—though that did add some incentive. Because it was all about control and trust. It was about me being able to control the circumstances, and not trusting anyone to do the job right. After all, if things got messed up, I could only blame myself. I nodded my head approvingly and decided to charge myself a pedicure for that qualified analysis.

The front door opened, and I was greeted by a young woman with straight black hair that glistened under the ambient light from inside. I had initially thought her to be Allison, but she was actually the babysitter for the two younger sisters. She welcomed me into the home and led me to the living room, where I was met with the disapproving glares of Joshua, Dan, and Sarah.

Allison and her parents were huddled on a large white sofa. Off to the side were two female plainclothes officers from the Anti-Crime Unit. I knew that part of Joshua's annoyed expression was also due to the fact that he had wanted detectives. Being a member of the NYPD's ACU gave you the same rank and status as the uniformed officers, only you worked in street clothes. And Joshua was being uncharacteristically elitist, but it made much more sense to me that our undercover officers were pulled from the ACU. This was the type of work that they were used to: blending in with everyday citizens, and keeping an open ear and watchful eye on all that went on around them.

I scanned the faces and read them quickly. They had already discussed the situation, and both Allison and her parents were adamantly opposed to it all. My guess was that they wanted desperately to make arrangements to send her away to a relative in another state. No one could blame them for wanting to run.

Joshua introduced me, and I politely shook everyone's hands, taking Allison's last. Her grip was warm but firm. She quickly withdrew it. Her actions were slightly timid, but her demeanor was friendly and surprisingly collected. I suppose I had expected someone who was frail, who made little eye contact and looked as if she were retreating within herself. But that's how she was feeling inside. How she carried herself on the outside was for the benefit of everyone else.

Allison was slightly pudgy, and wore faded jeans and a long-sleeve turtleneck with a brickred cardigan sweater. She sat upright with a confident posture, but more notable was her anxious habit of tugging on the edges of her sleeves.

"I'm sure you know what these people want Allison to do," Sandy said, scanning me like some kind of alien probe.

Jim began shaking head and laughing snidely. "This is ridiculous. I can't believe you folks would even have the gall to ask someone—a child—to do something like this."

Allison's voice was soft, and reminded me of Mrs. Miyaki's. "Daddy, I'm an adult."

"Barely."

"You're still our baby," Sandy cooed, as she pulled a somewhat resistant Allison closer to her.

Joshua sat up straighter on the footstool he was seated on. His voice was gentle and soothing, the same voice he used when speaking to his sons. "Allison, I would never ask anyone to place themselves in harm's way. I have two kids of my own, and I am very protective of them. You will be safe the whole time." He then added the two most dangerous words that anyone in the judicial system could ever say: "I promise."

He looked at me out of the corner of his eye, but I remained silent.

Sandy pulled Allison even closer. The more she did, the more her daughter resisted. "What do you think, Dr. Davidson?"

I stared at my lap, and then tentatively raised my head. I held my breath as Sarah watched Allison carefully.

"I think it needs to be Allison's decision," Sarah replied.

All eyes turned to Allison, and she looked at each of us hoping that one would have the right answer. When her questioning stare was met only with silence, she sprang from the sofa and ran down the hall. We all jolted when we heard the bedroom door slam.

No one said a word for what seemed like an eternity.

"May I?"

Everyone looked at me. Jim and Sandy looked at Sarah.

Sarah carefully eyed me as I nervously spun my watch around my wrist. "Sure, why not." But her gaze registered like a thunderbolt, serving as a warning to me.

I nodded, and walked slowly down the hall.

On Allison's bedroom door was a small wooden sign painted with flowers and birds, and her name spelled out in thin flowing letters. I rapped lightly, but knocked louder when I received no answer.

Her voice was quiet and shaky on the other side. "Leave me alone."

I shuffled my feet against the carpet and cleared my throat. "Please, Allison, just for a moment." When I placed my hand on the doorknob I received the shock of my life.

"Damn," I muttered. The air was too dry in the apartment.

There was a lengthy pause before the door stirred.

"Come on in," Allison welcomed me warmly. "It was open." She bounced energetically over to her bed like a kangaroo and motioned for me to sit wherever I desired.

I carefully walked to the desk chair, and smiled graciously as I sat. I found myself slightly turned off and mildly cautious of her seemingly forced and happy demeanor.

Allison's room was *almost* what I expected of a young

woman. On the walls were carefully placed framed photos of family and friends, and posters of Hollywood's current toast of teen idolatry. Her room was surprisingly neat, almost to the point of being anal compulsive. The closet door was ajar, and I observed that Allison had even organized her neatly folded and hung clothes in the order of the colors of the rainbow. On a chair in the corner of the room, a wrinkle-free pile of clothes had been neatly folded and rested comfortably, again, organized by the order of the color spectrum.

I looked at Allison stretched out on her stomach on her bed. The underside of her body all but sank into the soft mattress and disappeared into the plaid pattern of the comforter. Her chin was propped up against her two fists as she smiled happily at me. We sat in awkward silence, each of us waiting for the other to start the conversation. Then with one swift motion she sat up on the bed and grabbed a pillow then punched it into her lap.

"They say you're a professor."

"Yes."

"Psychology," she said almost disdainfully.

"And criminology."

"So, are you to pick my brain and try to figure why I'm so fucked up?"

My eyebrows arched and I was rendered speechless.

"Naw, you're not here for that." She nervously tugged on the ends of sleeves, and her mood became somber. "Do you know what it's like to be targeted?"

I think I had a pretty good idea, but I still shook my head.

"The cops and that FBI guy came here to tell me that someone wants to kill me." She clutched the pillow for security. "Me! What did I ever do?"

257

I frowned and closed my eyes. Joshua had kept his word; they didn't tell Allison anything. Still, what comfort did this provide?

"Why can't I just run away?" Tears began to roll down her robust cheeks. "Just go to my cousin's house in Seattle and be far away."

I was feeling warm, and realized that I hadn't taken off my coat. "You can," I said, pulling my arms out of the sleeves.

She looked at me in wonderment, as if actually fleeing had never been a real option.

I only hesitated for a moment. "But this person will just find someone else to lash out at."

"Someone else?"

I leaned forward and placed my hand on her shoulder. "Allison, we need you to help catch him."

She shrank farther into the bed and all but disappeared behind the pillow. "I'm scared."

"You would never be alone. Someone from the NYPD will always be with you to protect you."

Her body trembled. "No, I can't. I'll just go to Seattle. That seems like the best thing to do."

I leaned back and pursed my lips. We were approaching this the wrong way. Allison was a young woman who, for whatever reason, felt an undue pressure to be perfect. She felt as if the responsibility to be there for others was destroying her inside. When, in fact, she was looking for someone to be responsible for her.

I looked down at my watch and sighed heavily.

Allison watched me with curious interest as I unbuckled the strap and dropped the heavy timepiece onto her bed.

"What's that?" she asked, drying her eyes and pointing to the two-inch scar running across the underside of my wrist.

It was a quarter-inch thick and whitish in color. Small pale dots ran along the edges where the stitches had once been.

"A long time ago I accidentally put my hand through a plate glass window."

Ironically, Allison cringed.

"I was sixteen. I was chasing my brother through the house, and he ran outside. I ran out after him and didn't know the glass door was shut." I began to chuckle. "Our mother was a good cleaner."

Allison giggled, but her face quickly dropped to a serious stare. "Is that what really happen?"

I snorted. "That's what the doctors asked." I nodded my head. "And yes, that's what happened. Except, instead of calling for help, or carefully removing my hand, I let it fall onto the sharp edges."

My voice became hollow. I stared at the scar, and in my mind I could see the blood and I could feel glass again, pressing painlessly and easily through my skin as if I did not exist.

"I watched the sharp point draw this really light, harmless line across my wrist. It was strange. I was almost detached from it all."

"Like it was someone else's arm."

I looked up at Allison hugging the pillow and staring at my scar. She knew exactly what it was like.

"And then I began turning my wrist, slowly and methodically. And I kept doing that until I passed out." I picked up my watch and slapped it onto my wrist. "Next thing I remember I was waking up in the hospital. The doctors refused to believe my explanation of running through the door, which was only a partial truth. But my parents, wanting to avoid rumors and gossip, enthusiastically accepted my version of the story. And that's what the hospital report says."

Good thing, too, or they would never have accepted my application into the FBI.

"Wow," she said, gripping the pillow even tighter. "You tried to kill yourself?"

I smiled, charmed by her direct approach. "I don't know if I actually tried to kill myself. All I know is, at that moment I felt like I was in control. I didn't feel afraid."

Her eyes were like saucers as she nodded her head slowly.

"But I also decided that day, that I wasn't going to let myself be afraid again." I leaned forward and rested my elbows on my knees. "That I wouldn't let something like that control me. That I wouldn't let fear control me. *I* would control fear."

"I don't know," she said in a quivering voice.

I sat on the bed next to her and put my arm around her shoulders. I was somewhat taken aback when she fell into me like I was her mother—or, the mother she wanted.

"I know what it's like to be confused and to hate yourself," I said soothingly. "And what we're asking you to do is a lot to ask of *any* person." I rubbed her upper arm gently. "You don't have to do this. You can say, 'no,' and no one will think any less of you. In fact, we'll respect you because it's your decision."

Allison looked up at me and then down at her left arm. She carefully rolled up her sleeve, tears leaving light tracks along her face.

"I did this a couple of days ago." She pointed to a pink-ish patch that had already begun to bubble into a crusty scab. "I held it over a lighter. It felt good."

I gently took her arm in my hand and brought it closer

for me to examine. My face remained expressionless as I read her scars like a sad book of a young woman's life of despair.

"Are you angry?" she asked innocently, carefully watching my reaction.

"No," I said softly.

"Most people are." She ran her index finger along the lightest scar inside the crook of her arm. It was just barely a small, brownish line. "This was the first one. I was thirteen. I don't even remember why I did it. They didn't have to say it, but the nurses thought I was just a brat, and the doctors thought I needed to be institutionalized. That was before I met Dr. Davidson."

Allison rolled down her sleeve and pulled away from me. "I don't want to run. I feel safe in this room. It's the only place I do, and not just because it's where I hurt myself." She brought her hand to her mouth. "I want to help you. I'm tired of running."

There was a pained look on her face, a mixture of fear and exhaustion. But also buried deep within her expression was a mild hint of an inner strength: slight and subtle and barely noticeable, but struggling to break free.

I smiled gently and placed my hand on her shoulder. She was not going to run.

As I walked down the hall, a cynical frown spread across my face. Most of what I had said was true, and I really did feel a genuine concern for Allison's well-being. However, I felt somewhat guilty for even lying to her a little. But as long as Allison was a bit more comfortable and was willing to help us, then she didn't need to know how I really got that scar.

Chapter Forty-four

Later that night, as I stood in the bathroom doorway and watched Kyle brush his teeth, I realized that as confusing as my warped little world could be, I was actually very lucky in the relationships I had maintained over the years.

"What's so funny," he asked through a mouthful of sudsy toothpaste.

I choked on the last of my giggling. "I was just remembering the first time you ever stayed over. The next morning you brushed your teeth with that bitter-tasting toothpaste, except that it wasn't really—"

He waved his hand and spit into the sink. "Yeah, I remember." Kyle shuddered at the memory. "Sometimes a guy forgets that he has to be a little more into reading when he's in a woman's home."

My mind was lost somewhere in the lines of grouting between the tiles on the floor. I snapped to, when I caught him studying me in the mirror.

"What's going on?" he asked, his face buried within the soft cotton of a hand towel. When he put it back on the rack, his mouth had left white streaks of toothpaste along the edges.

"I don't know," I shrugged.

Kyle stepped over to me and put his arms around my waist. Then he placed a long, soft kiss upon my forehead. "What's going on?" he repeated.

"Have you ever felt like you were being used."

He smiled at me. "All the time."

I gave him a light tap on the chest. "I'm being serious. I feel like they're just using me."

Kyle frowned with concern and took half a step away from me. "This isn't that Joshua guy, is it?" He pulled me closer, and added in only a slightly joking manner, "I'll have words with him if you want."

I was touched, but I didn't need a knight in shining armor. My body collapsed in his strong arms. I was always softer when he was around me. That Irish blood Joshua often liked to remind me about somehow disappeared when I was with Kyle. When he was near, I easily became one of those cooing sentimental imbeciles whom I despised and found nauseating. For some reason I always felt safe within his hold.

"Have you ever felt like you were using someone?" I asked lightly, my face resting comfortably underneath his chin. The whiskers from his day-old beard tickled my cheek seductively.

"Let's go to bed. You're tired." With soothing words, we walked slowly down the hall and into the bedroom.

Kyle turned out the light and lovingly wrapped his body around me. I listened to nothing but the steady rhythmic sounds of his heart beating until I drifted off into a peaceful slumber.

Chapter Forty-five

There was a terrible odor in my office. I looked up from the files spread out in front of me of the three known victims. This afternoon I was particularly interested in the newly completed toxicology reports. If there was evidence that the victims had been drugged, then it would indicate a more lengthy seduction process before rendering them incapacitated.

My nose began to twitch like Samantha's on *Bewitched*. It really did smell in my office, like the gangrene often found on the homeless victims who I had watched being autopsied. I began a cursory once over of my shoebox of an office.

"Meredith?"

"Yeah!" I called out from underneath my desk.

"Could we talk?"

I banged my head on the way up. "Sure, I have a few

minutes before my lecture starts," I whimpered, rubbing the area near my frontal lobe.

"It won't take long."

Douglas Ford was the head of the Psychology Department at NYU. A chronically nervous man, with straggly gray hair and a goatee. Lucky for me, he had made it his personal duty to oversee the progress of all first-year professors.

"Please have a seat," I offered, quickly closing the cover on Sumi's lab report. "Does it smell like rotting cheese in here?"

Completely dumbfounded, he shook his head slowly.

"Meredith, how are things going?" he asked tentatively.

"Fine." I poked through the garbage can for any leftovers that should've been disposed of. "Is that a general question or are you more interested in how my classes are going?"

Doug smiled. "Yes, how are things going with your class?"

"Fine, as well. In fact today I'm actually looking forward to facing the little buggers." I looked out from behind the file cabinet, and grinned. "I'm just joking." I gave up my search and opened the window. "Why do you ask?"

"It seems that some concern has been raised—"

"Oh?" I said, my eyes becoming wider.

A blast of cold air shot into the room and I shuddered.

"Yes, um, some concern that you may be neglecting your duties here at the university."

I laughed casually and I sat at my desk. "That's ridiculous. I haven't missed a class, and I'm keeping all of my appointments."

"I know, on paper it all seems very well," Doug agreed,

nervously playing with his tie clasp. "But I think your students are feeling more neglected in respect to the lectures. The thing is—how do I say this? There have been some comments made, that in the last couple of weeks the quality of your lectures and attentiveness to your students' needs has declined."

My deliberate silence intensified the already awkward moment. We both concentrated on the crack of the Venetian blind banging in the wind against the window.

"No one's disagreeing with your style of teaching," Doug explained.

"Well, that's not exactly what I had inferred," I said, the irritation ringing clearly in my tone.

"Oh," he said meekly. "The general feel of the students is that the course had a strong beginning, but has seemed to have tapered off. They just want a little more attention from you."

I smiled cordially. "Well, then. The masses have voiced their opinion. If you would like, Doug, why don't you sit in on one of my lectures and you can make your own judgment?"

He flinched in response to my slightly abrasive tone. "I don't think that would be necessary, but just in case, when's your next meeting?"

"Today, but I'd prefer the next session."

Doug sighed, and stood from his chair, "I guess I'd better not hold you up any longer."

I stood. What had started out as a crappy morning was turning into a crappy afternoon.

"Hmm," I said as Doug left my office. "Doesn't stink in here anymore."

They were just as disinterested as I was. Ninety-six young faces staring at me with that blank expression meant to fool the teacher into believing they were paying attention, when in fact, their minds were daydreaming about the keg party from last Saturday night.

The words flowed from my mouth, but even I wasn't concentrating on them.

"The statistical rate of crime versus the economic status of a community, compounded with race, sex and family structure involves something completely different than the crime rate versus the unemployment rate."

I had no idea what I had just said, but I was positive that it sounded good. Denny wasn't in class. I hoped that he had just decided to skip today, but I feared that I had unjustly chased him away. I looked out into the sea of young men and women, and very few pens were moving.

The chalk was soft, just the way I liked it. It was easier to erase, easier to read, and it didn't make unsuspecting squeaking noises along the blackboard. I stepped away from the two words I had just written in large, block letters. Quiet murmurs rose steadily from the class—I had their attention.

SERIAL KILLER

Always a party favorite and undeniably irresistible. Sometimes I found myself disturbed by the way the general public, especially young people, seemed to be so fascinated with these gruesome crimes. I blamed it on the increasing glorification of killers and the disturbing depiction of violence in films and television. But my ideals did not harbor any support for censorship. A psychologist's interest was influenced not by the horrid actions of these monsters, but the science behind their motives. A violent criminal is an interesting character, not to be mistaken for some kind of celebrated hero.

I looked out at the stares concentrated upon me. They were filled with interest and wonder. Denny had been right. It was the only reason why most of these students were taking my class.

"That's all for today. I'll see you next session."

Blank expressions stared back at me.

"Go on. See you next time."

"Professor Brantley, it's only been half an hour," my graduate assistant whispered dutifully to me.

"Next time."

Everyone slowly gathered their textbooks and packed up their bags. I watched them file out, all voicing the same confused questions, but I just nodded and thanked them for coming. As the seats cleared, I looked out to the back of the room and saw Doug in the back row.

Chapter Forty-six

Joshua showed up at my door bearing a gift of two pounds of Starbucks Sumatra coffee. A little mild for my taste, but in no time at all it was brewing and sending its hypnotizing aroma throughout my apartment.

He was doused in Polo again, and I was surprised that the smell had remained on his body so far into the afternoon.

"I think I just got fired this morning," I mentioned somberly, pouring two mugs of coffee.

Joshua didn't respond. He just continued to flip through a legal pad filled with my notes.

I placed the half-and-half and a bowl of sugar on the counter. He enthusiastically poured half a mug of the half-and-half into his coffee and shoveled in two heaping teaspoons of sugar.

"I put on a poor showing for the head of my department." I looked at Joshua's unmoved expression. "It's nice to see that you're so apathetic about this."

"I'm sorry," he said, taking a seat at my dining room table covered with my notes and files. "But I didn't think the job was right for you."

I moved some color photos, where I placed a plate of day-old cinnamon rolls and a dish of butter. True to his Philadelphia upbringing, Joshua slathered on a chunk of butter before each bite.

I couldn't help thinking of Allison. She was being very brave. Braver than I had ever been.

"How is she?" I asked as I sat across from him.

His words were garbled by a mouthful of walnuts and raisins. "Fine."

"Her regular session with Sarah is tomorrow." I took a sip of my coffee. It was too weak.

"Yeah. She's nervous. But we'll be ready." He put down the remainder of the cinnamon bun. There was a fire in his brown eyes.

I reached for two files and handed one to Joshua. We began studying the charts in silence. They were break-outs of employee time sheets and duties for every day during the past two months. But we were concentrating mainly on the Tuesdays.

Two hours and one pot of coffee later, I flipped over the last page in my folder. "It's the same damn people working every day for the past two months. Except for this mural painter who started four weeks ago."

Joshua began scratching the point of his chin and looked up at me.

Before either of us could say anything more, the locks on the front door rattled—Kyle was done with his meetings. He dumped his computer bag and briefcase onto the sofa as I introduced him to Joshua. Like gladiators before battle, they both studied each other, comparing all outward physical attributes to their own. Joshua stood with a firm and elongated posture, giving him a good six inches over Kyle. But he awkwardly shook his hand, as Kyle intentionally flexed his biceps.

"So you're the infamous Kyle," Joshua said with stiff politeness.

Kyle could only manage a half smile.

As perverse as it may have seemed, I was taking great pleasure in having two men compete over me.

"Working hard?" Kyle asked with superficial interest as he wrapped his arm around my shoulders.

He gave me a gentle peck on the lips, and I inconspicuously eyed Joshua's reaction.

"Yeah," Joshua said, quickly averting his gaze and returning to the table. "Long hours. *Really* long hours."

This was getting to be ridiculous. Next thing I knew, we'd be passing notes in study hall. I gently pulled away from Kyle and sat down in my chair.

"What's this?" he asked, picking up the freehanded sketch of the unknown weapon.

Although I knew Kyle was harmless and could've cared less about anything we were doing, I eyed Joshua, not certain of how much information we were discussing with those outside the investigation.

He shrugged.

I think Joshua believed that Kyle was an imbecile.

"It's an item linked to the crimes we're investigating." I looked at the photos scattered about. "But we have no idea what it could be."

Kyle held the paper close to his face, and then began nodding his head. "I know what it is."

Chapter Forty-seven

Kyle handed me the chisel.

It was deceptively heavier than it appeared in the drawing. It was one thing to create the image of an unknown tool of death in your mind, and it was another to have a sketch placed before you. But it was a completely different experience to actually hold the weapon in your hand, to feel the weight and wrap your fingers around the solid wooden handle as the killer would have done. It was horrific, but I lost myself, and examined the chisel like a curious child.

"That sketch was pretty rudimentary," Kyle said, as he began poking through the small dark blue bins filled with an assortment of chisels, scrapers and sanders. "But it was close enough."

We had climbed the rickety wooden steps to the fifth floor of Pearl Paint, an enormous art store on Canal Street, and Kyle's favorite little clubhouse. He could spend hours going through this store, picking out expensive vellum, intricate pens or odd-smelling paints.

"What the hell is this?" Joshua was holding a metal spearhead-shaped object with a long handle. The triangular head had sharp raised pieces like a cheese grater.

Kyle was hidden behind one of the many boxes full of store inventory that needed to be put out onto the floor. He looked up and smiled.

"It's a rasp," he said with the perky delight of a kindergarten teacher. "You can use it for scraping plaster."

I stepped over to Joshua, and we both stared at it aghast. We then simultaneously scanned the aisle of the weaponlike tools. Kyle saw the sculpting tools for what they were, but Joshua and I were looking at them for what they could be—someone's sadistic torture devices.

I turned my attention back to the chisel. All the weight was naturally in the metal of the blade. And just as Anthony had predicted, three-quarters of it had a shovel-like quality. The tip was beveled to about half an inch. I pressed my forefinger into the U-shaped tip and ran it along the sharp edge, where it left behind a trace white line against my skin. Anyone could inflict so much pain with this.

I wrapped my long fingers around the octagonal shaped handle and began jabbing it into the top of one of the boxes. Even with a moderate tap, the chisel broke through half of the layers of corrugated cardboard. A woman nearby eyed us nervously, and then stepped away with small cautious movements.

It was then that we remembered where we were. There were only two of the larger sized chisels remaining in the display box. This type of chisel came in four more different sizes.

"Can I help you?" A young woman in a red apron tentatively approached us.

The cautious woman from before was watching from the end of the aisle.

"We'll take all of these," Joshua said confidently as he waved his hand over the bins containing the chisels. "And we need a manufacturer's catalog, if you have one."

"We do," the young woman replied suspiciously, her spikey black hair glistening under the fluorescent lights. "But it's only for the store."

"Let me talk to the manger."

"I'm the manager of this department."

Joshua looked around quickly, and when he spotted the woman at the end of the aisle, she quickly moved away to another part of the floor. He pulled out his creds and displayed them to the young woman.

"I guess we can let you have the catalog," she said quickly, hurrying us along toward the registers. "I'll ring you up over here."

The slow-moving checkout line of eight people angrily stared at us.

"I can't believe there was an elevator," I said once we'd gotten back to the precinct.

Five flights up the rickety stairs, and Pearl Paint had an elevator in the back.

Kyle looked at me and smiled. "I thought you'd want the exercise."

My stare was penetrating as he moved away from us and sat in one of the chairs by another detective's desk. That was twice in one week that someone had made a comment about my physique. With inconspicuous movements, I began squeezing barely a pinch's worth of fat around my middle. Maybe I was letting myself go a bit. I looked over at Kyle and his finely toned muscles. I thought of the fatty French foods that he liked to eat. Bastard. Why were men able to eat and drink like every meal was their last and still look like—well—Kyle?

Dan was clutching one of the two larger chisels. Even he was stupefied by the devastating nature of the tool. "How'd your boyfriend know about this?"

I frowned at him, not sure if I was more annoyed that he referred to him as my boyfriend or of the insinuating nature behind his question.

"He's a designer," I explained gruffly. "He knows what's out there."

Dan gave him the visual once-over and then placed the chisel on top of his desk. From his middle desk drawer, he removed a small Granny Smith apple. I think I was surprised that Dan actually ate healthy food. He placed it on the table and picked up the chisel. In five seconds I knew that I'd be picking pieces of fruit from my clothes. I stepped back just as he thrust the chisel into the apple. The blade went all the way through with the curved edge sticking out the other side. He held it up close to his face and examined it.

"Ouch," he stated simply, pulling the chisel from the apple. "We'll send all these to Toolmarkings."

He reached over and dragged a thick file closer to himself.

"After you called, I did a quick little check into this artist," he explained, opening it to the first page.

Joshua and I stared at the mug shot paper clipped to the first page of the arrest report. There was the artist, surprisingly handsome when not covered with paint. Six years ago he had been charged by the Westchester County prosecutor for one count of manslaughter. A mistrial was declared due to some technicality with his Miranda rights. That would only make him more of a target for Dan.

"Manslaughter is a lot different than murder," I commented, as I read how Eric Johanson had killed his young wife in the heat of a violent argument.

"The D.A. wanted to charge him with first-degree," Dan pointed out, taking a large bite of the mutilated apple. "His scumbag lawyer talked him down."

"There's a huge difference between killing someone in the heat of an argument and methodically plotting and strategizing three sadistic murders with malice." I caught a glimpse of Kyle nodding his head and watching me with an admiring grin. I think he was turned on.

Dan grabbed the file from us and dropped it with a heavy thud onto his desk. "Either way, he's got the drive in him." He began spinning the largest chisel between his fingers like a drumstick. "I'll have a little talk with him tomorrow. After Ms. Beauchamp's shrink session. All we need is some DNA and we can match him up."

Oh, yes, that easy.

"What makes you think he'll give you a blood sample?" Kyle challenged from across the way.

Dan stopped spinning the chisel and stared at him. "Why is he here?"

I stiffened like a lioness protecting her brood. "He was the one who did what a whole lab full of experts weren't able to do."

"Why do you think this man is going to just let you take his blood and extract DNA?" Kyle pushed further.

Even though he worked in corporate design, it went without question that Kyle was the epitome of the liberal-bleeding-heart-artist-don't-fuck-with-my-rights-give-the-arts-more-funding cliché, which I agreed with him on—most of the time. We often found ourselves on opposite ends of the argument regarding capital punishment. But then again, he never spoke to the kinds of characters I had, or saw how handy they could be with live jumper cables or rusty needle-nose pliers.

Dan put down the chisel and crammed his hands into his pockets. "He'll give us his blood so he can prove his innocence. If he doesn't, then he makes a good, strong suspect." He scrunched his face and his expression went sour. "Why the hell am I explaining myself to *him?*"

I looked over at Kyle. Dan had his suspect picked out, but what had me more concerned was that someone with this type of criminal past had been given access to the Juvenile Ward.

Chapter Forty-eight

The nineteenth floor of Bellevue was alive with activity before the sun had even begun its steady ascent. The idea was to be as discreet as possible. So things were done quickly and long before most of the city was waking. We were using the hospital's security cameras, but the NYPD had also positioned two of its own in Sarah's office. Manning the security door was the regular nurse, but a female nurse and one male aide had been added to the roster. A new female patient had also been admitted in the morning: a petite, baby-faced five-year veteran of the force, whose good genes were a huge asset to the NYPD. Officer Mills worked undercover in many juvenile situations: high schools, colleges, and more recently, pedophile investigations involving the Internet.

No one had told Sarah, Allison, or her family about the suspicion surrounding Eric. The official excuse was that the less everyone knew the better the performance.

However, I believed the real reason was that Dan and Joshua were afraid if everyone believed the "bad guy" had been discovered, they would feel that the NYPD had very little use for Allison's participation in the under-cover act.

I was a little uncertain as to why Dan felt the need to continue with this cloak-and-dagger routine since he already had what he felt was a strong suspect. However, I was glad that he hadn't put a freeze on the operation, since I was unconvinced that the painter was our UN-SUB. There were some coincidences, like him having blond hair, and blond hair was found at the last two crime scenes. And then there was the manslaughter charge. There had never been a reported incident of prior abuse, but that didn't mean things were hunky-dory in the Johanson household. According to the au-topsy report, Eric's wife, Emily, had died of blunt force trauma to the head, which she had received when she fell against the corner of a marble fireplace after he struck her. He had smacked her a couple of times before that, and she had hit him, too. It was an argument that was out of control with terrible consequences. I didn't feel that he had intended to kill her. Still, I wasn't writing him off too quickly. Not until I saw how he interacted with Alli-son. So we couldn't question Eric until *after* Allison had her session with Sarah.

Our small unofficial task force had more or less taken over the NYPD police liaison's tiny office down on the main level. Inside were small video monitors. A techni-cian turned to me and nodded as he began hooking up cables. I needed some coffee.

The tapping of my heels resounding off the walls re-minded me of the sterile basement corridors of the FBI Academy in Quantico. Normally, crowded and bustling with activity, they had their moments of desolation, late at night or during the meal breaks. I had always savored the times when those hallways belonged to me and me alone. It was always a calming feeling in an environment filled with chaos. Nowadays, those halls belong to the DEA.

The coffee from the café next to the NYPD liaison office was awful, but I drank it anyway.

Time was of the essence. We knew for certain that a murderer was going to be selecting his next victim at 2:00 PM when Allison Beauchamp had her appointment. We needed to watch what Eric did during those forty-five minutes, or if someone else was nearby.

The halls were now quiet, and upstairs was equally calm. With our people in position and the young patients still sleeping, the mood was pleasantly peaceful. There was concern for their safety, but our presence was merely for observation. The man we were looking for wouldn't strike out here—not in public. We were hunting the hunter.

I poked my head into Sarah's office. She was tapping away on her computer. The bluish-white glare reflected off of her reading glasses. Sarah looked up and waved me inside when she spotted me. I handed her a second Styrofoam cup I was holding.

"This coffee is like an experiment in nuclear physics," she said, cringing after the first sip. "They never get it right."

"Gives you that kick you need." I curiously eyed the computer.

"Just catching up on some e-mail," she explained. "My brothers and sisters have been wondering about me."

"I hope you're not discuss—"

She grinned. "Nothing about what's been happening

here." Sarah folded her hands and propped herself against the top of her desk. "You're a very driven person."

I sat down. "To the point of insanity, I think."

She smiled again and took another sip. "I'm not going to lie to you, but I don't like the fact that you're using Allison."

I studied Sarah's face. She was probably about the same age as my mother. What had my mother declared almost seventeen years ago in her stern, most disgusted voice?

This opprobrium is unforgivable!

I caught myself chuckling. When my mother had shouted those words, I had been more concerned with running and finding a dictionary than in the hateful tone she had used.

"Neither do I," I said, unconsciously spinning my watch around my wrist. I stopped when I caught Sarah watching me.

"But you really think you can catch whoever's doing this?"

I gazed at her pensively. "We have to."

Sarah looked down at the hulking watch on my left wrist. "Here's my card," she said, handing me a small piece of canary card stock. "My private practice is at my home over on York. My office hours are printed on the back."

Standing before the mural, I thought of Eric and his wife, and how they might have argued that night. How he had screamed at her and she at him. I checked my watch: two more hours to go.

Smiling, happy faces of children from all different ethnic backgrounds stared back at me from the wall. Some were painted above the others. Running and playing; tumbling through the clouds with joyous abandonment. Or were they floating? Floating toward heaven. I stepped back and absorbed the whole image. A tingling sensation crept up my spine. The faces depicted along the lower portion against a grassy green background seemed sadder. They played along the bottom of the mural as a female adult watched. Some gravitated toward her. And following the same fluid motion of the broad brushstrokes, some of the children drifted liked balloons into the powder blue sky.

I thought I was going to vomit.

"So what do you think?"

I whipped around, and was staring directly into Eric's painted face.

"N-nice," I managed to stutter.

He grimaced awkwardly. "You can be honest. It's not great. But they wanted something with a flat quality." He studied his work with a scrutinizing eye. "You know, no shadows or highlights."

"I was curious," I tried to say as casually as possible. "I was wondering what the theme is, aside from the obvious happiness of children?"

Eric carefully dropped the brush he was using into a dirty coffee can filled with murky brownish water. "Well, these kids down here are playing. They seem happy on the outside, but really they're hurting inside." He swept his arm to the opposite end of the mural and pointed to the adult. "That's Dr. Davidson, but I'll never admit it," he whispered.

I forced a smile. "So what is she doing?"

"Well, she's watching and making them feel good." He pointed to the children standing closest to her. "See, they're a little happier than the others."

I looked up.

"Now, these kids," he smiled proudly. "These kids are happy—elated—after visiting Dr. Davidson."

"Are they better?"

Eric contemplated this and shook his head. "No, they're just happier than they were before. And they feel safer."

Safer? I took a step away from him.

"You must have quite an admiration for Dr. Davidson."

"Absolutely," he said with devotion. "If you could see how the kids light up when she's around. It's like she's their medicine. They all love her. It's such a wonderful thing to witness."

I pointed to the kids floating through the clouds. "It looks like they're in heaven."

Eric nodded his head gently. "I guess in a way they are."

We sat in the NYPD liaison's office with the light brown blinds drawn.

The elevator doors opened, and we all held our breath. Allison Beauchamp, with her mother guiding her, stepped out onto the floor. In the monitor, she seemed surprisingly calm for someone sending an open invitation to her own killer. But she tugged more vigorously at the ends of her sleeves. I knew her heart was racing because mine was, too.

When Allison passed, Eric smiled and nodded his head. He said something to her, and she very nearly scurried back into the elevator, but Sandy held her wrist tightly and guided her around the corner toward Sarah's office.

We switched to the hall camera and watched as Sandy and Allison walked slowly toward the lens. As they neared, Allison said something that looked like,

"Mom . . . can't do this." But Sandy's reply filled me with even more pity for the young woman: "It's too late . . . promised."

I looked down at the floor. What the hell had I done to that poor girl?

Allison and her mother sat in Sarah's office with the door closed for forty-five minutes. And for forty-five minutes Eric painted one more child in the sky with a few birds flying in the distance. I didn't like it. And it had nothing to do with the painting.

For forty-five minutes no one else lingered in the area. For forty-five minutes we all stared, glued to the monitors, trying desperately to remain interested. Allison and Sandy headed for the elevator, and Eric waved good-bye to them. The doors quickly closed before either of them could respond. He shrugged and returned to putting some detail in the grass.

"I want to talk to him," Dan said with determination as he watched Eric mix some paint in a plastic takeout food container.

From the slanted angle of the camera mounted in the ceiling, I studied what I could see of the mural.

"It's not him," I said with a confident certainty.

"He's the only one nearby. And he made contact with her," Dan growled at me. Then he snapped his wrist at me. "Doesn't matter. I'm still questioning him."

I straightened and put on my coat. "It's *not* him."

Chapter Forty-nine

The light hazel circles darted back and forth, retracting and expanding in response to the shifting light. Eric Johanson's irises were a telling glimpse into the psyche of a man who had no idea that within the next decade he could quite possibly be the unfortunate recipient of a deadly potassium and barbiturate injection.

It was nearing the end of the workday when Dan had caught up with Eric. Even though Dan had assured him that the interview was simply routine procedure and that they just needed to clear up a few points of fact, Eric had been wary.

We had taken over a small interview room just beyond the secure entryway to the left of the nurse's station. Very simple: one table, four chairs and a mirrored window. It worked on the same principle as any police precinct's interview room, except with its eraser-pink walls this room was about one level higher on the cozy scale.

Joshua and I remained hidden in the observation room, while Eric sat nervously at the bare round table. His tousled blond hair was already beginning to mat against his forehead and clung to the paint streaking across his face.

"First of all," Dan said, as he remained standing, "thanks for staying late. This is all strictly routine."

"Okay," Eric said nervously, tapping his colorful paint-stained fingers against the top of the table.

When Dan looked down at the dancing digits, Eric quickly withdrew his hands and laid them on his lap.

"So," Dan began. "There anything I can get you? Want some coffee or something?"

"No, thanks." He nodded and glanced nervously at the mircocassette recorder resting in the center of the table. "I'm okay," he said, almost entranced by the hypnotic turning of the tape's wheels.

In a calculated move, Dan let silence fall between them.

"So, why am I here?" Eric finally asked uneasily.

"How long you been painting that mural?"

His eyebrows arched. "Uh, I guess a few weeks." Eric's tone had become more sedate.

"Now I don't mean to judge because I don't know the first thing about what you artsy types do. But isn't two or three weeks a long time to come up with, ah"—Dan chortled annoyingly—"what you've got?"

Eric's full lips thinned into a tight frown. "It takes time. You've got to discuss what whoever commissions you wants. What kind of image they're looking for. The theme they're trying to project."

Dan pulled out the chair opposite Eric and sat down. He looked as if he was about to fall asleep.

"Then I've got to present the ideas on paper. Thumb-nail sketches. Once they approve them, I've got to sketch it out on the wall. So I really didn't start painting it until about eight days ago."

"How long you been doing this art thing?"

I began shaking my head. I was happy to see that Dan disliked all artists and not just my boyfriend. I caught my expression in the window's reflection. It was the first time that I had ever considered Kyle my boyfriend. My eyes slowly panned to Joshua's reflection.

"All my life."

"What?" I quickly asked.

Joshua turned to me. "What?"

"All my life," Eric repeated.

I let our reflections disappear from my sight, and pulled my focus tighter on what was going on inside the interview room.

"You been doing this all your life," Dan said with a tinge of skepticism. "What are you, twenty?"

"Twenty-three."

"So you just paint?"

I watched Eric's posture and mannerism very closely. He was more relaxed, now. Probably comfortable with Dan's supposed interest in what it takes to be an artist, no matter how obnoxious and ignorant he was sounding.

"I do lithographs."

Dan scrunched his face as if he were reading a bad menu. "Litho-whats? What about sculpting?"

"Yeah, a little. Every once in a while. Mostly as a hobby because I haven't found it to be lucrative."

Dan reached down under the table into a corrugated box sitting on the floor. He held firmly in his hand the larger chisel purchased from Pearl Paint.

287

"Hey, I was wondering what happened to that!" Eric gleefully said. He quickly retreated into his chair when he absorbed the image of a burly police detective holding it like a knife, and quickly looked down at the tape recorder.

"You own one of these?" Dan calmly asked.

"I used to," he mumbled. "I lost it when I was planning out the mural."

"You lost it?"

Eric began rubbing his fingers nervously, and Dan studied his tar-stained fingers.

"Smoke?" Dan said, pushing an unopened pack of Camels across the table like he was dealing a pack of cards.

Eric eyed him suspiciously. "I thought you couldn't smoke in hospitals?"

Dan shrugged. "I won't say anything."

Joshua began licking his lips and they curled as if there was an imaginary cigarette dangling from his mouth.

"Do I look like an idiot?" Eric flicked at the cigarettes, and the box skidded across the table where Dan coolly stopped it with the flat of his hand. "I take one puff on one of those and you scrape DNA off the butt."

My mouth dropped when Dan's ears flushed. I couldn't believe that he was actually considering it.

Eric ran his effeminate fingers through his hair. "I just lost the damn chisel. One morning it was in my case, later it was missing."

"I see." Dan laid the chisel between them on the table. "Why did you bring a sculpting tool—and a sharp one—to paint?"

"I bring all of my art tools on site," Eric said impatiently. "You never know when a particular item will come in handy.

Dan's eyebrows rose.

"Just because it's made for sculpting doesn't mean you can only use it for that." Eric looked anxiously at the tape recorder, but then his gaze quickly shifted to the mirror. I felt as if he could see me watching him.

"Do you just use a screwdriver for tightening screws?" Eric said rhetorically. "No, you also use it for mixing things, prying open paint cans, chipping away—"

He leaned forward and grabbed the sides of the chair.

"Is this why I'm here?" Eric's voice rose, still staring at the window. "Because you want to know about my missing chisel. Is there some kind of missing chisel report you can fill out?"

"No, you're here because of this."

Dan reached back into the box and dumped a thick manila folder onto the table, and it landed with a silencing thud. Eric didn't have to open it to know what it contained.

"I know my rights," he quietly said, staring down at the folder. "You can't ask me anything without a lawyer." His eyes shot up at Dan. "There's this thing called Miranda."

Dan's stoic expression remained intact. "You're not in custody."

He looked at the tape recorder. "Then why the soundtrack?"

Dan shoved a piece of gum into his mouth and leaned his chair back. "So you don't say I did something that I didn't really do."

"Then none of this is admissible."

"So you're a lawyer. I thought you were an artist."

Eric looked down at the folder again. "I've had enough problems with your type in the past. I need to be a lawyer."

"Then I'd have to say, you're not a very good one."

Dan and Eric stared at each other, and I watched their showdown with an equally unblinking expression.

"Then I *want* a lawyer—a good one."

I waited down on the main level at the information desk for Joshua, while he used the men's room. The snippy man there eyed me with a condescending air, but never offered his assistance.

Eric had refused—declined—to give a blood sample. Even I couldn't convince him that having his DNA tested could only prove his innocence. He had his conspiracy theories. He babbled on endlessly about someone planting evidence once they had his DNA on record, and boy, wasn't he glad that he didn't fall for the cigarette trick. After an hour of cajoling and pleading, I came to the conclusion that Americans watch too much TV.

By force of habit, I checked my watch, but the numbers didn't register. What did Joshua have for lunch? Speaking of which, he owed me a nice big deli sandwich. On the other side of the lobby was a café, and across from that was a kiosk. I was torn—coffee or newspaper? I figured that my insides were probably a mess by now.

I had already read *The Times*, so I opted for *The Washington Post*. Something a little closer to—home? As I plopped a ten-dollar bill onto the counter, I recognized a frail silhouette making its way along the edge of the expansive corridor.

"Denny?" I shouted and arched my neck around the glass wall of the kiosk.

The figure did not acknowledge me.

"Hey, lady, your change!" the cashier yelled after me.

"Keep it!" I replied, bolting around the corner. I received no argument.

I quickly walked down the hall, my arms swinging ferociously as I dodged the dense traffic of people. If it was Denny, he was ignoring me.

"Denny," I called out after him.

But he had disappeared around the corner, and when I had made my way there, he was gone.

Chapter Fifty

The doors of D'Agostino's on Twelfth Street and University Place slid open and a waft of warm, dry air enveloped me. I grabbed a red plastic basket and carried it down the aisles. I quickly snatched up a bag of fresh spinach and a bag of shelled walnuts.

I owed Kyle for his stellar performance identifying the chisel. The lab had put a priority rush on our request, and after a barrage of tests, was able to determine that it was in fact the exact type of chisel that had been used. However, I didn't see how my home-cooked meal was going to be much of a reward.

Was that Denny I saw at Bellevue? I asked myself, as I picked up a small container of nutmeg. Did he just not hear me, or was he ignoring me? Or was it someone else. I had been tired and up since the crack of dawn.

At the deli counter my eyes and thoughts were drawn toward the trays of beef displayed in every possible configuration. The thin red fluid that oozed from the raw meat, settled at the bottom end of the metal trays lined with waxy paper. Sliced portions of cow's liver stared back at me. The dark organ reminded me of the case I had investigated in Cliffside. I stared at handsome cuts of lean steaks and quietly wondered: If cows could think on a higher level of consciousness, would they consider humans to be mass murderers or serial killers?

"Whaddah yah want?"

Such philosophical bovine questions would have to wait.

"Huh?"

"Come on, sweetheart, I got a line. What can I get for yah?" A paunchy middle-aged man behind the counter was dressed in a coat whose pristine white was covered in the crimson blood of dead animals.

"Oh, um," I stuttered, "A pound of veal scaloppine."

"One pound of veal cutlets." He reordered just like they did in Starbucks.

My brother, Ethan, had given me a gourmet Italian cookbook as a joke for Christmas one year. I was going to poison Kyle with a dish of Messicani di Vitello.

I watched the deli man plop my veal cutlets onto a sheet of white paper and wrap them tightly before folding them in a second sheet. My gaze was trained upon the thin blood marking the end of his sleeves. Rita had worked in a grocery story.

My red basket landed with a thud. And as I turned, my right foot caught on the edge, sending all of the contents shooting across the floor. I faltered slightly when I slipped on the small bottle of olive oil that had broken and slowly oozed across the linoleum. A young man in a red apron and holding a mop cursed at me as I raced down the aisle. I squeezed my way past one of the checkout lines and flew through the automatic door. Once outside I called Dan on my cell phone.

"The hairs on Rita Schaeffer's coat," I panted as I used the sidewalk to scrape the olive oil from the soles of my shoes. "They were unidentifiable."

"Yeah." His tinny voice echoed through my handset.

"Try this. Swap the coats. Say that Coat A is from Crime Scene B, and Coat B is from Crime Scene A. I bet you'll have two positive matches to the victims."

Chapter Fifty-one

While I was in the checkout line, Dan called me on my cell phone. They were confirming my theory with the coats, and I should be at the Forensics Lab in three hours. And, oh, yeah, they weren't waiting for anyone. There's gratitude for you. I stared grimly at the long, slow-moving line. The woman in front of me had a shopping cart piled high, and three screaming kids grabbing and tugging at the bottom of her jacket.

Forty minutes later, I raced home with my two plastic shopping bags full of groceries. I felt so badly for having caused such a commotion in the grocery store that I wound up buying extra things I had no intention of ever using. I tossed everything—paper and canned goods as well—into the refrigerator.

I quickly searched through my mail, then headed for the subway, nearly sprinting to the Broadway and Eighth Street station—the same station where I had ridiculed

Denny. I wished that I had listened to my instincts that day, but wishing was a waste of time.

At the corner of University Place, an elderly woman bent over a cane, hobbled slowly and unsteadily through the crosswalk. Like the rest of the crowd, I scooted around her and thought nothing more of her as she painfully made her way across the street.

When I reached the opposite corner, I saw the DON'T WALK sign flashing; the light was a few seconds away from changing. I looked back. The woman was about fifteen seconds from reaching the curb—four seconds from getting run over. I checked my watch. I checked her progress. She didn't look well. There was anguish in her eyes. I thought of my elderly landlady and how she complained of the arthritis in her knees and ankles. Walking was always a chore for her.

I backtracked and met the woman halfway through the crosswalk.

"Do you need some help?" My voice was loud.

She seemed startled, as if I was going to grab her bag. "Who? What?"

"Can I give you a hand?" I asked again. "The light's going to change."

She laughed. "Oh, don't you worry about me. I'll make it."

Unconvinced, I looked at her leaning heavily upon the cane and continued to walk alongside, using myself as a barricade between her and the traffic.

"Oh, I'm not that feeble," she kindly declared, when she noticed that I was still lingering about her. "You're very sweet and a darling, but I'm fine."

With a gentle flick of her wrist, she shooed me away.

Slowly, I continued to the corner without her, but waited and watched like my mother used to do when I first started walking to school on my own. My heart sank. Like Taekishi watched Sumi.

The woman stepped up onto the curb just as the electrical box for the traffic light clicked next to my head.

"See, young lady," she said to me. "I made it. Not bad for an old lady." She placed her hand on my forearm. "Your mother must've raised you well. Not many people take the time to be polite, especially to us old fogies."

I smiled and felt my cheeks flush.

See, see, Mrs. Brantley. You raised your daughter well. She earned her merit badge!

My mouth curled into a stern frown.

Hmph. She shouldn't have bothered that poor woman.

I watched the elderly woman make her way east along Tenth Street. She didn't seem so helpless and pathetic as before—before as I had originally seen her. In fact, she looked strong. She was strong.

Helpless and pathetic?

Helpless and pathetic, and in need of a guiding arm to help him across the street. The poor blind boy with no way of knowing if the traffic had stopped, or if the light was about to change. A cane—his prop. A cane—his weapon. What had Joshua said? *Perhaps the handle end of the sharp tool?* Or the handle end of a cane? The upper part of Denny's cane had to be sturdy, and folded up it was more compact and even stronger. But combined with a force filled with anger and hatred, it could become a dangerous weapon. So could a plastic spoon. Anything could.

I looked after the woman. She had all but disappeared into another crowd of pedestrians.

"Damn it!" I was late.

Chapter Fifty-two

The six envelopes were lined up along the counter. Two had a small folded card with the letter *K* lying on top of them. The other two had cards with the letter *Q*. The NYPD had adopted the same system of evidence classification that the FBI used in their lab. *K* for known, and *Q* for questionable. The two black wool coats were spread out on the opposite counter.

We already had the DNA profiles of all the hairs. The information was in our possession and processed. It was just a matter of comparing the correct Questionable hair with the correct Known hair.

Dr. Jade Frevere looked tired. Heavy, dark bags had ballooned underneath her eyes. She had spent the last three hours staring closely at too many charts and reading and comparing the radioactive fluorescent dye tagged bases of the DNA extracted from all of the hairs.

"Okay," Jade began, pointing to the bags labeled *K*.

"These are from the victims. Sumi and Rita." She pointed to another envelope marked *Q*. "This is from the first coat we're calling A—the Miyaki crime scene."

Jade moved down the counter to another bag marked *Q*. "These are from the coat we're referring to as B, from the Schaeffer crime scene. Upon Ms. Brantley's suggestion, we cross-checked them against the victims of the opposite crime scene."

Dan scrunched his face as he processed the information.

Jade pulled two *K* cards from the pocket of her lab coat. "Well, the hairs from coat A match Victim B." She dramatically snatched up the *Q* card and replaced it with a *K* before moving to the next group of hairs. "The hairs from Coat B match Victim A's." Again, another *K* card.

Dan eyed me, and I wasn't sure if it was distrust or admiration—or vexation.

"He swapped the coats," I said, staring at the two remaining unlabeled envelopes.

"I knew that kid was weird," Dan said.

I frowned at him. Weird did not constitute homicidal. But yes, it was looking as if he was homicidal.

"How come all of Sumi's hairs are short on Rita's—I mean—her coat?" I asked.

"They could've been torn or broken during the struggle," Jade explained.

"Why didn't you guys see this before?" Dan said in an accusing tone. "I thought under the microscope Oriental hair was clearly different than a white person's."

Jade's face tightened. "These darker hairs are of a short to medium length, unlike Victim A's *waist-length* hairstyle." She lowered her voice and turned slightly away. "We just didn't realize a connection, and, yes, an Asian's hair is noticeably different under the microscope, but we didn't have a chance to finish all of the testing. Besides, upon preliminary examination this particular victim's hair doesn't clearly exhibit these traits."

Dan's eyes narrowed.

"Excuse me, Sergeant!" she nearly yelled. "But no one suggested to us that the coats may have been swapped."

I stared out the windows. *Blame, blame, blame.*

"What about these?" Joshua quickly asked, pointing to the unlabeled envelopes.

Jade picked them up and held them in front of her face. "These are hairs that were found on both coats that can't be matched to either victim. However, they do match each other. Presumably the offender's."

"And what about the hair found on Sumi's body?" I asked.

Jade smiled with bemusement. "Now, there's a mystery. We thought it might've been part of this lot we're presuming to be the offender's, but the color was all wrong—too light. So, for shits and giggles we thought we'd check it against Victim B since she had lighter blond hair."

I held my breath in anticipation. It would have been an intriguing if not mind-boggling discovery.

"No such luck," she finally said after embellishing a long dramatic pause. "But could you imagine, Victim B's hair showing up at Victim A's crime scene—"

"That *did* happen!" Dan declared firmly.

"—on top of her bludgeoned body, covered in blood," Jade continued without missing a beat.

"Then where'd it come from?" Dan demanded.

"It was on top of the body?" she asked rhetorically.

He nodded anyway.

"Then I'm thinking you should have a look at your detectives and the officers workings in the CSU."

Dan's lips twitched, angered by Jade's insinuation that one of his men might've inadvertently contaminated a crime scene. But the fact of the matter was, just as the offender and victim leave behind personal evidence, so do the ones investigating it.

I stood by Joshua. "I think we've grossly underestimated him."

"Denny?" he asked.

"Even if it wasn't Denny. Even if we pretended that Denny didn't do this, if he was still a nameless, faceless unknown. Just the fact that he took the time to plan both murders at the same time—seeing far enough in advance to swap the coats—only means that he has always remained several steps ahead of us." I felt an almost genuine admiration for Denny's skill and intellect, and it sickened me. "There had to have been even more. I don't think Trina Williams was his first victim."

Joshua began shaking his head. "How does a blind kid murder and mutilate, and move a body?"

The answer was simple. Even Dan did not need it spelled out. Something told me that Denny didn't have a little brother to describe to him what the profilers were doing on that TV show.

On my way out I gently grabbed Jade by the elbow. "I use just a tiny bit of Preparation-H," I said, dabbing at the puffy skin under my eyes. "It really works."

She stared at me as if I was nuts. But when she thought I had gone, Jade's expression softened as she scribbled a note to herself.

A copy of Denny's general admissions application to NYU rolled out of the fax machine. I ironed the curled ends with the palm of my hand. I could not believe that some people still used thermal paper.

A check through the NCIC, the FBI's National Crime Information Computer, proved that Denny had never been arrested—or at least if he had, it had been for a misdemeanor that no one felt was necessary to process.

Denny had checked off the box for the Gallatin School, which was jokingly referred to by the other NYU students as the school for those-who-had-no-idea-what-the-hell-they-wanted-to-do-in-life, but had money to blow. He had printed neatly that his age was twenty, but I suspected that he was actually much older. Probably closer to twenty-nine, maybe thirty-two. He had also made a note of his blindness.

I grunted. He lived his charade in every aspect of his life.

Denny's primary residence was listed as 60 West 115th Street. The irony was as sharp as the chisel he used on his victims. Two detectives were sent over to the address, but I knew that they wouldn't find him there, or anybody who knew him. It was an arbitrary address that Denny had used. His mailing address was a PO Box in the Times Square Station post office.

Dan contacted the Postal Inspector, but the address Denny had used on the yellow application card for the PO Box was the same 60 West 115th Street. He had rented the smallest box size available, and it was overflowing with junk mail and magazines. For a blind man, he sure read a lot.

A detective was sent up to retrieve the unclaimed bundle of mail, and we rummaged through his collection of clothing catalogs, gun magazines, pleas for donations and credit card applications. Based on the misspellings that appeared consistently on sixty percent of the items, Denny was probably on every known mailing list in the country. I picked up one of the gun magazines: His name was spelled correctly.

A search for a driver's license also proved fruitless, which did not surprise me. Not many people in New York City had a license since owning a car was often impractical, cumbersome and a luxury only for those who could afford the expensive monthly garage rentals. Besides, a person didn't need a license to know how to drive a car. But one needed to have access to a car. I was fairly certain that Denny—the real Denny—had few friends if any. A typical nonsocial offender chose not to socialize. So he either stole a car, or he borrowed one from someone, like his—

Mother. Denny had mentioned his mother several times in his essay on the NYU application. It was filled with adoration and love, but he also spoke sadly of her "affliction," and how he thought she was brave for trying to overcome it, even though he thought she was nearing the end. To anyone in the Admissions Office, it would've read like a sad, but moving piece on a brave woman dying of a terminal illness. However, I was curious about the condition of her arms.

His thoughts, though disorganized, were eloquently stated—a far cry from the *pre-Madonnas* he had typed in the essay I had assigned him. When he referred to his mother, it was always in the present tense, so she was still alive when he wrote the essay. That would've been the previous spring.

My brain jumped ahead to the criminal court proceedings, to a line I had heard on far too many occasions.

My client wrote that essay believing in his mind that his mother was alive. He is obviously unfit to stand trial.

Denny was not mentally ill. It angered me when defense lawyers abused that strategy. It unjustly painted a sinister, evil portrait for those who really were mentally ill.

303

I checked the bottom of the application that was marked For NYU Admissions Use Only. Denny had been rejected. Strike one against society.

"Wasn't he in your class?" Joshua asked from across Dan's desk.

"Yes," I replied, completely flabbergasted.

The phone rang and Dan picked it up.

"But he wasn't a student?"

It was possible to attend classes without being a registered student, especially the large lectures where attendance was never taken. In the community of an enormous university it was far too easy for someone to exist without being noticed. And because my students' academic performances relied solely on essay work, which should've reflected their attendance level, their grades were calculated at the end of the semester. No one would have discovered that Denny was not a student until just before the Christmas break when his student ID was not on file.

"Being rejected from NYU only added fuel to the fire," I said, tossing the fax across the desk.

Joshua picked it up. "At least if he had been registered, we could've traced him through financial aid."

"It's interesting." I stared up at the ceiling tile. "I think he actually wanted to be a serious student."

"Thanks." Dan dropped the phone into its cradle. "I just got a tip from one of my buddies in the Sixty-second. He said they got a call the other day from some lady about her upstairs tenants. About a lady and her adult son."

My feet dropped to the floor. "And?"

"And she kept referring to the son as 'the strange blind boy.'"

Chapter Fifty-three

Denny and his mother lived on Seventy-third Street in Brooklyn, a residential neighborhood of mixed nationalities that still maintained its strong Italian roots. Given the circumstances of our situation and knowing that we were due for another victim on Thursday night, Dan had been able to acquire a search warrant for the Carter residence. Without any hardened evidence, an arrest warrant had been denied. Still, our trip to the Carter residence was of the utmost importance.

We turned onto the tree-lined street in three unmarked cars. But the dark Crown Victorias were a dead giveaway to anyone with an IQ that at least matched their shoe size. People in neighboring houses peeked through their windows, but drew the curtains as we neared.

The Carters lived on the top floor of a brick house with white shutters. It looked just like all the other brick

305

houses with white shutters on the street. The house was owned by a couple in their mid-sixties. After several days of anxiety, Mrs. Carralucci had finally called the police about a strange smell coming from her tenants' upstairs apartment.

We slowly made our way up the walkway, and I could not take my eyes from the Carralucci's once colorful grotto: a three-foot statuette of the Virgin Mary nestled within half of an egg-shaped shell. Her arms were gracefully extended before her, a soft expression of piety pointed toward the sky. Mary-on-a-Half-Shell is what I used to call them. I looked up and down the street; there seemed to be one on every lawn.

Two uniforms were standing in the foyer listening patiently to a short, roundish woman. In a thick accent, Mrs. Carralucci explained that her husband was at the nearby OTB betting away what was left of the rent money the Carters had paid last month.

"And no get me started with them." Mrs. Carralucci pointed to the ceiling. "They no pay me for this month."

She had short, curly hair, dyed reddish bronze, except it came out looking slightly purplish. It was styled in that puffy way, which seemed to be the standard among women her age. I was always under the impression that once women hit their sixties, they had their hair styled at the same salon.

"Are either Denny or Mrs. Carter home?" Dan's voice was gentle as if he were addressing his mother.

"No." With animated hand movements, Mrs. Carralucci told her tale. "I no see her for long time. The strange blind boy, he come and go all the time. He no come back last night."

I was tempted to ask her for some advice on preparing

the Messicani di Vitello I had brutally overcooked the night before.

Mrs. Carralucci began climbing the stairs to the second floor, a single silver key secured between her thumb and forefinger. The house had obviously been built as a one-family residence, and somewhere along the way someone decided to convert it.

My nose twitched. There was that odor again. Light, but definitely there.

"You know," Mrs. Carralucci said with round dark eyes as she noticed my reaction. "I smell for a bit."

Some of the detectives smiled and looked her up and down, but I knew what she was trying to say.

"When did you first notice the smell?" I asked her as we neared the top landing.

"Few weeks ago." She waved her hand in front of her nose. "I wonder if they no bring out the garbage. I ask the strange blind boy, but he always tell me, 'No, no, no. Everything okay.'" She leaned in and whispered to us. "But I know something not right." She tapped her forehead. "Something not right in here. I sense it for a long time. I tell my husband, but he say, no, I'm the crazy one. He just want the money."

Dan pointed to the door, and Mrs. Carralucci unlocked it. We all groaned and scrunched our faces when we were hit with the smell, not overbearing, but definitely more noticeable. The detectives wasted no time in snapping on Latex gloves and pulling the place apart.

The living room was dressed in a drab olive color, with protective plastic pulled tightly over the furniture. One lone armchair positioned next to the TV was missing its cover. Bluishwhite light from the outside streamed in through thin sheers covering the only window. The room was spotless. Off the living room to the right was a short hallway with a door on either side. At the end was the bathroom. To our left was the kitchen. I poked my head in. A detective was already rooting through the cupboards. The smell wasn't coming from there.

I looked across the way toward the hallway and motioned to Dan.

"I come in here before to find the garbage," Mrs. Carralucci explained when she saw me looking around. "But I no find it."

Dan gently took her by the arm and walked her to the front door. "Ma'am."

"I think maybe in one of the bedrooms, but that blind boy gone and change the locks. He not supposed to do that. I tell my husband to make him unlock it, but my husband—eh—he don't care."

"Ma'am," he said more firmly. "Why don't you go back downstairs?" He nodded toward one of the uniforms standing in the doorway. "Officer Gilbert will go with you."

"Okay, okay, I go with her."

Dan closed the front door, and it was suddenly a lot quieter.

Detective Wilson was struggling with one of the locked bedroom doors. "Hey, Bernie. See what you can do with this."

A technician carrying a small leather case bent down in front of the doorknob. From the black case he selected a thin pick and a double-ended pick. In two seconds the door swung open.

"Crappy lock," he said, unimpressed with his own handiwork.

Inside was a mess. Food wrappers and empty soda cans

littered the floor. The curtains were drawn, so someone flicked on the lights. Clothes were scattered about and smelled dirty.

"This ain't the odor," Dan said, as he stepped over a pair of crumpled checkered boxers and white tube socks wound into a tight ball.

It was a stale smell, but no, it wasn't *the* odor. The bed looked as though it had been slept in several times without being made.

"Why does a blind man need a reading lamp?" I asked rhetorically, pointing to the nightstand.

"Or a camera," Joshua added. He was holding a basic point-and-shoot 35mm in his hand.

I looked around the room and didn't see Denny's white cane. He was hunting again.

On the end of the bed was a brown shoebox. I opened it and slowly picked through its contents. Pictures of Allison from the other day—I recognized her red sweater. Pictures of Rita when she was alive, pictures of Sumi when she was alive. These were taken from a great distance with a 35mm and some kind of zoom lens. I dug deeper. Pictures of Trina when she was alive. All of them were alive and appeared to be unaware that their pictures were being taken. My muscles stiffened when I found photos of women I did not recognize. More victims of varying ages, but no more older than Rita Schaeffer. I counted them. There appeared to be five.

I fanned through a set that had been bound with an elastic band. They were closeups of the victims' clothed arms, and just their arms, as they moved about in public. I watched Wilson pull an expensive-looking camera and zoom lens from the closet.

There was another box sitting on the desk near Joshua.

I dropped the photos I was holding back into the box and went over to him. The second box was filled with more snapshots. This time Polaroids of Sumi, Trina and Rita. They were dead. Photos from the known crime scenes and some of crime scenes we knew nothing about. Dan joined us as we flipped through them like we were casually looking at someone's vacation photos.

I handed one to Joshua. It was of Sumi, lying in a pool of blood in the corner of her secret apartment: her safe place. There were several of Rita's lifeless body sprawled out in the back seat of a car: a clean, practical, domestic car. And still more of Trina lying on the dusty ground of what appeared to be a baseball diamond.

"There's a softball field over by the FDR, isn't there?" I said to Dan without looking up from the photos.

"Yeah," he grunted.

There was one of a woman sprawled out on a sandy ground. There were no outward signs of trauma. She almost looked like she was sleeping, except her body was not right. It seemed disjointed and lifeless. She had not been dismembered, and based on what we knew of Denny incorporating this detail into his signature, this young woman was probably one of his earlier victims.

"Another ball field?" Dan asked, looking over my shoulder.

I studied the photo some more. "No. The sand is orange-red and white. That's indicative of the southern Midwest."

"Look at this." Joshua held out ten of the photos like he was playing gin. "Just the arms."

Just the arms, tied and dangling in space after Denny had removed them from his victims. When we had finished, the boxes were bagged and marked. So were both

35mm cameras and all of the accessories. We never found the Polaroid camera.

Joshua looked around at the disheveled room. "This is uncharacteristic of this type of offender. Someone who fools the whole world into believing that he is blind in order to seduce his victims into feeling safe around him is not a disorganized mind." He pushed his hands out into the air. "*This* is a disorganized mind."

I carefully picked up some of the food wrappers and examined them. And as odd as it may seem, I counted the three pairs of underwear. "Three days."

"What?"

"This probably covers about the last three days, not including today." I placed the food wrappers back on the floor where I found them. "He wasn't always like this. We're driving him to this mental state." I looked up at Dan. "He knows the end is near, and he's panicking."

"Good," Dan said in anger. "Then he'll break. And we'll get the bastard."

I was frozen, standing in the middle of the room and felt as if the clothes and garbage were consuming me.

"He stood here unable to control the elements," I said with passion. "Unable to control us, he cannot maintain the order in his life anymore."

I watched as the clothes were bagged, so were the bed sheets. Once the rug was visible, it was picked at and vacuumed for any possible fiber evidence. We all left and found Bernie across the way working on the other locked door. Like Denny's room, he easily unlatched it. When it swung open we were immediately overcome by the rancid smell. *The* rancid smell. I covered my mouth and nose with my hand, and Bernie ran to the bathroom and vomited into the toilet.

311

"Oh, my God," Joshua winced.

The stink was overwhelming and it stung our eyes. We knew what the odor was. We had encountered that fetid stench on many occasions.

"Uggh," Dan wiped his watering eyes. "Find it, wherever it is," he ordered his detectives.

I heard Bernie letting loose into the toilet again.

The bedroom was small, so there were very few places to look. Drawers were pulled, the closet searched, and aside from four pairs of house slippers, underneath the bed was clean.

"I guess Mrs. Carter didn't go anywhere," Joshua commented, his head buried inside the tiny closet. "No shoes."

Dan stared at the carpet, and all I could think of were images of the Gacy crime scene. But this was the second floor. There would be very little space to hide anything underneath the floorboards. I looked up at the ceiling, but it was pristine white. If anything were hidden up in an attic space, there would most likely be a stain on the poorly constructed ceiling. Either way, the smell was coming from somewhere inside the room.

We all walked the square footage of the bedroom, our noses twitching in the intense silence that had enveloped us. The stench was equal in all four corners.

I stared at the slippers and crouched under the bed. Four pairs of slippers and no other shoes. I shined my Sure Fire underneath and found nothing except for a gray dust bunny in the corner. Something just did not seem right. Turning the intense beam upwards, I began tracing the outline of the underside of the box spring. Even with the obvious age of the furniture, the fabric of the box spring seemed displaced. With sweeping motions, I ran the flashlight along the length of the bed. There was a barely visible, light brownish stain in the middle of the gauzy fabric.

I quickly scurried out from under the bed. My heart was racing a marathon.

"Help me with this," I said in short breaths, as I pulled on the mattress.

Dan moved quickly and grabbed the bottom end. The odor grew even more intense. Bernie had returned. His face was ashen and he kept his head low attempting to hide his embarrassment. Once the photographer had taken his obligatory shots, Bernie took a flat head screwdriver and began removing the staples from the gauzy top fabric of the box spring. When he rolled it back, everyone leaned in, but quickly took a collective step backwards.

The body was unrecognizable, but it appeared to have been female. I figured that it had been Mrs. Carter. She was laid out along the 1×3 supports of the box spring, partially wrapped in one of the plastic furniture covers. Half her face had been smashed in, and the other half was sunken in from decay. She had probably been there since before Trina Williams was killed.

"Where are her arms?" Bernie asked, desperately trying to control his gag reflex.

I leaned in and studied the warped outline of the corpse. It was difficult to tell, but it did appear that her arms were missing and probably removed long after she had expired.

"Practice makes perfect," Dan with disdain.

The corners of his mouth were turned downward as he chewed slowly, but firmly on a piece of gum.

"Got any more?" I asked.

He gave me a piece and didn't chide me about having a weak stomach. Then he graciously handed out the rest of what he had to everyone in the room.

"Get the ME here," he instructed. "Where the fuck are the arms?"

Everything was silent save for the light sounds of cracking gum.

I removed my gloves and stepped into the living room. Standing by the window, I punched eleven numbers into my cellular phone.

"Psychology," someone answered.

I got Doug on the phone. He didn't sound happy.

"Where the hell are you?" he scolded. "You're supposed to be teaching right now. That neophyte of a GA is handling your lecture today. Half the class walked out in the first five minutes."

I remained calm.

"Doug," I said, gazing at the armchair without a plastic cover. "Could you go into my office and pull the files in the bottom drawer?"

"I don't think you understand the trouble you're in."

I drew back the edge of the sheer curtains and stared out at the small neighborhood crowd that had gathered along the sidewalk.

"I understand. Could you please just do that?"

"Fine," he huffed. "By the way, it really smells in there now. The other professors are starting to complain."

I heard him put down the receiver, and the clinking of keys jingled in the distance, followed by his barely audible cry of, *"Oh, my God!"*

I pulled the phone away from my ear and snapped it shut.

Joshua was looking at me.

"Well," I said, "I know what happened to the arms."

Chapter Fifty-four

"Allison still needs the protection," Joshua argued with me.

We were in the Tenth precinct's interview room.

"You think Denny's long gone?" Dan asked me, making no attempt to hide his skepticism.

"No," I said, my voice rising to an uncharacteristically high decibel. "At least not until he's ready to kill tomorrow."

Dan slipped a piece of gum into his mouth. "So he's gonna kill tomorrow."

"He has to," I said with wide eyes. I thought of Sandy and what she had said to Allison as we watched them approach Sarah's office. "There's no turning back."

Joshua chortled. "Then he still has his sites set on Allison. She's next on the list."

"No, no. He's too smart for that."

"You said it yourself, that his state of mind is degenerating. He's being forced to act irrationally."

I began lightly wiping the top of the table with my hand. "The rational thing to do would be lay low. He's irrational, so he'll continue with his attack, right on schedule. Except it won't be Allison. He needs to find a new victim."

Joshua tried to roll his eyes inconspicuously. "Then who's next on the list."

"Catherine Eckert," Dan read from a computer printout.

"No, he's not that stupid." I stared Joshua right in the eye. "Remember, he's always several steps ahead of us."

Joshua firmly straightened the knot in his tie and asked me point blank, "Why did he put the arms in your office?"

I thought for a moment, and knew he was trying to trip me up. "I think he wants us—me—to catch him."

He leaned forward and got into my face. "Then don't you think he would go about things as he had originally planned, knowing that we're on to him?"

I did not have an answer. We had encountered sociopaths in the past who were sometimes conflicted between the desire to evade the police so they could continue with their murderous reign and wanting to be captured so their celebrity star could shine for even just a brief moment.

"All I know is that he's angry, now," I said. "And when people are angry, they try to make you hurt. To make every action memorable." I thought of Doug finding the gruesome discovery in my file cabinet, and of his quick and inevitable departure from NYU. "Believe me, the arms were memorable."

Joshua's voice softened. "We can't risk abandoning Allison, especially since we have no leads otherwise. We can't leave her unprotected."

I looked at Dan.

"We're sticking with Allison Beauchamp," Dan said. "I'm not taking any chances."

"Well, then," I said angrily, leaning my elbow against the table. "I guess we'll be finding victim number four late tomorrow night."

Chapter Fifty-five

Thursday morning I woke as if it were like any other day. I dragged myself out of bed at 6:00 AM, drank a mug of coffee, showered, dressed, read *The Times*, and drank three more mugs of coffee, all before 7:30. Yes, just like any other day, except today we were supposedly going to catch a killer. I put down the Business section—my investments weren't doing well—and rested my mug on a pile of crime scene photos. I no longer cared if they got ruined.

Denny's mom had been dead for nearly five weeks, Anthony had told us late last night. Her arms had been cut off, perhaps two weeks ago. Just before Denny had begun incorporating that element into his signature.

"Kyle, honey," I said with a casual air, as I watched him in the kitchen pouring a cup of coffee. We both liked our coffee the same way.

"Yep," he managed to grumble.

His hair was sticking straight up in the front, and it made me smile.

"Tell me something."

"Mm." He stepped around to my side of the counter and leaned up against it.

He was so damned cute in just his pajama bottoms.

I looked back down at the newspaper. "What do you think of Virginia?"

He didn't respond.

"Northern Virginia."

"Uh, nice scenery," he said in a groggy morning voice. He dug a fist into his eye and wiped away the sleep.

"Why do you ask?" He rubbed the other eye. "Do you want to take a vacation, or something?"

I smiled and returned to my paper. "No, just wondering."

Lunchtime came and went without me eating a bite. If I was too figure out what Denny's next move would be, I had very little time. I looked at my watch three times in a row, and had to check it a fourth before the time actually registered in my brain.

About five or six hours to figure it out.

An APB was put on Denny. He was to be considered dangerous. Small checkpoints had been set up at all the bridges and tunnels. The Port Authority police were also on full alert, which meant that both La-Guardia and JFK airports, as well as the Port Authority bus terminal were swarming with undercover and uniformed officers. Still, I didn't believe that Denny was going anywhere beyond the boundaries of New York City.

Allison tried her best to go about her business as if none of this was happening, all the while the plainclothes officers kept a close eye on her. I called in to Joshua and Dan on regular thirty-minute intervals. Regularity was important in these sorts of matters. If I was off in the slightest, Joshua would immediately know that something was wrong on my end. However, by the eighth call, I think he was sick of hearing from me, as was evidenced by the ten times he allowed his phone to ring before answering it.

According to Allison, she would have gone to an Eighteenth-century Poets class at City College, then stayed home for the rest of the day and night. If we hadn't been involved, how would Denny have managed to get her out of the house? Sumi had her private club house where she often escaped to at night. Rita worked until 8:30 PM. And the night that Trina had disappeared, she had taken the PATH train to her mother's house in Jersey City; she just never made it.

Who was Denny hunting? His mother's arms in my file cabinet: Was it a warning or an invitation? Or both?

At 5:00 PM I got on the subway and took the N train to Queens. At the beginning of the rush hour commute, it was standing-room only in the packed cars. The air was thick from everyone's body heat, and I was having difficulty breathing. The day I had confronted Denny about the coat, he had taken the N uptown. Had he stopped off at Times Square to pick up his mail, or did he take it to Queens to find out where Allison lived? How far in advance had he planned everything?

The train pulled out of the 59th and Lexington Avenue stop. It rattled and shook, and everyone swayed in unison with the jerky motions of the car. I had maligned Denny—embarrassed him in public—and thirty-three hours later Rita Schaeffer was found dead. I could not help but feel somewhat responsible for the brutal nature of her attack.

As the train came above ground and we neared Queensboro Plaza, I watched the orange sun fill the empty dusky sky. It was beautiful. A sun sets and then it rises. Those were the only two things in life that you could rely upon.

Chapter Fifty-six

Sandy answered the front door and hurried me inside before quickly locking the deadbolt and drawing over the security chain. Joshua waved off an officer who began patting me down.

"They're a little jumpy tonight," he whispered in my ear, leading the way into the living room.

I did not have to breathe too deeply to smell the nicotine on his breath. "They're not the only ones," I said pointedly.

Dan was setting out four large pizzas from the Greek restaurant on Thirtieth Avenue. Two plain cheese and two pepperoni. A large pie in New York City took on a completely different meaning in terms of a big pizza. New Yorkers never did anything in small amounts, especially food.

Allison's younger sisters had been sent to an aunt's house in New Haven. Allison and her parents sat with us staring at the untouched pizzas. No one was in the mood to eat. Four uniformed officers, two plainclothes, a detective, an FBI agent and one psychology professor—ex-professor—sitting with a frightened young girl and her parents, staring at the best pizza the neighborhood had to offer. It was the stupidest thing I had ever seen.

"He's not coming," I said, blowing my hair from my face.

Joshua nodded his head lightly.

Allison looked up at me and looked as if she was about to cry.

I checked my watch.

8:47.

What was Denny up to? Maybe he was going to wait. Maybe I was wrong, and we had frightened him into hiding. The investigation would continue for another year, but Denny and any victims bearing the same signature would never appear, until three years later when the story was repeated on one of those true crime shows and one of his friends ratted him out for the reward money.

9:09.

Dan finally leaned over and grabbed a slice of pepperoni. When he picked it up, the hot cheese slid off the crust and landed with a greasy thud into the box. He looked up and his eyes scanned everyone. Then we all broke out into a burst of laughter, which rose to a pitch of near hysteria. I watched Allison as she fell into her parents' arms. It was nice to see her smile.

9:14.

My heart skipped. Sumi had left her apartment at 9:14 that night. I stared at the floral pattern in the rug. Mom, Trina, Sumi, Rita—and then there was Allison. We had broken the chain. It was always bad luck to break a chain. Mom, patient, patient, patient. The image of the painter's mural flashed in my head.

9:18.

The patients—the children—all running to Sarah—to Mom.

My head popped up like it was on a spring. I couldn't breathe. Everyone was still laughing. Laughing about the damn cheese.

"Sarah."

In the middle of a laugh, Joshua lazily turned to me. "What?"

"Sarah," I repeated a little more loudly. "He's going after Sarah."

Allison's face dropped to a pale pallor. "Dr. Davidson," she barely managed squeak.

No one questioned or challenged me—there wasn't time. Dan sprang from the sofa and grabbed the phone.

"Her number. I need her number," he yelled.

Sandy faltered and then ran from the room to get her address book. I quickly thrust my hand into my coat pocket and pulled out Sarah's tattered business card.

"No one's answering," he said angrily. He grabbed one of his officers. "Keep calling. Get me on the portable if you're able to get her on the phone."

Maybe Sarah was in danger, or maybe she was enjoying a lovely Sauté de Poulet aux Crevettes at the newly renovated Russian Tea Room. Either way, none of us wanted to find out tomorrow morning in Anthony's autopsy suite.

One of the plainclothes dressed in beat-up jeans, black combat boots, flannel shirt and carrying a portable radio ran in from the kitchen.

"Sergeant, you said to tell you if anything peculiar came over the portable," he said, dialing down the volume on the scratchy voices coming over the small amplifier.

"Yeah?"

"Well, a situation is developing over in the Nineteenth."

"What is it?"

"I'm not sure," the young officer stuttered. "It came in first as a ten-ninety, but was just upgraded to a Level Three *and* the ESU was just called in."

"That's a pretty severe jump for a simple domestic dispute," I commented, already shoving my arms into the sleeves of my coat.

"Some big shit is going down," Dan said, quickly putting on his own coat.

"There's a lot of cross-talk, but I think shots were fired," the young officer continued.

Dan checked Sarah's business card.

"Her apartment is in the Nineteenth." He grabbed his coat. "Stay with them!" he yelled at the others as we ran to the front door.

I looked for Joshua, but he was already waiting in the backseat of Dan's car.

Chapter Fifty-seven

The red beacon clung stubbornly to the roof of the car as we swerved to miss the oncoming traffic. Lights and sirens were of very little use on the congested streets of this city. I always hoped that if I were ever to be mortally injured, it would not be in New York City. The suicide rate was high among paramedics because of the mounting frustration in losing so many lives in the backseat of an ambulance that didn't make it to the hospital in time.

"Bridge or the Tunnel?" I asked.

Dan radioed for assistance, and we were quickly told that at the moment, the Queensboro Bridge was the fastest.

He looked at me.

We weren't buying it. The Queensboro Bridge was never the fastest. However, the bridge was closer and farther uptown. I popped my head out the window and yelled to a gypsy cab driver who was sitting in his silver-gray sedan smoking an herbal cigarette.

"The Tunnel," he said in broken English over the blare of the siren. "Take the Tunnel."

This time I looked at Dan. We also knew that cab drivers and the police did not always get along.

Dan pressed down heavily on the gas, and we headed for the Queensboro Bridge.

The bridge was slow, but probably just as slow as the Tunnel. It did not matter. The bigger problem was the traffic on the streets in Manhattan. Sarah's apartment was on York Avenue and Ninety-first. We were only at Sixty-fifth, stuck behind the M31 bus.

"Shit." Dan pounded on the horn.

There was nowhere for us to go. We were boxed in.

Dan got on the portable and confirmed that the incident was in Sarah's apartment building. A possible crisis situation. Which at this point could have meant anything.

I switched on the car's radio to 1010 WINS AM. They were doing the traffic report.

Heavy police activity on the Upper East Side, which could be a problem early on in the morning commute depending on how long the police will take. And the Dow Jones fell another two hundred points to—

Depending on how long we took. I shut off the radio.

We hadn't made it very far. The street sign above us—Eighty-third.

"Where you going?" Joshua shouted out the back window as I began sprinting up the avenue.

"One of us will get there first!" I shouted back.

Well, obviously. Logic was not always a priority in times of crisis.

I assumed a sprinter's crouch, keeping my body bent and my head low. It seemed that I was doing a lot of running these days. My knees hurt. So did my shins. I was keeping my breathing controlled. Something wet fell against my forehead, and I smacked it. Water. Another drop. I looked up at a street lamp. I could not tell if it was rain or snow. It was falling so lightly in the orange light, moving gracefully in the wind like a shimmering curtain.

"Hey, you idiot!"

The horn blared and the front end of the cab grazed the back of my leg. The sign said, DON'T WALK. It did not matter. I was running.

I checked the next street sign—Ninetieth.

It was a tall, modern high-rise. Two unmarked and three of the newer white marked police cars filled the circular drive in front, their light bars flashing an ominous red that grazed the building's beige façade. A light blue ESU truck was positioned in the middle. It wasn't the biggest mobilization of law enforcement I had ever seen, but it was certainly an attention grabber. There had been a larger more spectacular scene last winter when ice was falling from the new Reuters Building in Times Square. Residents had been cleared, and they were huddled in jackets and coats, far from the chaos.

Just as I was sprinting along the edge of the driveway looking for an opening, I saw Dan pull up. Damn. Well, everyone had been hinting to me that I needed the exercise.

A uniform put out his arms and blocked my way.

"She's with us!" Dan yelled over. His detective shield was dangling from his lapel.

The officer waved me through and stepped aside.

I had to give Dan credit. As much as he seemed like an imbecile and his prejudices were unbearable, he was effective in times of crises. He knew how to act and react, and he certainly commanded an authoritative air. Dan was a good cop who was just doing his job; that was all that could be asked of him. That was all that could be asked of any of us.

I caught up to him.

Dan and Joshua were standing next to a man in full SWAT regalia. He wore a black jumpsuit and Kevlar vest and helmet. A speaker, shaped in an ear mold, was attached to a portable secured inside a Velcro pocket of his vest, and ran up through his uniform and into his right ear. The whole contraption allowed him to communicate with others in a whisper and in high-noise situations without the threat of detection.

The ESU was the unit the NYPD called when they needed help. An elite team of officers, they were the police department's version of the FBI's Hostage Rescue Team. Trained not only in tactical maneuvers, but paramedics and a touch of emotional TLC. I had seen an ESU team take down ten men in a drug bust, and five hours later talk a suicidal man in his underwear out of jumping from the suspension wires of the Brooklyn Bridge.

I made my way over to them, and was introduced to the on-scene commander, Lieutenant Chamberlain.

"Who called it?" Joshua shouted over a nearby siren.

"Some neighbor," Chamberlain shouted back over the commotion. "Said she heard some noise. The desk sergeant thought it was a domestic dispute. Two uniforms went up to the apartment, but they didn't make it too far. He fired off a round into the air. Said he had a hostage. That's when they called for backup. When he started shooting at *them*, the backup called us."

"Has he made demands?" I asked in an authoritative tone.

Chamberlain eyed me warily.

"It's okay," Dan said. "She's working with us."

When Chamberlain spoke, rain water sputtered from his lips. "No, ma'am."

"Brantley," I said.

He nodded his head. "We were trying to call on the victim's phone, but he's not answering. Most of the time we get a busy signal."

Dan guiltily bit his lower lip. His officer back in Queens was probably tying up the line.

"We got the phone company to clear it."

"Who's up there now?" Dan asked him.

"Two teams, one in each stairwell." He guided us to the back of the ESU truck, where he showed us an architectural drawing of the building with a plan view of the floor.

Sarah's apartment was outlined in a pink highlighter. A small *X* had been marked in the area labeled *Living Room.*

"She hasn't moved from here," the lieutenant explained. He pointed to the two stairwells on either end of the floor. "Entry teams in both." He jabbed his finger into the far stairwell. "Sixty-two feet to the front door. The other's ten feet."

Dan spit his gum onto the ground. "How many rounds total?"

"Fourteen." He seemed a bit annoyed as he pointed toward the building.

"Casualties?"

"Negative."

Chamberlain paused and nodded his head in response

to some voice that was unheard by the rest of us. He adjusted his earpiece and then depressed the key button taped to his index finger.

"Copy," he said into the mike. "Chamberlain, out."

I was surprised when he looked at me.

"He's asking for you."

"Me?"

"Brantley, right? Professor Brantley."

Joshua nodded, but there was concern blanketing his face. "Get him on the phone."

"Like I said before. When we can get through he won't take it."

I looked up at the front of the building. "I can go talk to him from the hallway."

Both Joshua and Chamberlain shook their heads.

"He just wants to talk to me," I said, trying to assuage not only theirs, but my apprehension as well.

My eyes shifted from face to face as we remained huddled in the wet cold. I was not sure why Denny wanted me specifically, but I was willing to find out.

"Let her go," Dan finally said. I was surprised when he added, "I know she can talk him outta there."

Joshua shook his head defiantly, but it was Chamberlain who had the last word. This was his situation.

"You'll have to take the stairs," he explained, reaching into the back of the truck and handing me a Kevlar vest and helmet. "Every time he hears the elevator ring, he fires off at least one round."

"What floor?" I asked, already heading to the lobby door.

He matched my quick pace. "Eighteen."

I stopped in midstride. "Good," I said simply before continuing and entering the lobby.

"We can take you up to the tenth, but you'll have to climb the rest of the way."

Joshua and Dan followed close behind me, as an officer led us through the lobby carrying a KV4 Rectangular Ballistic Shield. In the elevator we took off our coats and secured our Kevlar vests and helmets. It was odd to look down at my chest and see the word POLICE spelled out in white letters instead of FBI.

Somewhere around the fifteenth floor, I began to curse the overpaid architects and the wealthy developers who made these high rises with twelve-foot ceilings. The eight flights of stairs we climbed were actually twelve. Never in my life had I been so happy to see the number eighteen painted on a wall.

In the stairwell nearest to Sarah's apartment, we crouched beside the scout officer of the first entry team, positioned low and closest to the door.

"He's got a handgun," he quickly explained while adjusting his MP5. "We can't see what it is. But from the way it's firing, I'm guessing a semi."

"Rounds fired?" Dan asked.

"Seven."

Chamberlain had received erroneous information, and that had me worried. What was really going on inside the apartment? I did not doubt that Denny was dangerous, the bullet holes were evidence enough. But did this crisis truly demand a commando-style of offense?

"Then he's got a ways to go." Dan ran his finger along the doorjamb. "Hope the blind guy doesn't have more mags."

"Blind? He's got a pretty good shot for a blind guy. He's missing us because he wants to." He stopped and was listening to someone through his earpiece. "Okay, we think he's opening the door again," he said for our benefit.

We peered through the crack in the door, careful not to accidentally touch any of the sharpshooters and set off some trigger-happy onslaught. Denny's leg poked through the front door of Sarah's apartment, but he quickly withdrew it when four minute red dots from the sharpshooters' laser sites landed steadily upon it. I did not have to hear what was being said to know that the command was "green light on visual."

SWAT Teams were highly skilled and I respected their abilities, but I sometimes found their tactics a bit bombastic. Joshua and I came from a different school of training, and our negotiators were often at odds with the Ninjas and their MP5s. In this case, there was no need to give a green light. At least not yet.

"Yes, that's a negative," the scout officer replied grimly into his mike. "Just his leg."

"Professor Brantley, are you there?" Denny called out through the heavy oak door. "I don't want to shout to you."

"This is Professor Brantley," I shouted back. "Answer the phone, Denny. I can talk to you that way."

"No. In person."

"He's calling for her again," the scout officer whispered. "He wants her inside. Yes, sir."

"Let me go in," I said in a commanding tone.

He ignored me.

"No way," Joshua said to me. "It's too dangerous."

"He's been firing off rounds like it's New Year's in Brooklyn," Dan added, studying the holes riddling the hallway.

I stared angrily at the two of them. They had been willing to put Allison's life in jeopardy, and yet, for me this was too dangerous? No, it was never a good idea to offer a potential hostage in a crisis situation, but I did not get the sense that Denny wanted to hurt me. He just wanted to talk with me face-to-face.

"Yes, sir. Confirmed." The scout officer still kept his aim concentrated on the apartment door. "Twenty minutes, that's all you got. Then we're *making* him come out."

He motioned over his shoulder to an officer behind him, who quickly landed next to him with a thermal imaging camera. It detected heat. The fire department used them to search for fires within walls and behind closed doors, and to search for trapped survivors in smoke filled rooms. The ESU owned eight of the small handheld units, and they were all in a state of grievous disrepair. The one being slowly pushed out into the hallway in the cautious hands of the young officer looked as if it had been around for centuries. Though the NYPD and FDNY had been using them since the mid-eighties, this particular camera was a newer model and had probably seen a lot of action.

The officer held it up to the outside wall of the apartment, and immediately, two bright white images appeared on the small screen. One was stationary in a seated position. The other moved about at a lazy pace. A small oblong-shaped image appeared and flickered lightly.

The officer with the camera spoke. "No change in position. But that must be the kitchen, he's cooking something, now."

Kitchen to the left, I stored in my brain.

Sarah looked to be only a couple feet from the images of the burners' flames, and she was much too small in proportion. She was being held far on the other side of the apartment, away from the front door. I wished I had studied the architectural drawings more carefully.

"Denny!" the scout officer called out. "This is Jason."

I looked down at the top of his head. It was kind of odd to finally know his name.

"We want to send in Professor Brantley."

There was no response, but the figure in the camera stopped moving.

"Did you hear me? We're going to send her in like you asked."

We heard a muffled, "Okay" from inside.

As I stepped into the hallway, I caught a glimpse of one of the holes in the doorjamb left by one of Denny's rounds. It was a deep hole, very clean with very little plaster chipped away. I began undoing the Velcro on my vest.

"What are you doing?" the officer with the camera asked in disbelief.

"I need him to recognize me as Professor Brantley," I said. "Not Agent Brantley."

Joshua bent down and scooped up the vest where I had tossed it back into the stairwell. "Are you nuts?"

I ignored him and tossed the helmet at him.

"I'm not going to be responsible for you," he said in hoarse whisper.

"Trust me on this one." My eyes locked on Jason. "No matter what you *think* you see happening through that camera, promise me that you'll give me twenty minutes."

He stared at me as if I was insane. Jason did not know who I was and he didn't care. He took his orders from someone else.

I deferred to Dan. "Please."

His expression was stone, but he finally nodded his

head. "I'll give you your twenty minutes. Unconditional. But one second over and these guys are coming in after you."

I smiled my thanks, but knew that we were all screwed and heading for disaster. Twenty minutes was nothing, and even Dan did not have the authority to make such calls.

An officer led the way carrying a ballistic shield. When we reached the apartment I waved him away. My actions were not the symptoms of some heroic bravado, but I believed that Denny would have perceived me as a threat and a betrayer if I showed up looking like I was ready for guerrilla warfare.

My palms sweated as I neared the apartment. I rubbed them together and slowly inched my way along the hallway to the hinge side of the door.

"Denny," I called out in a moderate volume. "It's Professor Brantley. I'm going to come in now. It's just me, and only me."

I looked back at the stairwell door, and the officer with the camera motioned through the crack that someone was moving toward the door. My insides were gripped with fear and I was sweating profusely.

"Calm, Meredith," I whispered quickly to myself. "Must remain calm. Do not let him smell fear. Do not let him have control."

The doorknob turned, but remained still after it clicked open. I stared at it for a while, uncertain if Denny was just waiting for me to open the door so he could lay the remaining rounds into my chest. I looked back at the stairwell again and wished that I hadn't given up the Kevlar vest or my human shield so quickly.

The officer with the camera motioned, but I could not

tell what he meant with his hand gestures. I just knew that Denny was doing something different now. I crouched and placed the flat of my hand against the door. Slowly, I pushed it open halfway. I cautiously poked my head inside and remained low as I crept into the foyer. It was dark, but a light was on in the living room. I could only see part of the living room. Sarah was sitting calmly on the couch, watching me. Her arms were weird, and I figured that they were tied behind her back.

"Close the door," she commanded mechanically. Denny must've instructed her to do so. "Lock it. All three locks."

I did. I poked my head into the kitchen.

No one. The kettle was beginning to whistle.

I rose tentatively, keeping my back to the wall and slowly making my way toward Sarah. Denny was probably standing across the way with the gun trained on her. But I was still waiting for an ambush. I made it to the end of the short hallway and cautiously peered into the living room. Sarah was alone and her feet were also tied. Two words flash through my mind: AMBUSH DROP.

Sarah tried to warn me with her eyes, but by the time I turned and saw the shadowy figure behind me, it was too late. He lunged at me and I felt the chisel stab me in the thinnest part of my upper arm. It easily cut through the sleeve of my blouse, and I instantly knew some of the pain that Sumi, Rita and Trina had felt.

My other arm instinctively shot out like a catapult and my clenched fist landed in his chest, knocking him against the wall. Before I could reposition myself, I saw his folded cane sailing toward me. The top end of the handle landed squarely across the left side of my jaw, sending me plummeting into a heavy oak table where my head bounced off the corner like a rubber ball. I fell to the floor with a deafening thud, and Denny's heavy boots muddying up Sarah's expensive Oriental rug faded into a hazy image of colorful dots. I tried to pick myself up, but my body quickly collapsed and everything around me disappeared into the squelching sounds of the tea kettle and boiling water.

Chapter Fifty-eight

I was floating. No, I wasn't dead, or at least I did not think I was. Or at least I hoped that I was not. Everything around me was white. Bright white. Subtracted. There was no up or down, left or right. Then I saw a figure in the distance: a child. It was a little girl, coming toward me. I knelt down before her. The girl was pretty, her blond hair flowing in soft waves. I stared curiously—it was myself as a child. I reached out my hand, and she did, too. She was trying to say something.

"What?" I pleaded. "What are you trying to say?"

The little girl was right in front of me, but I could not hear. I could only see her lips moving.

"Please, what are you saying?"

"Please, what are you saying?" the little girl's voice finally sounded in a too cute lisp.

"What do you want to tell me?" I asked.

"What do you want to tell me?"

I began to frown, and the little girl followed suit.

"Stop it," I said.

"Stop it."

I quickly let go of the girl's hand and she mimicked my angry gesture.

"Stop it!" I ordered.

"Stop it!"

I'd had enough. I turned to leave, but there was nowhere for me to go. The space around me was nonexistent. I spun around to confront my younger self, but I froze at what I saw. The little girl was no longer there, instead I was looking at Sumi—and she was looking back. I bent down so that I was eye level with her.

"Sumi?"

She nodded.

I smiled, tears streaming lightly down my face.

Her eyes were so clear and full of life.

"What are you doing here?"

She smiled a big grin. "What are *you* doing here?"

I squinted slightly, hoping that Sumi wasn't going to start playing this annoying game.

"I belong here," I said matter-of-factly.

I wasn't sure why I had said it, but it seemed right.

"No, you don't," she replied in a sweet singsongy voice.

"Don't I?"

"It's time for you to go, Professor Brantley."

"What?" I panicked. "No, wait!"

The phone was ringing loudly in my ears. I opened my eyes, and when I tried to focus a sharp pain shot through my skull. I tasted blood and curiously began rolling my tongue along the inside of my mouth, looking for a cut.

"Oh, God," I groaned.

Okay, so I was wrong, damn it. He did want to hurt me.

The phone stopped ringing.

I tried to move in order to assess the situation, but I could not. I mean, I really could not. If my vision was still a little cloudy, my brain was working sharply in overdrive. I was bound. My hands were tied behind my back. I tried working my wrists, but my efforts were met with resistance. The ligatures were digging into and scratching my skin. Denny was using the same brown twine he had used on his three dead victims. His mom, he didn't bother tying.

Things around me slowly became clearer, and I could see that I was seated next to Sarah on the couch. If not for having our arms bound, anyone could've entered the room and thought we were having a friendly discussion about—oh, serial killers.

Where was Denny? My eyes scanned the room, but he was not with us. I made another effort at carefully maneuvering my wrists, but he had made several passes with the twine and the knot was tight. He had studied me well, knowing that he could not skimp on the ligatures as he did with his other victims.

My lower arms began to tingle.

I squinted and focused on the green digital numbers on the VCR. It was too far away. I blinked hard and focused on the numbers again. They were flashing. I did not need glasses to read what the clock said. It was always 12:00 AM in this apartment.

How long had I been out? If it had been a while, there was no telling what the Ninjas outside were willing to do. I began biting at the collar of my blouse, making a futile attempt at pulling it up toward my mouth and nose. Tear gas grenades could be a viable option. Talk about your chemicals. Six sections—ninety-four grams of gas—was not a pleasant experience. I looked down at my collar, and wasn't certain if the stain was from my lipstick or the injury in my mouth.

"Welcome to my home," Sarah said with a dry delivery.

I quickly turned to her and then we both smiled. Even though our predicament was of the utmost severity, it was comforting to know that we could keep our sense of humor about things.

Still slightly dazed, I pulled myself up with my tied fists, using the back of the couch for support.

"Where is he?" I asked, tasting blood again.

"In the kitchen, I think," she replied with a surprising casualness.

"How long was I—"

"Oh, probably three or four minutes. He just finished tying you when you started to wake up." Sarah looked at me with half a smile. "You've got a really thick skull."

I chuckled quietly, but the pain seared through my forehead like a hot knife. I studied what was available to us. Absolutely nothing. No pewter picture frames, or letter openers—no sharp objects.

"Did he bring the gun with him?

Sarah stared guiltily at the ceiling. "No. It's mine."

I could not hide my surprise.

"It was my husband's, and I just kept it after he passed away."

"What kind is it?"

"Oh, I don't know. Silver and shiny."

I sighed. "Is it a revolver?"

"No, one of those semi-automatics, I guess." Sarah became sullen. "I'm sorry for being flip, but I'm just a little PO'd that someone's come into my home and is holding me hostage." She fell back into the couch. "It's just been a really lousy two weeks."

I nodded my head in agreement. "So, just the gun and the chisel." There was a throbbing along the left side of my jaw and my lip felt red-hot. "And the cane."

"And whatever he decides to find in the kitchen."

We listened as he banged drawers and cabinet doors.

"How many magazines?"

Sarah looked at me with confusion. "Eh?"

"Uh, bullets. How many bullets does he have?"

"Just whatever's in the gun."

"What's his state of mind?" I continued to grill.

"Mm, nuts."

A grin spread across my face again, but I recognized the fear that Sarah was trying desperately to hide. I sat up straighter and leaned toward her. We did not have time to practice our comic act.

"Does he seem suicidal?" I asked.

She considered this briefly and shook her head.

"Good." I looked toward the kitchen. Things had quieted down, so I knew that he would be returning soon. "Has he said what he wants? Why he's here?"

"Nothing." She began to race through her words. "Whenever I try to talk to him, he just tells me to shut up. He keeps saying the system failed him. He doesn't want to talk."

"Mm. He wasn't answering our phone calls." I began to slip into the sofa and I pulled myself back up again. "Has he been abusive, or directed any violence specifically toward you?"

"None."

I fell back against the cushions. If no one knew what his agenda was, then we were not in a good position. All I could figure was that Denny, realizing we were closing in on him, was doing what he felt he was being forced to do. We were driving him to do this.

Denny walked into the living room carrying a cup of tea and half a sandwich in one hand, and the semi-automatic in the other. I studied it quickly: a Smith & Wesson, 9mm. The NYPD baseball hat that Dan had given him was pulled back on the top of his head. His movements were smooth and elegant, unlike the awkward way he carried himself when he was "blind."

We never made eye contact as he sat in the armchair directly across from us. With slow methodical bites, he consumed his snack before taking the first sip of tea. He looked up at me after polishing off the rest of his hot drink in one large gulp.

"Thanks for coming," he said, projecting the image of a gracious host.

He put down the cup and trained the gun on us. He studied me, searching for some kind of approval or permission for his actions, but I remained silent.

"You're kind of stubborn, aren't you?" he said, waving the gun at me.

"Irish blood."

He smiled.

I was unnerved with the way his eyes moved about. With his free hand, Denny reached into the pockets of his jeans and removed three Polaroids. He held them up to us. They were of Sarah. Blurry and grainy, since they were taken from a distance, but undeniably her as she was entering Bellevue from the smaller parking lot in front of the new Psych Building.

I looked at her through the corner of my eye, and wondered if she realized what Denny had meant by taking her picture, or was her horrified expression because she just figured that he was spying on her? Did she know that he had chosen her to be his next victim?

Denny grabbed the remote off the coffee table and

flicked on the TV. Each of the three major networks had the same late breaking story—*Live!*

"Cool, I'm a celebrity," he said with a wide grin.

An old photograph of Denny appeared on the TV.

With the gun still trained on us, he reached over and picked up a Polaroid camera that was resting on the floor at his feet. Denny smiled and took his self-portrait. Then he licked the back and stuck it to the TV screen.

"That's better," he said, satisfied with how he was now being represented.

He clicked the mute button on the remote and sat back down.

"I knew you'd figure it out," he said with admiration. "I was hoping you would." Suddenly, his expression drained of all life. "I needed you to."

With my long fingers, I carefully grappled with the knots on my ligatures. The pain shot through every joint in my hands.

"I can't stop it myself." Denny began breathing heavily and fighting off the uncontrollable emotions building inside him. "I am *not* a nobody!"

I froze. I was uncertain whether this was genuine, or a performance simply for my benefit.

He squeezed his eyes shut. "I can't stop myself."

Denny jumped up from his chair and moved over to me. He slowly knelt before me and stared at me with unblinking eyes. The barrel of the semi-automatic was pushed far into my abdomen. He was close, and it made me uneasy. I smelled tuna fish. He was too close.

"L-leave her a-alone," I heard Sarah stutter.

"Shhhh," Denny barely uttered in a light whistle.

I immediately withdrew to a time that seemed so long ago. It was another man—a boy—who had breathed his sweet angry breath into my ear. It had been hatred that had flowed from his mouth. It was anger that had driven him to hurt me: to steal all of what I was. His rage had taught me to hate—to hate myself. I began unconsciously twisting my left wrist and the scratching twine dug further into my skin. Just as I had tried on that night to use a broken beer bottle to cut my way free from his leather belt, but wound up slicing my wrist instead. But the pain from the dirty shards of glass that had littered the upstairs bedroom had been my escape. I had felt nothing, and I knew nothing of what was happening.

For the first time in such a long time, I closed my eyes and began to pray. The words came back to me so easily, as if I had never stopped saying them. Perhaps in some unconscious part of my mind, I never did.

I could feel Denny's hand reach around my waist. I remained rigid, but inside I recoiled and retreated to someplace far away.

Years ago I had made a promise to a young woman: that I would never again be overpowered—by anyone, and most certainly not by fear. And I had given that same lecture again, a few days ago, to another young woman.

My eyes sprang open, and Denny flinched like a cockroach does when you flick on the kitchen light. My body tensed and pain raced its way along my face as I clenched my jaw. He pulled away, but the semi remained imbedded between my ribs.

I began moving my wrists again, spinning them quickly and covertly behind my back. The twine was scratching my skin raw, but the knots were stretching and loosening.

"I *have* to kill you," Denny said frantically, but in an apologetic tone.

Damn. The twine was caught on my bulky watch, and my right wrist was still tightly bound.

"I wanted to cut you up, but I reserve that ceremony for those who earned it." He looked slyly over at Sarah. "You have to understand that I can't let you live—either of you."

My watch had just begun to squeeze through the loop.

Our eyes were locked on to each other. Denny pushed the semi further into my side, and I moved my left hand faster as it threaded its way out of the ligatures. I quickly pulled the twine from my right.

Sarah trembled. "Denny, there's a lot of police outside."

That was the wrong thing to say. I still held his stare, but I wished that Sarah had kept her mouth shut.

"Yeah. Which is why I gotta kill you. If I don't kill you, then they won't give me the injection."

I dropped the twine somewhere against the sofa cushions. "That's what you want? You want to die?"

"With dignity." He looked at the TV as the camera pulled out for an aerial shot of the parking lot swarming with dark uniforms. "Not like an animal being hunted." He looked back at me. "Not like they died."

I could hear Sarah's breathing grow more rapid.

"It's the only way I can be stopped because I just can't help it anymore." He pushed harder, and it felt as if the semi was deep inside of me. "Sorry."

How pathetic. Center stage even in his final minutes of life. Strapped to a table with an audience of reporters, lawyers and law enforcement watching his grand finale. The little twit.

I clenched my fists. "You've already killed nine—"

"Twelve."

"You've already killed. They can give you the death penalty."

Denny began shaking his head. "No. You're my guarantee. You're one of them. If I kill you, they'll come after me. After all," his smile was smarmy, "who really gives a crap about the others?"

My eyes narrowed. I was pissed. I was pissed that I had let Joshua talk me into this whole mess in the first place. I was pissed that one of my students was murdered. I was pissed that I was fired. I was pissed that I was being held hostage. But I had to maintain whatever bond it was that had developed between us, or neither Sarah nor I would be alive to see tomorrow.

For a moment Denny eased up on the gun. And as if daylight had suddenly shifted to night, he looked old. His eyes were devoid of all life and he stared off into empty space.

"For in that sleep of death, what dreams may come," he muttered in a garbled voice. "When we have shuffled off this mortal coil."

Denny had startled and surprised me. My tone was distant as I finished the line from *Hamlet*: "Must give us pause—there's the respect that makes calamity of so long life."

There was nothing noble about him.

He looked over at the TV. The self-portrait had slid down the front of the screen and glided across the hardwood floor. Denny pulled the cap down over his eyes and half his face disappeared behind the bill, like an executioner's hood. "They're going to fry me. That's just the way it is."

The hell it was.

He thrust the semi into my side again. For an instant, I thought I heard his finger tapping lightly on the trigger. Denny looked up from under the cap, and for a moment I saw the young awkward man who sat in my lecture hall.

My eyes never left his as I tracked every movement, every intention. In the dark void that glossed over his face, there was a flicker of desperation, anger and deadly victory. I had to act—NOW.

A rush of adrenaline consumed me. My left hand grabbed the wrist of his shooting arm, turning the semi down toward the floor and away from both Sarah and me. I thrust my right side at him and my leg behind his. The heel of my hand slammed hard against the bridge of his nose, sending him reeling backwards over my hip. As he fell to the floor, a firecracker exploded near my ear. I saw a quick flash followed by the smell of gunpowder. I dropped to the floor on Denny's right side, my legs up near his head and sprawled over his chest, his right arm pushed against the inside of my left leg as I pried the semi from his hand. He grabbed, but I slammed the point of my elbow into his abdomen and he grunted before easily surrendering.

Things were a blur again. There were lots of people. Black uniforms, Kevlar vests, boots thundering against the parquet floor, people shouting orders. They descended upon Denny like a pack of wolves. They flipped him onto his stomach and cuffed him, and everyone relaxed slightly, MP5s trained on his still body.

Where had the shot gone? I looked back at Sarah. She was lying on her side and crying. Dan was undoing her ligatures. I saw blood, but not on her. It was dripping down my face and stinging my eye. I wiped it away, but it filled my vision again. My fingers moved quickly and frantically tracing the hairline along my forehead.

Nothing.

They moved lower, and still nothing. My fingertips moved more rapidly. They stopped in something sticky directly above my left eye. Just a graze? I pulled cautiously and the skin seemed to move beyond its natural boundaries. An air bubble caught in my throat and my breathing was short. Though the wound protested, I quickly felt around the inside of the skin and mentally outlined the path of damage. It was not so bad, right? A couple of stitches, I'm sure. I'd be okay. But I could not hear Joshua as he spoke on that side of my face. I turned my head three-quarters.

". . . *never* going to be responsible for you again! What you did was stupid . . ."

I turned my head back and, thankfully, his voice disappeared.

The ESU had entered the apartment with precision and speed, and Denny was arrested without further incident. Someone kindly gave me a dishtowel to press against my forehead. It had a rooster on it with the sun rising in the background. Denny was carted out of the apartment, but not before Dan nearly ripped the baseball cap from his head. After some brief questioning, Sarah and I left her apartment and rode the elevator in silence with Joshua and Dan. There would be more questioning at the hospital.

Outside, we saw Denny being hurried through a crowd of reporters, the bright glare of the lights washing out his already pale complexion. He mugged and sneered at the cameras for the benefit of the public. Inane questions were flung at him, like: "Do you feel like you've been wronged by the system?"

And of course he had. His replies were consistent with what we expected from a conceited, intelligent sociopath who could not take responsibility for his actions, unless of course, it garnered him the attention and fame that he so desired. Either way it was always someone else's fault. But I watched the theatrics, and remained unconvinced that even this was the real Denny. I did not think that any one of us had actually been allowed to see his true self, and we never would.

The axe used to mutilate his victims would never be found. Nor would the eight other women he admitted to killing in the same brutal manner. Of course he would never divulge their locations. That was the only thing he had left that was his and his alone. The only thing remaining that he controlled.

As Denny was driven away into the rainy night, Joshua helped me into the front seat of Dan's car. By the time he had locked his seat belt, the news vans and reporters had all but disappeared. I looked at the Polaroid I was clutching in my hand. I did not remember it until now. Denny had handed it to me before the ESU entered Sarah's apartment. I never even realized that he had taken my photograph. It was a closeup of my face while I sat on the couch. My eyes were shut tight.

I touched my right hand to my forehead. The blood dripping down my palm was the last thing I remembered before falling against the dashboard and blacking out.

Chapter Fifty-nine

The doctors at Bellevue had told me that I would be fine, but it was necessary for me to be admitted for a few days of observation. I had stubbornly demanded that under no circumstances would I remain imprisoned in a hospital bed. My wounds were only superficial, and I was conscious and alert. The exhausted intern had finally negotiated an overnight stay. The doctors and nurses tiptoed around me and spoke in amateurish code, as if I could not figure out that I had been drifting in and out of sleep for more than a day and a half.

Kyle had slept by my bedside the whole time, curled up as best he could in a stiff chair with nothing but a flat pillow and a polyester blanket. But when I woke this morning, he was gone. I knew that he had a very important business trip in Chicago scheduled months in advance, and I would never ask him to lose an account over a meager bump and a cut on my head. As I had slipped in and out of consciousness, I remembered hearing him whispering to Joshua. Kyle did not want to leave, but Joshua promised that he would look out for me and assured Kyle that everything would be fine. I think I loved them both.

Thirty-nine hours after I had first passed through the emergency room doors—leaning on Joshua's arm with my head bleeding and my lip swollen—I had just about had enough of the institution. At the first signs of the daylight, I dressed and relocated myself just outside the emergency room entrance, where I was surprised to find Sarah making her way around the corridor.

"Good morning, Meredith," she said pleasantly—a bit too pleasantly for six-thirty in the morning, and for someone who was just getting over being held captive by a violent murderer. "I was just coming down to see how you were doing."

I tried to pull off an acceptable smile, but I suspect that it looked more like a sneer. The hearing in my ear had returned, but a light ringing remained. I was told that it would disappear in few days.

"Well, you're looking healthier than you did when Joshua first brought you in," she said.

"I'm feeling much better, thanks." As much as I liked Sarah and appreciated her concern, I wished that she hadn't bothered to check up on me. I wanted to be alone.

From somewhere in the ER a woman screamed hysterically. "Get these IVs outta me! You're killing me! You're killing me!"

Two doctors chuckled as they walked by—apparently, one of their regulars.

"I bet you're really going to miss this place," Sarah said with a wry grin.

* * *

The bandage on my head was irritating the stitches underneath and I had to struggle to restrain myself from scratching at it. I could not decide which had been more painful: the actual injury or the needle and syringe full of Lidocaine that had been injected into the open wound four times. A throbbing pain still shot through my skull like an electric shock, but I wanted desperately to go home. Detached from everything around me, I fingered my hospital bracelet and it spun easily around my wrist. Then it suddenly dawned on me that my watch had been removed. I carefully studied the almost two decade-old scar barely noticeable under the burns left from the ligatures. Joshua had asked me about it once, but I had managed to sidestep the issue. Kyle never mentioned it, but I would often catch him studying it as if he were searching for the theme and symbolism behind it.

I felt so tired. I thought back to what Cheryl had said to me in the bathroom last week. I still didn't have the answers. My face fell. Was *that* the answer? Was that why I was so obsessed? Was it a journey: a search for answers?

I cursed under my breath. Romanticizing my problems to the glamour of some Gothic novel was just as pathetic and not nearly as clever as a pathological killer masquerading as a young blind man.

Joshua sat down next to me, holding two paper cups from the coffee shop inside the hospital.

"I thought you might like this," he said, handing me one of the steaming coffees as he sat next to me.

"Thanks," I whispered. My lips moved awkwardly and were still sensitive. "I probably shouldn't be drinking this, but if you don't tell, I won't."

I took the cup carefully in my left hand; my right was still a bit stiff. Apparently, I had slugged Denny a little harder than I had thought.

Joshua looked at me thoughtfully, gently running a finger along the point of my chin: the only part of my face that didn't ache.

I shivered at his touch. "I guess I won't be winning beauty contests anytime soon," I joked nervously.

His expression remained serious as he gently held my face near his. "You're always beautiful to me."

I wanted to cry.

The glass doors of the entrance to the ER slid open, and a man with his arms handcuffed behind his back was led into the hospital by a member of the fire department, followed by a pair of uniformed police officers. Joshua and I pulled away from each other and looked up in time to watch as the expressionless man was taken down the hall for psychiatric observation. He would be held for seventy-two hours and released, only to be readmitted the following week. This was the way of life for the stranger who remained nameless to us. The man's ghostly stare was all that was needed to tell a tale of despair.

"You know, NYU is probably going to fire me," I said shaking my head as if I even wanted to go back. "Actually, I think they did."

"You were in the hospital," Joshua declared. "Anyway, maybe it's for the better. You need to come back to Virginia. New York's too crazy for you."

I smiled and the pain raced its way through every nerve ending in my face. "So when are *you* going back to Virginia?" I asked, enduring another jolt from the piping hot coffee.

He looked down at the black scuffs marking the tiled floor. "I'm leaving in a few hours—"

"Good," I said with a smile, trying to hide my disappointment. "You should get back to Kirsten and the boys. I'm sure they really miss you."

Joshua looked at me through his thick eyelashes, and I melted inside.

"Meredith, I'm worried about you."

"Well, the doctors say that I'll have a nasty headache for a few days, but I'm sure the pain killers that they gave me will be great." I retreated into my words when I noticed that his expression never changed.

"I want to know that you'll be okay, not just tomorrow," he said, seeking the reassurance that I couldn't give him.

"What can I say, Joshua? I don't know what things will be like in one hour, let alone next week. All I know is that I've made it this far in life and I'll keep going. Nothing's going to stop me from trying."

I could see it in his reaction that it was at this moment Joshua knew for certain I would not be returning to the FBI. And how could I? I had not figured out anything in my life.

He smiled and gently kissed my hand.

"Maybe we'll see you for Thanksgiving?" He started toward the sliding glass doors. "I'll save you the wishbone."

I watched as he disappeared through the parking lot and out of my sight.

"Save us both the wishbone," I whispered. "We need it."

My head dropped toward my knees.

Beside me, where Joshua had been sitting, lay a large package wrapped in white paper. It was stinking of cheese and meat.

I brought it to my nose. "Genoa and provolone." I squeezed it and smiled. "On a hard roll."

Chapter Sixty

Winter had finally set in as puffy flakes of snow dusted the morning sky and settled gently along the landscape of the FBI Academy. Nearly seven miles south on Route One, I could only appreciate the splendor of the scene from my second-floor office, through a small window in desperate need of a thorough washing.

The New Year had arrived with no more grandiose expectations than any other day. This particular holiday held no special place in my heart since it was merely a mocking reminder of passing time and unsolved cases, a simple reinforcement of the harsh reality that more were to come. Perhaps, in some childlike fantasy, I believed that by not acknowledging the New Year, there would be no more victims to be found.

I took a slow sip of coffee and grimaced at the sludgy mess that the nearby sandwich shop had concocted. A few drops dribbled down my chin and trickled along the face of my ID badge. I stared at the numeral "2" boldly printed under my picture, clearly identifying me as a member of the NCAVC. My thoughts were interrupted when I felt someone's gaze studying me.

Joshua was leaning against the doorframe, a thick file tucked under his arm. There was a look of disbelief blanketing his face, and I made no attempt at maintaining eye contact as I wheeled my chair out from my desk. I felt like a lost runaway who had just found her way home. As I sat and began nonchalantly shuffling through the photos of society's latest statistic, I stated flatly, "I'm back."

ANDREW HARPER
RED ANGEL

The Darden State Hospital for the Criminally Insane holds hundreds of dangerous criminals. Trey Campbell works in the psych wing of Ward D, home to the most violent murderers, where he finds a young man who is in communication with a serial killer who has just begun terrorizing Southern California—a killer known only as the Red Angel.

Campbell has 24 hours to find the Red Angel and face the terror at the heart of a human monster. To do so, he must trust the only one who can provide information—Michael Scoleri, a psychotic murderer himself, who may be the only link to the elusive and cunning Red Angel. Will it take a killer to catch a killer?

NOWHERE TO RUN
CHRISTOPHER BELTON

It's too much to be a coincidence. A series of computer-related crimes from different countries, all linked somehow to Japan. Some are minor. Some are deadly. But they are just enough to catch the eye of a young UN investigator. As he digs deeper he can't believe what he finds. Extortion. Torture. Murder. And ties to the most ruthless crime organization in the world.

It's a perfect plan, beautiful in its design, daring in its execution, and extremely profitable. No one in the Japanese underworld has ever conceived of such a plan and the organization isn't about to let anything stand in its way. Anyone who tries to interfere will soon find that there is no escape, no defense, and...nowhere to run.
